.⁻ PRESS

ABLE WAS I

ABLE WAS I

A NOVEL

DREW BANKS

.— PRESS

•⁻ PRESS

Dot Dash Press
270 Liberty Street
San Francisco, CA 94114

Printed in the United States of America.
10 9 8 7 6 5 4 3 2

The characters and events in this book are fictitious. Any similarity to real persons, living or dead, is coincidental and not intended by the author.

Book design by White Space, Inc.
Author photograph © Duane Cramer
Cover photograph © Tracie Klein
Map inserts illustrated by Fernando Martin del Campo

www.dotdashpress.com

ISBN 1-59113-793-4
ISBN 978-1-59113-793-1

PALINDROME

\pal'in-drōm\ n (1629) :
a word, number, phrase,
verse, sentence, or poem
that reads the same forward
or backward. From the
Greek word *palindromos*
(*palin*, meaning again, back
and *dromos*, meaning running),
the literal translation is:
running back again...

ELBA 1985

August 15, 1985
Before I saw Elba, there was nothing but sea and sky. Then it appeared,
small on the horizon, an insignificant fleck just below the vanishing
point. On the water, perspectives are not forged from hard angles. No
perfect square is centered on the edge of the sea. The imminence is the
same, yet the path, variable. Nascent and amorphous, the island bobs
up, down, right and left as the boat stays its course.

Let it go, he told himself. Hot sea air streamed past as he made his way to the bow. There was a crowd but that didn't matter; he was alone. He spread his feet wide across the deck's planks and rode the water's pitch. Arm's length from the rail, he leaned into the wind, balanced gravity against resistance and released his grip. For an instant he was weightless, a buoyant extension of the ship. His shoulder-length hair floated behind, fanning out upon a plane of air. It felt epic and empowering, and his mind began to calm.

Ahead, the division between sea and sky stretched as far as he could see; the little dot of land a flaw in its harmony. "Elba." The rush of sea and wind were so loud he couldn't hear his own whisper; he wasn't even sure if he had said it out loud. It was funny to think of it as their destination, this island about which he knew nothing. Whether it was his release, the solitude or simply the sea, he didn't care; something had dispelled his anxiety. He would deconstruct the moment later but now he was grateful to give in to it and allow his racing thoughts to slow. Discomfort settled like fine silt, a delicate mask. As Elba grew larger, its form began to take shape, the edges not rigid but soft and muted. The Mediterranean faded upward like a variegated rose.

2

Grey and his father stood together, silent.

This trip was one of the few times, apart from their annual Christmas tree buying ritual, they had ever spent any solo time together. While there had been many enrollment and apartment-finding logistics, most of the time it was just the two of them—driving together, eating together and making some uncomfortable attempts at conversation. Now the handoff. Grey took in the moment, aware of both its promise and discord.

An hour earlier in the university cafeteria, Grey's father had ordered two beers with their pizza. "Good luck, son," he toasted. In raising the frosted mug to his mouth, Grey grimaced and struggled to swallow as he checked out the students at the surrounding tables. With unusual perception, his father commented, "It takes a bit a gittin' used to. D'ya wanna Coke instead?"

"No thanks, this is fine." Unbeknownst to his father, Grey had been drinking for over two years; he loved fruity drinks and often shared a glass or two of white zinfandel with his mother. But he hated beer. Smiling with assurance, Grey forced another long draft.

They were in the first afternoon orientation session and by the looks of the crowd, many had partaken far more than he and his father. It was an opportunity to start college off right—drunk. The general jocularity failed to infect Grey. He wanted it over. This finality was the culmination of three years of planning. He had deferred enrollment, saved his every penny and filled out copious loan forms to attend a college that none of his friends would consider and at a distance too far for frequent familial visits. A few more hours and he could start anew.

The couple in line ahead of them turned around. At five-eleven, Miriam was just shorter than six-foot Grey and towered over his five-eight father. She wore black, plastic-rimmed glasses with a full head of dark hair pulled up in some kind of bun. Neither eyewear nor hairstyle masked her femininity but instead gave her a disguised Lynda-Carter-in-the-first-scene-before-the-bad-guy-appears voluptuousness. Her stature, hair and glasses weren't the only things she had in common with Lynda, nor did she try to conceal the other two, not even with the slumping thing that girls her size often do. Nope, she stood shoulders back, chin and breasts out, smiling and talking to everyone like she had no idea that she was the hottest girl there. Her friend was a shorter, less exuberant fellow named Pete. From what Grey had picked up eavesdropping the past half-hour, they were childhood friends from Charlotte who knew the ins and outs of the Raleigh scene. For the last ten minutes they had been discussing which would be their first bar of the night.

"Are you from around here?" Miriam asked.

Grey was too eager. "No, I'm from Tennessee . . . Memphis." Miriam's attention was distracted to someone in line behind them who called her name.

Pete smiled and extended his hand. "Cool. I've always wanted to go to Graceland." Pete's eyes did not stray; his palm was warm and smooth. He asked, "So, why State?"

With an intensity Grey had rarely before experienced, Pete listened—really listened. It was the first conversation unencumbered by his past. With it, Grey began to reinvent himself. His father, smiling beside them, was unaware or unconcerned that this would be the last of their attempts at father-son bonding. From here on, their interactions would be of similar disregard but born from a vastly different relationship. Yet Grey's father would always ask, unconsciously marking the moment, "How's that guy ya met with Miriam on the first day of college? D'ya still see him?"

Four years later the spontaneous decision to go to Europe was the ultimate testament to Grey's metamorphosis. It was the fall semester of their senior year. On his way to the bathroom Grey passed the open door of the study where Pete was sitting—his atlas open before him—reciting capitals to himself. Grey held his bladder in an about-face straight to the kitchen to call Miriam. The three had been roommates since they were sophomores. Somewhere along the line Miriam moved into Grey's room and her former room became *the study* although rarely was a book opened there unless it was Pete, depressed, poring over his atlas.

"Babe, cancel tonight and pick up a case of beer on your way home." Drinking turned to chugging turned to beer bongs turned to sentimentality as each confided his post-collegiate aspirations. First, Miriam with her New York dream, and then Pete's Peace Corps plans. When it got to Grey, he speculated about a job offer from the Research Triangle firm where he had worked the past three summers. Stopping mid-sentence, he would realize that he, the obsessive structured one of the three, had never given serious thought to life after college.

Silence lingered too long. Miriam was now the one staring at the atlas; her long blond hair fell to its pages. After Grey and she started dating, Miriam stopped dyeing her hair and started wearing contacts; she gave into the blond bombshell she had spent years eschewing in favor of the quirky intellectual. Now she had so embraced her beauty that she was ready to up and move to New York to become a model. Who needed another geophysicist anyway? The night's mood was about to downshift when Miriam looked up, smiling and clear-eyed.

"Let's go to Europe."

Miriam's sister and a group of girlfriends had bought a beat-up VW bus, spent a month driving from Paris to Rome and then sold it, making enough money to pay for half the trip. It was a story of carefree decadence that antsy, yet-to-be-encumbered college seniors couldn't resist. Miriam's enthusiasm invigorated the merrymaking and the three returned to the topic that had captivated all of Raleigh since State's miraculous NCAA championship victory the previous spring: could Valvano do it again?

Somehow, through the memory loss of much that was said that night, Europe stuck.

Grey had spent a year arranging the trip. None of them had ever traveled outside the U.S. so every choice required research. Not that he minded doing all the legwork; it was a great way to avoid confronting the uncertainty of his future.

When, at the last minute, Pete asked if Tom from his church group could come, even Miriam was unsure. Grey and Miriam had discussed it in private. How could they say no? Miriam knew Tom from the couple of times she went with Pete to his church bowling night and said he seemed a little pissy. On the other hand, a fourth person would make the trip cheaper, and besides, this was the first time Pete had ever asked anything of them.

Grey met Tom two days before their departure. He tried to dismiss his initial reaction yet couldn't shake a bad gut feeling. Tom was nice enough but something kept him distant, aloof. It quickly became obvious that he was also cheap. Even though everyone had agreed to splurge on a pre-departure weekend in New York, Tom started in before they were out of the airport.

"I'm not paying for a cab. Y'all can do what you want; I'm taking the bus." Which of course meant they all took the bus, saving a whopping two dollars between them.

Each expense became a debate. They were all pinching pennies with years of school debt ahead of them but this was their graduation trip. Having spent months cost-comparing every detail, Grey had pieced together the least expensive trip possible but a beer here and a museum entrance fee there, that was part of the deal. Tom refused to spend a dime on anything. He just wanted to take a few pictures, bitch about how much things cost, and move on. It was as though he preferred photographs to life. Manipulated experiences rendered and sorted, imperfect ones discarded. This is what bothered Grey the most—this controlled detachment. It was too familiar.

For Miriam it was his constant harassment of women. She was no activist and had, her entire life, laughed off comments about her breasts, but by the time they landed at Newark she was fuming. "He will not be sleeping within ten feet of me."

It all fell apart in Italy. Grey hadn't realized that most of Europe took August off. For Chrissakes, how could an entire continent vacation at the same time? Pisa was a nightmare. The wait for the tower was unthinkable. They argued over whether to wait or not. Tom made a stink. Grey held their place in line while Miriam, Tom and Pete went to tour the church across the square. The priest taking donations told them that they couldn't go in wearing shorts. Thank God it was Tom who flew off the handle and not Grey. And in a church no less. It solidified Grey's position that Tom's pettiness was ruining their vacation.

The week before in Venice when Grey exploded at Tom, it was Grey who came across looking like the bad guy. His own words rang in his memory: "You fuckin' asshole. Do you fuckin' care about anything but that fuckin' camera? I hope you don't get a decent fuckin' picture outta the entire trip." Now he felt vindicated. At least he hadn't called a priest a "spineless faggot." Even though Tom had said it out of the priest's earshot, they all, Pete in particular, were appalled.

Tom demanded that they leave Pisa immediately. Miriam and Pete didn't protest but were passive-aggressive with no suggestions when Tom asked where they wanted to go. The Pisa bus ride hadn't been short and it would have been an empty day if they turned around and went back. Tom had to scramble. On the walk back to the station, his insistent gait slowed. What would they do now? Grey reveled in watching Tom grapple to find an activity for the group.

Though most employees of the Pisa bus terminal spoke English, Tom struggled. "What're our non-Pisa options?" he asked the portly, bespectacled ticket vendor.

"Options?" the man responded.

Oblivious to the absurd at play, Tom added irrelevant detail. "Yeah, where can we go insteadda back to Florence?"

The man peered down through his bifocals, considered his schedule and then back up, still bewildered. "Anywhere," he answered.

Tom raised his voice and became the self-righteous American. "I mean, where can we go today? Where can we go to see somethin' before sunset?"

The man adjusted his glasses and again consulted the ferry timetable as if it might provide divine intervention. Grey was amused, certain that Tom would never ask for help. Nor would Grey offer. It was perfect vengeance—watching a foe drown in his own inadequacy.

Out of either civility or her own impatience, the girl waiting in line behind them took up Tom's cause. She was tiny, maybe five-feet tall, with a waist no bigger than Grey's thigh, a bare tanned waist against which her equally tanned thin-wristed arms crossed. The white tips of her long fingernails tapped against her protruding ribs. Grey had never seen a French manicure before and wondered why one would be so garish as to draw attention to the dead part of the nail. "Go to Aelba. Eesa beery near." Sensing their indecision, she added, " . . . eend *multo bella*."

"Elba?" Miriam questioned. "Isn't that the island that Napoleon was exiled to?"

The girl rolled her eyes. (Few women liked Miriam.) "*Sì*, et ees de island but et ees also de most beeutiful island en de Medeeteranean. End de ferry es cheep." Sensing their collective doubt, she added, "De beaches are de best en alla Europe."

A half-hour later they were on a bus heading even farther west. This was their first time off plan and they were all a bit uncomfortable, Tom most of all. What if it was a bust? A detour could be expensive. But it was his obstinacy that had prompted this deviation and his resulting distress was pure pleasure for Grey—enough for whatever it cost to spend a day on Elba.

Piombino was not the beautiful Mediterranean port town they had imagined; it was far more port than town. The bus dropped them off in a parking lot fenced in by billboards advertising competing ferry lines. Their doubt redoubled when they discovered roundtrip tickets cost twenty thousand lira. It was only twenty bucks but the two-thousand-to-one exchange rate made everything seem more expensive.

There was a quick conversation and tentative agreement that they should stay in Elba overnight since there was no way to get back in time for the last bus. This required paying for two rooms—their hostel in Florence and wherever they ended up in Elba. Tom squirmed. "Maybe we should just go back?"

Winking at Grey, Miriam argued that an impromptu adventure would add to the whole of the trip. She donned Tom's vibrato, "C'mon man, beach, babes, boobs."

Even Pete agreed. "What could it hurt?"

Tom couldn't risk taking the opposing stance.

The ferry was crowded but not with tourists. At least not with American tourists. Most passengers appeared to be Italian, their conversation and laughter a cacophony to the unaccustomed ear. The foursome made their way to an interior cabin and grabbed cross-aisle seats—Tom and Pete in front, Miriam and Grey behind. Waiting for everyone else to board, each settled in for the two-hour journey. A well-dressed family of five *scusi*'d themselves by Grey and sat down next to him (except for the good-looking mid-twenties son who crossed the aisle for the open seat next to Miriam). Grey leaned back, resting his head against the hard plastic seatback. He closed his eyes and enjoyed the dull vibration from the boat's engines.

At sea, Grey's victory was diluted; he lost his sure footing. What if they couldn't find a hotel? He hadn't packed his Dopp kit nor, he suspected, had the others. They probably hadn't so much as a toothbrush between them. It was the first time on the trip he felt ungrounded. It wasn't just that they had veered from his plan but the incoherence of the situation made him feel out of control and incompetent. He was at odds with the group and surrounded by unfamiliarity. He knew his restlessness was triggered by long-held encumbrances, but that didn't make him feel any better. Six months of preparation freed him from such anxiety. Now the sudden lack of structure was oppressive.

Grey spied the family beside him. The father, like son, was handsome with a strong profile. He was around fifty but with a full head of black hair slightly graying at the temples. He wore a pair of gold, wire-rimmed reading glasses and directed his attention to the paper in his lap. The mother was of similar esteem, her stylish hair, short, colored to that indistinguishable tint of muted blond common for women of her age and class. She herself was also indistinguishable, with her shapeless, pampered skin; pearl-encrusted earrings; and a predictable beige skirtsuit two shades darker than her cream, silk blouse. She was just so. She sat motionless, fixated on the ceiling-mounted television a couple of rows ahead. The two teenage girls, one or two years between them, were allowed to wear the fashion of the times, in moderation and from the right stores. They each had the long, straight, jet-black hair of their father, and probably mother. Both wore tight jeans with their eyes shadowed and nails painted to the exact shade of their respective colorful but tasteful tank tops. They giggled in whispers, their eyes darting in unison to Grey, and then back to each other. His return smile was vacant.

In front of him, across the aisle, sat Pete with his head down, reading his third novel of the trip. He was focused, distant. The few feet of red carpet between them seemed, as always, impassable. Pressure welling in his chest, Grey got up with the pretext of scoping out the boat. At the cabin door, he glanced back. Tom was fiddling with his camera, Pete, reading and Miriam, chatting with the son who, by the looks of it, was practicing more than his English. There was a balance of sorts. Maybe Grey was the outsider now.

On deck, he vied for a position at the rail from which, for a time, he contemplated the empty seascape before him. And then the island appeared in the distance, a speck of land upon the horizon.

Elba was indeed beautiful and the beaches were packed. Everyone's mood lifted, even Tom's. There was a collective spark, as if this could be the story of the trip— a day on a Mediterranean island which none of their friends had ever visited. Grey stopped and surveyed the landscape to get his bearings. He scanned the row of buildings ahead of them. "I'll catch up with you; I'm gonna find a room." He wanted to secure their hotel as well as bypass the embarrassing hunt-and-peck. Choosing a restaurant was bad enough but deciding a spot on the beach would be painful. They were all wearing T-shirts boasting some American product, event or institution. Until landing at Heathrow, Grey was unaware just how American the T-shirt-as-fashion was. But it was all they'd brought. He thought at least his '79 *Spoleto Festival* was, in its obscurity, more fitting. There was also Tom's damned camera that hung prominently around his neck. No, better they divide and conquer.

Grey expected Miriam to come with him and was taken aback when she decided to hang with the boys, especially since the Italian hunk had split off from his family and was tagging along as well. Not that he was jealous—Miriam was beyond trustworthy—but still.

"David, this is my boyfriend, Grey." She didn't say *David*, but *Daveed* like the statue.

"Nice to meet you," Grey said as they shook hands. David's response was more sneer than smile. Or so Grey thought. Yes, the sooner he found a room, the better.

He set off following a group of sunburned Germans who looked like they were in search of shade. Their hotel perhaps. As the path from the beach narrowed into a street lined with restaurants and shops, the crowd thickened. A quiet Mediterranean island Elba wasn't, at least not in August. It was apparently a popular vacation spot for Europeans. Of the throngs that surrounded him, none were speaking English. The dissonance was disorienting; he was unable to lock into anything. The Germans turned into a *farmacia*, probably to slather on some sunscreen and head back to the beach. Grey placed his palm over his forehead, pressing his thumb and middle finger into his temples, and then pushed his hair back by running his hand over the full expanse of his scalp. It was an unconscious gesture, one that he always did to force himself to pay attention to his surroundings. How was he going to find a hotel? He didn't even know where to begin. The streets vibrated with motion as far as he could see. The intensity reminded him of New York, the origin of their journey that seemed as distant in time as Elba was from their carefully mapped itinerary. He perused the street's signage, listening to the crowds for anything familiar.

He drifted. Even the congestion of New York City was more organized than this mob scene. Maybe it was because of New York's predictable grid of avenues and streets. Or maybe it was because New Yorkers didn't create such a commotion. New York crowds, in general, didn't speak, much less speak over one another. There might be a backdrop of street noise but that was weighted against the directedness of intention.

Grey recalled how they had been so quick to adopt Northern self-reliance, not asking anyone for help as they set out to hike from their Forty-second Street hostel to JFK. Any New Yorker and most tourists could have told them this was a bad idea. Pete had wanted to see the Village so they started off in the opposite direction of Brooklyn, hugging the Hudson while navigating the pedestrian-unfriendly West Side Highway. There was no shade and the midsummer heat radiated from the concrete and asphalt. They turned westward onto a tiny street and within steps, the heat faded. Trees stretched across the road; patches of filtered sunlight danced across the pavement. They sat on the cool sidewalk sharing a box of cinnamon rolls that Grey had picked up at a corner store by their hostel. Across the street, two handsome men in their mid-thirties were planting purple geraniums in urns that flanked their gate. *A Separate Peace,* Grey thought, an idea that was dispelled as soon as they resumed their journey and, at the end of the block, entered the Village. All of them, even Miriam, later confirmed their discomfort at the men with earrings who passed holding hands, and women with batik skirts and no bras who appeared lost, a decade out of step. At last they made it across the city to the Brooklyn Bridge. It was noon; they were behind schedule but still had time.

Six hours later they were lost and exhausted. The daylight and the neighborhood darkened. They became uneasy, glancing at each other, each hoping that one of them would acknowledge their misjudgment. Their silence was broken by a Brooklyn suburban housewife, one of four playing bridge on a card table erected in the middle of the sidewalk.

In Grey's mental reproduction, the scene was embellished with artistic license as the foursome stopped in mid-play and looked up at them in disbelief. He envisioned a frozen canvas of overdramatic bewilderment, a modern day Norman Rockwell painting that would be titled something like *A Curious Encounter.*

The reality was much less precise but infinitely more comical. Betty, a Brooklyn-born and raised townie who had no time for feigned NYC indifference, had stopped them as they tried to skirt around the obstructing table.

"Where d'ya think you're goin'? Three white boys and their big-tittied girlfriend, cruising down Flatbush with those neon mug-me-please backpacks at seven-thirty at night?"

When they told her they were headed to JFK, she promptly laid down her cards, rose to her feet and led them into her brownstone. They followed her through the hallway into the kitchen. As she picked up the receiver and dialed a cab service, she mulled them over, tapping her soft pack of Virginia Slims Menthols, ejecting three from its torn opening. She took one and pushed the other two back in. "People say that New York is dangerous. But it's not really, unless you're stupid." She crooked her head to shoulder the receiver so she could light her cigarette. As she waited on hold, she exhaled her words with spurts of smoke. "I fear that for you four, any city's going to be a bit of a risk."

5

"*Mon Dieu, tu es un idiot.*"

Recognition jolted Grey back. He looked around him, no idea what to search for, but zeroed in on three men sitting at an outdoor café. They were in the middle of some passionless debate. Grey first noticed the unmistakable shrug-pout and then he heard one of them speak.

"*Parlez vous anglais?*" Grey's French was limited to the classroom; his words were diffused with breathless nervousness.

The one in the middle considered Grey with ostensible bemusement and replied, "*Non.*"

Enlivened by a real conversation in French, his follow-through, to his and their surprise, was exact. "*Savez-vous où est un hotel?*"

Their smirks disappeared. The Frenchmen didn't feign indifference like New Yorkers; theirs was a birthright. The one on the left took a leisurely drag from his cigarette before responding, "*Quel hôtel?*"

Grey's confidence evaporated. He stuttered, unable to recall the word for *any*. Losing his tenor and accent, he lobbed. "*Un hôtel avec une libre chambre?*"

His opponent winked at his companions and attacked without mercy. The velocity of his reply was impossible. "*Ça va être dur de trouver un hôtel en cette saison, mais vous pouvez essayer la rue juste derrière. Il y'en a plein a bas.*" Fortunately, Grey understood much better than he spoke. Though the speed caught him off guard, he didn't fall for the confusion tactic of the long sentence. He caught the phrase "street behind this one" but acted as though he understood everything. Ending the conversation with "*Merci, au revoir,*" he sliced short, leaving no possibility of return.

Anger blurred his perception; he hated this situation, this dependency. He rounded the corner and scoured the street, oblivious to any of the three hotels in the block to his right. Next to him stood a rail-thin woman, lugging a massive Louis Vuitton trunk.

"*Scusi.*" Usually Grey was a Southern gentleman but his displaced anger had found a target. He glared at her with her white jeans, clingy low-cut white blouse, white stiletto heels, oversized Jackie-O sunglasses and a neck plated in gold.

"*Scusi,*" he heard in surround—the second squeaky plea from this Italian moll beside him accompanied by a gruff baritone from behind. When a broad, muscular arm elbowed into his side, Grey spun around to see attached to it, a broad, muscular middle-aged man wearing a broad, unequivocal scowl. As the man grabbed the trunk, he pushed Grey aside. That Grey was blocking an entrance did not dawn on him and if it weren't for the porter's intimidating size, things could have turned ugly. But a contemplative pause allowed a moment of undefiled consideration. In front of Grey was a reception desk above which a sign read, *Crystal Hotel.*

Sunglasses perched atop her head, Ms. faux-Versace was now at the counter waving her hands in the burly clerk's face. In his short three days in Italy, Grey realized that Italians checking into hotels had to argue over the rate. It was a cultural thing. He was in no mood to wait the requisite ten to twenty minutes. He became Tom, the entitled American tourist asking in defiant English, "Excuse me but do you have any rooms available?" They looked over, stupefied by the interruption. Grey notched up the volume and elongated each word. "Doooo you-uuu haaaave aaaaa roooom fooooor ooooooone niiiiight?"

They eyed him without regard until they assumed his diatribe to be complete, and then returned to their ritual. Grey had no choice but to see the scene through. His anger defused, he turned his attention to the lobby. It was a typical European *pensione* with white, gray-veined marble floors and dark paneled walls. *Even on a beach . . .* His musing was interrupted by a teenage girl who emerged from a back room behind the desk.

He pounced. "*Parlate inglese?*"

"A leettle."

Over the past few weeks, Grey had discovered that, though in the U.S.

speaking *a little* of a foreign language meant two or three words, in Europe it meant semi-fluently. In his excitement, his voice pitched higher than normal. "Great! I need a room for one night."

Her accent was thicker but with a softer, more velvety lilt than the girl at the train station. "No eesa poseeble en eeny otel onna de eesland. Today ees Asoompsione Day. Alla day otels eesa close-ed or eesa feel-ed seence day beegeennin of da year. Ima soorry."

"You've gotta be kidding. There's nothing?" She shook her head, redirecting her attention down to some loose papers she was holding.

"Can you call around?"

"*Per favore*, eef you wheet fer ze meeneger." She pointed her now-stapled papers toward the porter-registrar-bellhop-and-apparently-manager who, trunk in arms, was following his newest guest up the stairs.

Grey sighed. "Sure, I'll be right outside." His adrenaline was spent; he walked out and sat down on a bench next to the hotel's entrance. "Stupid, stupid, stupid," he mumbled to himself as he dropped his head into his hands. His long hair draped across his face, exaggerating his defeatism.

6

Grey felt someone's eyes upon him.

A man carrying a toolbox stood before the bench. Behind him, the overhead sun was so bright that he was shrouded in opposing darkness, a hallowed shadow. "Wunna rum?"

Grey's response was immediate and respectfully Italian. "Sì." As he raised his hand to his brow, the man's aura faded.

Still blinded, Grey could distinguish only the movement of the man's lips. "Fur you ulone?"

Grey paused and answered in a slow Spang-Ital-ish, "*Per me and tres amigos,*" which devolved to fast English, "but we can all sleep in one room." The man tilted his head to one side. Allowing no time for rebuttal, Grey added, "We can sleep on the floor."

The man's face began to come into view. There was something odd about his eyes but he turned too fast for Grey to get a good picture of him. He was already walking; his sonorous voice projected behind him. "Come."

Grey hesitated but resisted his cautionary nature and asked no further questions. Instead he followed rather than joined. In rationalizing this etiquette, he convinced himself that, without being able to speak Italian, he would make the man uncomfortable by his side. His lag was just a few steps.

Like this they crossed town, Grey maintaining his guarded distance, staring straight ahead at the stranger whom he followed. He had been on Elba for over an hour and if pressed, couldn't describe the island in a broad sense. He could outline the crag of land as pictured from the ferry, the crowded street, the café table with the three Frenchmen, the lobby of the Crystal Hotel and the backside of a man carrying a toolbox. From peripheral awareness, he also knew its narrow side streets, the desert-like dryness and the presence of the sea. But for the most part, his hour on Elba had been one of myopic resolve. Now his central focus was the languid movements of his intended host.

Antonio's walk was as hypnotic as the distant Elba had been on the edge of the horizon, its cadence as reassuring as a well-articulated argument. His stride was open and long, without reserve; his hips swayed with no resistance, an undulation almost feminine but so natural it was utterly male. There was fluidity in the way he moved, like he was floating on land. With every step, Grey trusted him more.

"Mari!" Antonio called as he entered the gate of a nondescript single-story house on an even less descript street. A beautiful porcelain-skinned woman emerged, not much older than Grey. Trailing behind her were two young children. Antonio set down his toolbox, bent onto one knee and extended his arms. The children ran to him. Grey admired this open affection; it had not been an element of his youth.

It wasn't a *pensione* as Grey had expected, but a small family home. At first Grey wondered if there might be an adjoining guesthouse though he saw no indication of one. Maria was reticent when Antonio introduced the idea of opening their home to strangers. Their strained discussion was evidenced not as much by their tone as by the reactions of the children who retreated behind their father's legs. Grey stuck his hands into his pockets and looked away.

From what he could see, the room in which they stood served as foyer, kitchen, living room and playground. Other than a corner of kitchen appliances, there was little delineation. The entire terracotta floor was bare, its octagonal tiles the only element that brought a semblance of order to the space. Two tables dominated the area in front of sliding glass doors that extended across most of the back wall. The glare of the bright afternoon sun, reflecting from the doors' glass smudged with small handprints, filled the room with sunlight. There was a half-finished toddler puzzle on the table closest to the kitchen and on the other, two plastic eating bowls, one blue, one yellow. All the chairs were pulled away from the table in disarray. Neither the tables' design nor their incongruous placement helped define a separate space yet their combined expanse with the scattershot of chairs was overcrowding even in such a large room. The antithesis of this disorder was the institutional front half of the room with a couch, armchair and old console television set, all backed to the wall as though they had been moved for some sort of group exercise.

Grey's attention returned to the family, a stark contrast to the bland decor. Antonio and Maria were a striking couple. In the context of the familial setting, Grey could now see the man before him. The olive of his skin deepened in juxtaposition to Maria's pallor. He was about five-ten with a head of dark curls framing face in a casual manner that reminded Grey of old photos he'd seen of flower children from the '6os. His sinewy body was a rich network of long banded muscles honed from a life of manual transport and labor. His eyes were indeed odd: translucent green ringed by a single dark band of cobalt blue, gilded with small flakes of complementary colors like Italian glass tiles. They seemed to shine from an internal light source, reminding Grey of the young Afghani girl who had just appeared on the cover of the National Geographic, whose burka-askew image had so mesmerized the world that, overnight, she had become a haunting international symbol of the repression of beauty.

Maria's eyes of brown-black absorbed the delicate rays of Antonio's with a fierce gravity. That she ruled this household was clear, not with an aggressive dominance but a mutual assumption of her domesticity that resonated through her every pore. Grey could see that Antonio was presenting the idea, not the decision. The decision was Maria's to make.

At five-eight she stood a little shorter than he, tall for an Italian woman. Like Grey's mother . . . or Miriam. Waves of deep brown hair fell just past her shoulders, its thickness drawing an exact hairline that bound her pale, elongated face—a Modigliani harvest moon against a starless sky. Erect, arms crossed beneath her breasts, she was standing right foot angled in front of the left in a dancer's third. The children tugged at Antonio's pants legs—unspoken support of his position—and waited for their mother to succumb. There was familiarity in this scene that made obvious the inevitable outcome.

She glanced over at Grey and locked her eyes onto his for just an instant, and in that instant, Grey felt her power, and her judgment. He tried to hold her gaze but instead, eluded scrutiny by concentrating over her shoulder to the wall behind. She turned back to her husband.

On the wall hung seven or eight photographs—a typical family picture wall, a cross-cultural touchstone on which he focused to avoid the awkwardness of the situation. In the center, side by side, were two individual wedding photos.

They married young, eighteen perhaps. Maria wore her hair up. Maybe it was the absence of color around her pale skin or maybe something else, but her eyes, black marbles against her white oval face, appeared distant and sad. Antonio, on the other hand, looked ready for his wedding night. He was downright gangly, all arms and legs, but it was easy to see the man he would become. His curly hair was long and fell around his shoulders. He seemed uncomfortable in a suit but in it, he was even more handsome. In the black and white photo his green eyes were gray, ablaze with expectation.

Grey thought of the photographs his mother had featured in the hallway of his childhood home. It was a short expanse broken by doors leading to the three bedrooms and the main bathroom. The walls were covered with white vinyl wallpaper upon which green Victorian lovers wooed under a willow tree, repeating their courtship every three inches or so. On the only unbroken stretch of wall big enough, hung four photos. Dale, Steve and Grey peered out from a triptych frame, all shaven-headed and smiley, each with a different plaid shirt over a solid dickie—the faux turtleneck swatches of fabric that enabled middle-class Southern children that suave sophisticated '70s look without having to wear a real sweater. The swollen appearance of Grey's stubbled head in relation to the other two boys' slimmer, more normal heads had been a joke that Dale and Steve would taunt him with throughout his childhood, even into their teenage years, until the photos mysteriously vanished when they moved to a new house.

The fourth picture was of her. She was very young and Grey thought, astoundingly beautiful, a glamorous movie star in a fitted suit and white gloves with an enormous orchid pinned on her wide lapel. Leaning against an old-fashioned armchair, she stared into the camera. Her eyes radiated from the frame with a noble serenity that Grey had never seen on his mother's face in real life. When alone in the house, he sometimes took the picture from the wall and pored over its every detail, trying to conceive the woman she once was.

One day Grey overheard his mother tell a visitor that it was her wedding picture. He didn't consider it odd that his father was absent from the photo, or even from the picture wall itself.

Silence brought him back. He returned to find Antonio gone and Maria studying him. She wore a look of courtesy; she had decided but was not convinced.

The back of the house was more plausible; there was natural flow and relationship from one room to the next. Through mostly demonstration and gesticulation, Maria covered the basics with Grey. She led him to a small room with two twin beds, a bathroom that she insinuated was for more than just them (he assumed it was the only one in the house) and then explained that dinner was at five. Afterward, on the front doorstep, he leaned down to shake the two limp hands of the children who had been shadowing his tour.

"*Il mio nome è Grey,*" he uttered, one of the three or four Italian phrases he had picked up from his Berlitz pocket guide. They shied farther behind their mother.

When he rose, Maria's demeanor had shifted. She was transformed from household matriarch to young mother, appreciative of attention given to her children. From the interior side of the open doorway, she smiled for the first time since his arrival. "Giuseppe e Juliana."

7

With their accommodations secured, Grey relaxed. What had been, in his quest for a hotel, the undecipherable chatter of the streets was now joyous laughter. Dusty heat became the arid breeze of an unexplored arcadia.

He stopped at the ferry building to check the schedule for the following day. There was a twelve-ten and a two-thirty; either would work for them to catch a bus back to Florence before nightfall. Having determined where they were staying and when they were leaving, he could now let Elba wash over him. The blue-green of the Mediterranean took on more luxurious hues.

The beach was overwhelming; even at four in the afternoon it was packed, a sea of flesh. The skimpiness of most bathing suits and toplessness of many women lived up to the stories all-American male, college-aged tourists regaled of European beaches. Grey smiled, wondering how Miriam and Tom were able to conceal from their Italian guest their opposite reactions to public nudity. Tom probably wouldn't; he would ogle and guffaw, and it would infuriate Miriam not to be able to take him to task for it. But she would do her best to ignore him; she would be cool and collected, acting like it was nothing new. Grey would hear about it later. Come to think of it, there was no urgency to get back. Instead he looked out to the sea.

As usual, eyes turned toward him. It wasn't his inappropriate clothes or good looks, not that he couldn't turn a few heads with either. It was his dreaminess. He seemed unaware of people around him. He moseyed his way down the beach, stopping every now and then to gaze out to water or to analyze any random insignificance that caught his eye. He wouldn't bend over; instead he planted his feet and dropped his body straight down. His broad shoulders would lodge between open knees, a gymnast about to tumble, as he remained steadfast, squatting, fixated on some stone or shell as though it were a precious jewel. His hair, the same color and fineness of the sand, hung down, shielding his face from the bathers on the beach. It was as if he were searching for something in that stone, something that he had lost, or never had. People stared. They always stared.

He knew they were watching him and it made him withdraw even further. It was in crowds that Grey was the most alone. He would distance himself from everything human, choosing instead to focus on inanimate details around him, if he made it out of his head at all. He continued to search down the endless strand past the inquisitive faces to the ever-changing border where the sea met the sand. Even amidst his distraction, he had no fears about finding the others. He did however fear what he found: a loud, embarrassing Tom sidled next to two unfortunately accommodating Texan girls. Unfortunate in that they were accommodating and unfortunate that they were unmistakably Texan. SMU. The three of them were on the beach what a panhandler was on the New York subway—an intrusion that made itself known regardless of collective avoidance. Miriam, Pete and David were sitting a good disassociated five feet away.

Grey approached without calling attention to himself. He quietly sat down by Miriam and relayed to her the details of their lodging.

" . . . a nice family." His last words were amplified by a break in Tom's conversation.

Tom followed the girls' eyes and rubbernecked back over his shoulder at Grey. "Dude, ya finally made it! Whudja find?"

Grey kept his reply short and unobtrusive. "Probably the last room on Elba."

"Cool." Tom returned to his audience.

An attractive Marcia Brady-blonde, sporting, in character, a yellow polka-dot bikini, smiled up at Grey. "Hi, I'm Katrina." Her companion, similar in appearance but somewhat less so in every cutesy category, an obvious Jan to Katrina's Marcia, followed her lead. "And I'm Daniella."

"I'm Grey," he said, extending his hand. "Pleased to meet you."

Miriam was already to her feet before the second hand was shook. "Grey do you mind walking me to the house; I need to go to the loo." Two days in London and Miriam now said *loo.*

"Sure." Grey held out his arm. She reached past his hand to his forearm, a more intimate touch. He lifted her to him.

Unabashed, Katrina winked at Grey. "Come back soon." She raised and protruded her shoulders in practiced innocence that accentuated her polka-dotted cleavage. She did not look at Miriam when asking her to "tell Grey about tonight" but locked her polka-dot-matching blue eyes onto Grey's. "We're gonna rock this rock of an island." She shot up her one free arm, punctuating the moment, her elbow hyper extending as cheerleaders' elbows so often do.

They hadn't walked two feet, still well within earshot, when Miriam ranted, "You have got to be fucking kidding me." Miriam never cussed, much less used the F-word. And as an adjective to boot—she sounded like a pro.

Grey grabbed her hand. "So what's Dav-eed like?"

Miriam turned to him with an askant look that said *how do you always know the perfect thing to say?* Then she tightened her grip and pulled him headlong toward the surf. He didn't resist; they ran until they fell laughing into the water. He grabbed her before she could regain her footing, pulled her to him and kissed her. The warm, salty water tasted good on her mouth. Walking back to shore, hand in hand, people again stared, but the only ones looking at Grey were filled with envy. Her red scalloped silk bra though her clinging transparent T-shirt was sexier than any flat-chested European bare breasts could ever be. And she knew it.

Miriam instantly won over Giuseppe and Juliana. Upon meeting them, she dropped to her knees, stuck out her bottom lip, and rolled her eyes upward. They giggled with acceptance, leaving their mother's side to follow Miriam back to the transformed guest bedroom.

There were now two additional pallets encompassing almost the entire floor space and a towel on each bed. It was close quarters but better than they had had in Amsterdam. At least they didn't have their backpacks to clutter the room or hashish smoke seeping through every crevice. Some type of potpourri was scattered on the windowsill around a small statue of the Virgin Mary. Grey didn't remember it being there before.

Twenty minutes later Miriam returned after being shown both the bathroom and Juliana's goldfish. "How adorable is this," she said, shutting the door behind her.

"Ain't it though?" Grey was lying on one of the pallets reading his journal.

Miriam walked over to the window. "I'm so glad you're actually using your gift. Now at least there'll be some record of what goes on inside that head of yours." Without skipping a beat, she added, "Hey, can I wear your shirt until mine dries?"

She looked around. Grey lay with his eyes closed, the journal resting on his chest. "Babe, are you okay?"

Miriam had given Grey the journal in New York. Pete and Tom bowed out of the evening, both claiming exhaustion, and she tricked him into getting dressed by saying she wanted to check out the Ford modeling agency and who knew who might just walk out as they were passing by, maybe Eileen herself. Instead she took him to a new, swanky restaurant called Café Luxembourg, a stylized Deco place with a zinc-countered bar on which sat trays of miniature gherkin pickles and little stainless trees of hardboiled eggs. She had read about it in *The New Yorker* and had called two months ahead to get reservations. They ordered Tom Collins, the only real cocktail that Miriam would drink. After dinner the waitress served a gift wrapped in a colorful map of the world and an old-fashioned ice cream sundae with one white birthday candle atop. Understated. Miriam's purse was too small; she must have either mailed or had someone else bring the present to the restaurant. She couldn't have brought it in herself; they hadn't been apart since they landed.

Instead of appreciative, he was glib. "What's the occasion?"

"Life."

Miriam wore the simple string of pearls her mother had given her before she died. They were a family heirloom that went back three generations. Miriam worried so much about their being stolen that she rented a safe deposit box just for them. There was no way that she was going to bring the pearls to Europe and so she must have some way to get them back to Raleigh, maybe the same way she'd got his present here. This evening had taken a great deal of planning.

The journal's leather was soft and worn; upon its pages, words were meant to be serious, meaningful. He opened it, and on the inside cover was pinned a simple silver chain. Below, two handwritten lines:

In these pages will be memories and around your neck this chain will

forever remind you.
Love, Miriam.

He reached across the table and grabbed her hand. "Remind me of what—this night or how absolutely incredible you are?"

Her eyes searched his for something, something she didn't find. "That's for you to decide."

She stepped over the other pallet, knelt beside him and cupped his cheek in her hand. "I didn't mean to sound bitchy; it really does feel great to see you using the journal. You're so private and sometimes I think it'd be great if you had a confidant besides me." He opened his eyes.

Her thick hair was almost dry and had begun to frizz into a Bardot dishevel. A thin line of mascara had trickled down her cheek and disappeared under her chin, reemerging to ride her collarbone downward until it faded to the color of her skin. She was the sexiest woman he had ever seen.

"And I'm sure as hell not gonna let that be another woman."

In his eyes she now found what she had been searching for. She straddled his waist. "Do you wanna make a memory?"

Grey pulled himself up onto his elbows and nodded toward the door. "I think we've got company."

Giuseppe was standing, silent, in the doorway with the taller Juliana behind him peeking over his shoulder.

8

Miriam stood at the sill, looking out the window. "Let's get back; the boys are gonna wonder where we are."

Grey craned his neck to respond. She had pulled her hair back in a ponytail; Grey's T-shirt covered her bathing suit, reaching all the way down to her mid-thigh. "Go on, that ferry ride made me a bit queasy. I'm gonna read a while."

She picked up the Virgin statue and turned it over to examine the forger's mark. Miriam collected European ceramics, mostly Hummels, but in the past year had branched out into Lladros. She was now in search of an Italian master. "Are you sure? You're not still mad about the journal comment, are you?"

He turned back around and grabbed the journal from the floor where it had fallen during their abbreviated interlude. "I was never mad; c'mon, you know me better than that."

She bent over him from behind and kissed him upside down. "I know you well enough to know that ya wanna be alone."

"Dinner's at five—we shouldn't be late," he told her as she was walking out the door.

She turned back and cocked her head. "Babe, I'll be back long before then. Think I wanna hang out with Tom and that ridiculous pair of bimbos?"

Maria stopped Miriam in the hallway and in broken English apologized for not having a separate bedroom for her. "Puhlee-eeease, you have done so much." Miriam's response was muffled through the closed door but its Southern deference rang clear. Until Maria asked if Miriam would mind sleeping in the living room. While there was no mention of what Giuseppe and Juliana had seen, it was obvious she knew. Miriam's solicitude became obsequious; Grey was certain her cheeks burned red with embarrassment. That they had crossed propriety in this woman's home would mortify Miriam. He fought the urge to go out and comfort her but knew it would only make things worse. Miriam would want to pretend it never happened and do everything she could to win this woman and her children's favor. In a week or two they could discuss it but not now. Grey opened the journal to the first page.

> *Don't know what I'm supposed to write here. Who knows maybe my grandkids will read this some day so I probably should keep it clean. Grey Tigrett III, if you are reading this, let me first say that your grandmother was a babe in her heyday (in case "babe" doesn't stand the linguistic test of time, it means a captivating, cultured woman with a great rack).*

Serious words, these weren't. He was tempted to cross it out but figured that it went against the rules of journaling. He flipped through the pages and skimmed some other entries.

> *Eight hours into the flight and haven't slept. Pete and I talked until he finally drifted off a couple of minutes ago. Can't believe that in a few hours we'll be in London.*

> *Who knew the white cliffs of Dover were really white? Actually made of chalk. Two hours early to hydroplane. The others are killing time in a pub while I climbed up here. Up here alone—just me, the cliffs, and the English Channel disappearing into the fog that hovers just off shore. It's a bit desolate. I feel like Heathcliff in Wuthering Heights. God that sounds so gay.*

Gradually, from Calais to Rome, the journal became less chronicling and more introspective.

> *Tom is such a prick. I'm not going to let him ruin this trip. He will not wedge us apart. I feel Miriam slipping from me but I think it's because everything here is so . . . foreign. I'm sure things will be OK once we're back. But Pete feels miles away. We can't seem to get past this stupid*

*awkwardness between us. I was hoping we would on this trip. I'm sure
we will if Tom quits butting his f_____ nose in.*

He had written his final entry on the ferry as he stood upon the deck and
watched the island emerge into view.

*Before I saw Elba, there was nothing but sea and sky. Then it appeared
small on the horizon, an insignificant fleck just below the vanishing
point. On the water perspectives are not forged from hard angles. No
perfect square is centered on the edge of the sea. The imminence is the
same, yet the path, variable. Nascent and amorphous, the island bobs
up, down, right and left as the boat stays its course.*

*What would it be like to live on the water—the lack of rigidity, a
respectful coexistence with impermanence? The sea, the weather, even
the coastline. I've never been on an island . . . unless New York counts.
But then New York denies, or rather has overcome, this ambiguity. It
is, like the American culture itself, with its uncompromising perennity,
the consummate example of nature in defiance.*

He couldn't concentrate. What did he want to say about Elba—that he was
a loser for holing himself up inside while the others were on the beach enjoying
the sun and meeting new people, even if they were annoying Texan teases? He
thought about all the times, as a child, he had stayed inside and read, even when
his mother tried to shoo him outdoors.

Sometimes she nudged: "It's such a beautiful day." Others, she threatened:
"Well, if you stay in you're gonna have to help me clean this sty of a house."
Often Grey would do just that. In truth, these times working together as a mother-
son team were some of his best childhood memories. She would be on her yellow-
latex-glove-covered hands and knees, hair tied back in a scarf, scrubbing the
bathtub with Comet, while he was her gopher for whatever she needed—bring
her a roll of paper towels, change the music, listen to her prattle. She would tell
him of her youth, stories that he cherished, stories that he preferred far more than
his book or the kickball game his friends were playing down the street.

Again, Grey felt his stare. He looked up. As before, Grey was blinded by an aura, but he couldn't figure out the source of the light. Then it was gone. Antonio stood dripping in the doorway. He was wearing a bikini-cut bathing suit, a style that on a man Grey dismissed as contrived and vulgar. The wet suit clung to him, its red silk accentuating both copper skin and masculinity. Yet it was not vulgar nor was Grey dismissive. Antonio shut the door. Grey's breath became shallow, his senses magnified. His heart was pounding in his ears. The sunlight from the room's window shimmered against Antonio's wet body. Every pixel of color and light dilated. The visual gestalt was assaulting; Grey was forced to look away. He heard Giuseppe and Juliana outside playing. Wetness pressed against him, smeared over his body. Antonio's breath was hot and dry like the Mediterranean breeze. Grey tried to open his eyes, but they were glued shut. His breath quickened. With all of his concentration he strained to force his eyes open. His eyelashes fluttered. Antonio's hand pressed against his lower stomach and slid down into his underwear. Grey's clenched body began to spasm.

"Grey!" Grey's eyes snapped open. Pete was in the doorway, dry and fully dressed. Grey was drenched in sweat, shaking with unfulfilled desire. He faked a yawn and rolled over with a stretch. Pete continued, "It's four forty-five and Miriam said we were eating at five. I didn't see anyone in the kitchen—are ya sure?"

Grey replied through a second feigned yawn, "That's what I was told. Where's Miriam?" His pretend sluggishness squandered enough time for his erection to subside.

"She went to the drugstore for something, said she'd be back by five."

Grey put on Miriam's now-dry T-shirt. It was too tight and outlined the athletic build he usually hid under baggy clothes.

They went back to the common room and found Maria. Grey attempted the introductions but Pete took over. Aligning with their respective foreign language studies, Pete had brushed up on his Italian; Tom, German; and Grey, French with the belief that limited conversational ability might be required in some situations. Until Elba, every tricky scenario included someone who spoke enough English for them to muddle through. Within twenty-four hours, all three of their language skills would be tested.

After a successful interchange, Pete told Grey that dinner was at six, not five and that when he asked what they could do, Maria suggested they buy a bottle of wine. Pete glowed at his conquest, becoming unusually talkative as they walked into town. He apologized for inviting Tom. They discussed how Tom's presence had spoiled something, had disturbed their special camaraderie that was, in part, shared expectations but mostly due to their deep friendship that had grown over their four years together. An intimacy in which Tom played no part. Grey was happy to discover that Pete had also anticipated this trip as an unforgettable cap to their college experience. And now, with Tom, it was less meaningful. Pete paused before adding that it didn't need to be less fun.

They walked in silence for a few minutes with a familiar tension building between them. Pete then began to reflect on their adventure to date. They laughed about backpacking to JFK, the hashish incident in Amsterdam, and the hundred-and-one-degree Rhine River trip; agreed about the magic of Salzburg; and then turned serious when Pete shared his reaction to the Venice blowout.

Grey listened, interjecting "uh-huhs" and "yeahs" to keep the conversation moving. It was times like these, alone, Pete advising him on this or that, when his attraction would surface full-force. As Pete's monologue expanded and contracted, as it jumped from one random non sequitur to the next, they merged into a sort of natural unison, a common to-and-fro. It was no coincidence that Pete's presence in the doorway had triggered his dream. But it was the memory of Antonio's image that forced Grey to readjust himself mid-stride.

"Man, you need to get laid." Pete guffawed, sounding like Tom. "You're hard all the time." But his laugh was good-natured. "I, of all people, can understand your two's waiting until marriage but puh-leasse." Grey stopped. Pete grabbed his arm and pulled him forward. "Hey c'mon, we're not kids; you're way too sensitive. Boners and sex are no longer taboo." He leaned in and whispered provocatively. "Or jerking off for that matter." Pete paused long enough to make Grey wonder if this was a rebuke, a tease, or both. His final comment didn't just sound like, it was, dead-on Tom. "Hey, don't be such a priss."

Grey was hurt but managed an it's-no-big-deal performance. "Which one do you think Tom will sack?"

Pete was certain. "Are you kiddin'? Katrina for sure."

Grey raised an eyebrow. "I wouldn't be surprised if he has that *Summer*

Lovers European three-way he went on and on about on the plane."

On their return to the house, Grey applauded Pete's navigation of the wine purchase with a frat-boy congratulatory slap on the back. When they arrived the two tables had been pushed together and were already set except for one seat where Miriam was helping Giuseppe and Juliana finish their puzzle. "Where's Tom?" Grey asked.

"He decided to skip dinner and meet Katrina and Daniella for a drink instead," Miriam replied while pretending she couldn't distinguish between the remaining few puzzle pieces and being spurred on by her adoring helpers.

Maria stood at the sink cutting either a zucchini or a cucumber for a stew she was making that smelled fantastic. She called it something like *gurglingone*. Pete tried to translate Grey's joke about the boiling pot's "gurgling on." Maria smiled politely. Antonio was sitting in the middle of the room, watching some TV news program, but when Maria signaled dinnertime, he pushed his chair back against the wall and walked over to his place at the head of the table. She had trained him well. Grey avoided Antonio's eyes, ashamed that he had not yet purged his dream. There was an uneasy moment as they sat down but it was soon dispelled as Giuseppe, sitting between Grey and Miriam, reached up and grabbed their hands. Everyone followed suit. Maria's hand, still hot from the kitchen, was small in Grey's; it felt almost as much like a child's as Giuseppe's. Antonio and Giuseppe exchanged a father-son look that confirmed Giuseppe would say grace. Breathless with reverence, Giuseppe managed to turn what started as ten or so word prayer into a full minute recital that Pete later told them was basically the Italian version of "God is great; God is good; let us thank Him for our food" but that Giuseppe had lopped on special blessings for everything from his parents to Juliana's goldfish to a lot of things Pete couldn't understand. Before everyone released hands, Antonio added, "And God bleess our geests." The meal was short; after grace, no adult spoke unless responding to one of the children. The quiet didn't seem normal but it didn't seem tense either, probably the natural result of the language barrier or the distraction of the stew's savor. After dinner Grey and Miriam helped Maria clear as Pete, with newfound confidence in his Italian, tried initiating a conversation with a disinterested Antonio about America's European foreign policy.

With the last dish dry, Pete set out to meet Tom for an evening with the girls, and Maria invited Grey and Miriam to join her and the children for the Feast of the Assumption festival in town. Grey bowed out, telling Miriam that his stomach still wasn't quite right and he thought he should rest. She said she would stay with him, but he urged her to go alone.

"Anyway," he lied, "I promised Pete that I would join him and Tom later to give him an excuse to leave early. Who knows, maybe I can talk Pete into peeling off and coming to the festival with me." They joked that if they could orchestrate an entire night without Tom, Grey's stomachache was worth it.

9

Grey collapsed onto his pallet. He cringed at the memory of Pete's words.

Miriam and Grey had been sleeping together for over a year but had told no one. When she moved into his room, she was adamant to him and everyone they knew that this did not mean they were going to have sex. She was waiting until she had a ring on her finger. "And not just an engagement ring." In the beginning she was charmed by his restraint. Then she was appreciative. After a few months of not even drunken attempts, she was dubious. Finally, it was she who made the first move. She was still the initiator. Not that, once prompted, he didn't get into it; he did. He just never thought about it. His fantasies were triggered by another member of the household—Pete. He was hoping that on this trip there would somehow be a transference of this desire. But to Miriam, not another man.

Beside his pallet his journal lay open. He picked it up and read,

August 15th, Elba—What am I doing

He must have fallen asleep while writing about the Pete incident. The words appeared less an unfinished thought than an existential life quandary. *Was that what it was?* Grey shut the journal and put it back in his suitcase. He got up, determined and antsy.

He went into the common room, to the glass doors. The sun was lower in the sky and not so glaring. There was a terrace off of which extended a small olive grove. Light streamed through the olive trees. Sunlight through trees always calmed him; Grey could lie for hours under a sun-basked tree, exploring myriad shapes and shades of green the sun made as it migrated across its branches.

Outside, his distress waned. An ungrouted stone wall extended back from the outer edges of the terrace and sloped up the hill to create the narrow grove. Orange plastic netting lay beneath the trees to harvest the olives. The adjacent homes also had backyards—some with vegetable gardens, some with flowers, one other about three houses down with a similar grove. Neither the street nor the house had given any hint of this charm.

Grey wandered into the trees, sidestepping the netting so as not to tear it. The orange plastic glittered with what little light penetrated the tree's canopy. Not too far up the hill was the back wall that stretched across the lot to the grove's farthest corner from the house. Here, it was as tall as Grey; he couldn't see over it. Away from the terrace, the stones were larger, less ornamental. Between them, easy footholds. Grey climbed on top. He gazed across the rectangular parcels of land down to the sea. Unlike the horizon from the ferry, there was no destination, no singular vanishing point—just the shoreline and the open sea.

He began to cry. His world was one of fantasy caught in a time and age past where his desires could be contained in the realm of imagination, where reality had not yet contaminated the purity of unrequited dreams. He did not want to let go; yet he could not continue to live the life of the child he no longer was. He decided to join Miriam. As he climbed from the wall, the sea disappeared.

Antonio stood inside, behind the glass doorway; he seemed surprised to see Grey emerging from the trees. He smiled.

This time they walked side by side, their silence no longer disquieting. They walked toward the beach. The pre-dusk sun was not strong but still hung over the island. For a while there were others, a crowd joyous and laughing, the music from the streets ahead pulling them forward. They branched away, down, alone again, to the shore, to a rowboat docked on a small pier. Antonio nodded for Grey to get in. Grey sat facing the water; Antonio did not correct him. Grey shut his eyes and enjoyed the warm sea air against his face.

They stopped at a buoy near one of the larger rocks just off the remote end of the beach. Grey turned around to see Antonio hoisting the buoy's rope into the boat. Antonio's hands were covered in red splotches, an allergy or skin condition. Grey looked down through the water, surprised at how clear it was. The sandy floor was spotted with some sort of seaweed or plant. It appeared to be only ten feet deep but it was an illusion of perspective. He knew this because the cage attached to the rope was almost imperceptible. Then, as it came into view, there was a disturbance in its smooth ascension. Trapped inside, a crab struggled as the cage swelled, rising into the lighter waters until, at last, it reached the surface. Antonio pulled the cage into the boat. The sun met Elba's highest peak. Everything turned orange—the air, the sea, the crab. Antonio's eyes. The boat drifted, and with it, the sun. It was now behind Antonio. For the third time, Grey was blinded to him. He heard a splash and turned back to the sea. The sun had dropped behind the peak; orange faded to ochre. The cage lay empty in the bottom of the boat. Antonio was nowhere to be seen.

The water glimmered with ambient light. The situation was absurd—his dreams invoked reality and now his reality evoked dreams. Antonio appeared just off the bow. He splashed Grey and called out, "Sweem?" His voice broke the proscenium; reality challenged the surreal. Like a morning dream integrating the surrounding sounds of daybreak, the moment expanded to include Antonio's spoken word. Grey didn't move. Staring across the water into Antonio's eyes, he tried to absorb their light.

Antonio dipped again under the water. The contrasting movements of the surface above him refracted as a prism, a Guernica of geometries. He disappeared beneath the boat and came up next to Grey. Resting his arms on the boat's edge, he lowered his head and closed his eyes. Grey remained still, listening to Antonio's slowing breath. He looked past him into the water. Without the sun's direct light, its clarity was even more astonishing. Antonio's naked body hung limp, surrendering to the water's sway. Grey averted his eyes into the boat where he now noticed Antonio's clothes neatly tucked beneath the plank where he had been sitting. Grey tuned back to him. Antonio's breathing had calmed, no longer visible against the hair of his forearm. All was quiet except the sea's gentle lap against the boat's hull. Antonio opened his eyes. "Sweem?" he asked a second time.

Either *Yes* or *No* would have broken the tension. Grey's mouth was dry; his voice cracked, "*Freddo?*" a question that conveyed both his ability to swim and maintained the power structure in play.

Twilight receded to night; ochre faded to red. The water enveloped him. Tendrils of diffuse light spiraled upward, framing the boat's hull, its darkness floating like Elba but the water met no sky. The image dimmed; the outline of the boat collapsed and merged into the sea.

Antonio's forcefulness belied the sensuality of the Mediterranean's embrace. He pressed into Grey's back from behind, wrapping his arms around Grey's chest. His knuckles slid down against the ridges of Grey's stomach as he reached into Grey's pants and yanked them from his body. For the first time since he entered the water, Grey realized motion as he watched the mangled phantom of his jeans entangle with the crab cage and sink away. His eyes burned with salt. Antonio scissored his legs around Grey's waist, driving his pelvis into Grey's back, freeing his hands to grab the rope and pull them to safety. The rope's coarse cord buried in Grey's neck, bore into his skin.

As they broke the surface, so did the dream. But this time it was no dream. Antonio was just being playful when he pulled Grey overboard. It wasn't until he heard the rope sliding down over the boat that he realized something was wrong—the cage had snagged Grey's pants and was dragging him down to the sea floor. He was already twenty feet deep before Antonio reached him.

Back in the boat, Antonio was frantic. "*Mi dispiace, mi dispiace. Come siete?*"

Grey started to answer, amazed he wasn't gasping for air. His eyelids were heavy. Only a few rays of daylight remained. He looked into Antonio's frightened face. Dilated pupils dulled his eyes, extinguishing their light. The drama, the metaphor, the intoxication of near death flooded over Grey. He tried to say he was okay but shock overtook him. He rolled his head to the side and laughed. He laughed at fate; his dramatic interpretation of his life had caught up with him. His laughter was silent. Red faded too fast to black. He heard waves splash into the boat. He was vomiting seawater.

10

Grey lay in the bottom of the boat. He had stopped coughing but was still gasping for air. He stared up into Antonio's rekindled eyes.

He wanted to remember this day not as a symbolic dream of intangible desire but as a triumph of risk and discovery. He wanted more than the story of a generous stranger who took him on a sunset boat ride. He wanted more than just a dream.

Antonio was sitting on top of him, naked, unconscious of how the texture of his skin rubbed against Grey's thighs, how the only thing between them was Grey's underwear soaked, revealing. The seawater that mingled with sweat and dripped from Antonio was real as was the shift of their bodies that would have been imperceptible had it not brought further contact, further weight such that the sexuality between them could not be denied. Grey could not restrain his arousal. Antonio's eyes were no longer fearful.

Grey pulled Antonio on top of him, further depriving himself of the oxygen that every cell in his body craved. Antonio's lips were warm and still salty from the sea. Like Miriam's, but virile, powerful. Antonio did not resist, as though a kiss was a natural consequence to their heightened emotional states. It could have been a gesture of gratitude, but they both knew it was more.

Nor did Antonio repress his body's natural reaction rising against Grey's stomach. Emboldened, Grey opened his mouth, allowing his tongue to explore as his limbs did the same. He slid his hand down Antonio's back, stopping at a small triangle of wet hair that bordered the base of his spine. His fingers hesitated but then followed the hair downward. Antonio shivered. Grey continued, pressing his fingers until he came to where there was more warmth, less resistance. He stopped. Antonio lifted his torso but kept his hips pressing into Grey's. He did not remove Grey's hand. His eyes beckoned, ablaze with renewed brilliance. This time Grey held his eyes, absorbed their light.

The night's darkness was still incomplete. The power shifted one last time.

Still on top of Grey, Antonio sat upright, bringing his erection into full view. He lifted Grey's upper body to remove Miriam's shirt. As he lowered Grey back to the hull, he left one hand beneath the small of his back. Grey arched to the pressure. Antonio's energy intensified; they now kissed with much more determination than exploration. With his free hand, Antonio tore at Grey's underwear. There was nothing between them now and they pressed into one another with insistence. Antonio's finger did not stop as Grey's had—it penetrated. There was an instant reflex of pain. Grey winced as he forced his body to relent. He gave into it. Pain became pleasure. Grey lifted his legs and placed his heels on the boat's cross bench. He slid down to elevate his legs, drawing Antonio's finger deeper inside of him. "Uhhhhh," Grey exhaled through his mouth, tightening his butt and abdomen to hold off for as long as he could. His entire body shuddered, still weak from depletion. He was just about to come when Antonio placed his other hand on Grey's chest and carefully withdrew his finger. Grey's heartbeat quieted; his muscles relaxed. Antonio traced his palm from Grey's chest down the center of his body, slowing as he encircled Grey's erection, opening his hand once again at its base. There he stopped, massaging, stretching Grey's skin onto his own, and then sliding across Grey's testicles to his own erection, which he pulled back against himself, closing his eyes as he rolled his uncut skin up and down, over the head and back. He opened his eyes once more into Grey's. He searched for resistance. There was none. He lifted his hand to his mouth adding his saliva to their sweat. It was a starless night; distant sounds of celebration floated on the air. Antonio entered Grey with tenderness respectful of their mutual lack of experience. Grey did not know that they came together. He did not feel, as he always thought he would, the exact moment it happened. What he felt were the muscles under Antonio's shoulder blades relax into his hands and the rocking of the boat against the sea.

They walked the same path back to the house. Tension stretched between them but unlike the earlier adrenaline rush, this was more of an aching throb, anxiety accentuated in each step. Having given Grey his pants, Antonio wrapped his shirt around himself like a sarong. They went to the back, to a faucet at the edge of the terrace. Antonio turned the hose onto his naked chest; the water was almost silent, a slight trickle. The orange netting glowed against the dark ground. Miriam's pallet lay a few feet away on the other side of the wall. She was a heavy sleeper except when she was worried. Grey prayed this was not one of those times.

He looked up at the stars overhead and wondered where they had been earlier. Antonio wrapped his wet arms around Grey's shoulders, pressing their bodies together once again. "Open," he said as he placed his hand on Grey's forehead, "No here," and then moved it to his heart. "Here." Antonio held the hose over them. The water was warm and sweet, cleansing. He drew Grey to him, rinsing the sea from their bodies.

Grey could no longer avoid his eyes. They were indeed remarkable. He wondered if part of their intensity was not their reflection of light but of honesty. Maybe they seemed brighter because they did not filter—no internal processing, no second-guessing, just the totality of the moment. Their bodies aroused each other once again. Moonlight and shadows flickered against them, less diluted, more rigid than beneath the water's surface. Antonio's passion was no longer contained by timidity, Grey's body no longer softened by the sea. Hard angles cut into one another. The netting sank into his back. Grey stared up into the tree canopy; the dancing shapes were darker in the moonlight, more secretive and illusive, more profane. Pleasure retreated to pain. He closed his eyes and waited for the light.

Miriam's blanket was thrown to her side; she lay curled up in the fetal position, still wearing Grey's T-shirt. She was snoring her little whistle that Grey thought was so cute. Grey knelt and brushed a loose lock of hair behind her ear. She smiled. He pulled the covers around her, bent down and kissed her on the cheek.

She instinctively reached for him; her hand was warm with sleep. "Didja have a good time?" she said without opening her eyes. She wouldn't remember this in the morning.

Grey's throat was so tight he could barely get the words out. "It woulda been better with you."

She smiled wider for a few seconds but then her grip loosened and her smile slackened back into her dream world.

Grey opened the door to his room. Pete was alone, spread across one of the beds, his underwear-clad body exposed in the heat. It was an image that, before tonight, would have flustered Grey's libido. Grey stripped nude and lay on the pallet beneath Pete's bed. He rolled onto his side and pulled the sheet to his waist. The moonlight from the window illuminated his back. It was reddened, still imprinted from the netting, like a map of New York City. Its grid was broken only by the curve of Miriam's thin silver chain that cut diagonally across his distended shoulder blade. Like Broadway. As he sank into sleep and his markings vanished, his dream self began to recompartmentalize—reality from fantasy, experimentation from discovery, structure from desire—even as Antonio's semen remained inside him.

They arrived early. The heat was suffocating so they sat outside for the entire ferry ride. Tom and even Pete took off their shirts. Grey didn't. Miriam was chatty, still giddy about the Feast of the Assumption procession where they carried a life-size statue of the Madonna from the church to the port. While she was intrigued with Grey's fishing trip, it didn't hold her attention in comparison to her truly local experience. Pete sat beside her, reading a tourist pamphlet he found in his seat. Next to him was Tom who, true to form, was doing his best to bring the group down. He was furious that Grey had insisted they all four split the cost of the room, even though he had neither eaten nor slept there. The real reason he was mad was because he got no action and was swindled to boot. After paying for an exorbitant night of dinner and drinks with the girls, he woke up hung-over on the couch of a very expensive and very vacated room. Upon leaving the hotel, the desk clerk stopped him. The clerk spoke no English but Tom, through broken German, discovered that the girls said he would pay for the room. At first he was indignant about "not forkin' over a fuckin' dime" but recanted when it was obvious that the manager was going to call the police—a word that sounds remarkably similar in any language.

Paying for three rooms in one night after sleeping on a couch pushed Tom way over the edge. He sulked while Miriam elaborated every detail of her evening. Pete listened, splitting his attention between Miriam and his pamphlet. Tom, pissed at her good humor, lashed out. "I don't see how you can sit there and smile."

Miriam tried to lighten him up. "Come on, it's a good story."

As he unlocked his camera case, he muttered, "Katrina and Daniella—they even used fuckin' foreign names." The mood became somber and Tom commenced his morning camera ritual. Even Miriam became reticent as Tom removed the cap, blew dust from the lens and began checking it over for damage.

Pete tried to draw the group back by reading aloud from the pamphlet:

> *"In 1814, the allied armies of Britain, Spain, Portugal, Russia, Prussia, and Austria captured many French possessions and some of France herself. Napoléon was forced into exile on the island of Elba and Louis XVIII was restored to power."*

Miriam leaned over Pete's lap to read it for herself. "I told you. Look at me, a physics major and one-upping y'all on European history." Pete continued, "Not only that but . . . hey, listen to this:

> *Napoléon was born during the Feast of the Assumption on a couch in the living room of his parents' lavish house."*

"So yesterday was his birthday; how weird is that?"

Elba was again a craggy rock in the distance. It was just a little over a day since, on this same ferry, the similar circumstance had instilled Grey with calm. He chuckled, thinking how he'd wanted to deconstruct the reasons for his letting go. His laugh was muffled by the wind. He was reminded of *The Count of Monte Cristo*, which he had read in high school. Monte Cristo, a similar insignificant rock on the Mediterranean, an island of unimagined riches. Now he remembered it was in this novel where he had read of Napoleon's exile to Elba, where his class had spent two days discussing the impotence of power. Long after Elba had disappeared from view, it was the memory of that discussion that lingered. It would be a topic that Grey would revisit throughout his life. As he would the island itself.

Grey watched Elba bob up and down on the horizon. As it receded, so did he. He realized that, after this trip, he and Miriam would part ways. Pete too. He didn't connect this to his experience with Antonio. That would come later. Instead, he let his mind float out to sea.

From the silence, Miriam's voice boomed, "Ow! Babe, what'd ya do to your neck?"

That morning Grey had found his pants neatly folded beside his pallet; there had been no need to explain. Grey flinched when she touched the scab. "A stupid accident."

When he now recounted an abridged version of the accident, Miriam put her arms around him, placing her hand softly over the wound. "That must have been terrifying."

Grey replied, "You have no idea." He did not hug her back and she soon pulled away.

As soon as the ferry docked, all four of them were restless to disembark. They stood next to one another, bound in the expectant huddle of other passengers. They were quiet, each in his own mental space. Throughout the rest of the trip, there would be no mention of Elba; they would not veer again from the itinerary.

They began to unload, crossing the boat's makeshift bridge to shore. The water glinted up through the planks, sunlight reflecting against its blue-green. Grey stopped for a moment, but the crowd pushed him forward. He gave way, running his hand through his wind-tangled hair that he had spent the better part of a year growing out for this trip. When he pulled it away, strands of long hair clung to his fingers. He decided that as soon as they returned, he would cut it back short.

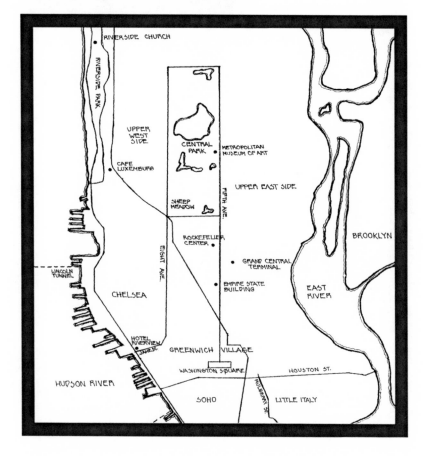

12

He shivered. It was unseasonably cold, but then autumn was always spent by the end of October. Although Grey had lived in New York for fourteen years, he continued to be surprised by the extremes. One day the city sweltered with equatorial humidity and the next, the trees were bare, fallen leaves swept away by an army of nocturnal street cleaners. Tonight a cold wind blew off the Hudson. Yes, autumn was done; tomorrow the city would awake to a dewy, wintry gray. He grabbed the deck rail with both hands, closed his eyes and leaned back, letting the tension in his arms support his full weight. And then forward, slowly bending over the waist-high railing, imagining his weightless freefall to the street six floors below. He relaxed his shoulders and tilted his head from side to side. The cracking of his neck soothed him, as did the minute shifting of the wind around the contours of his face. He stood back upright and opened his eyes to the river. From inside he heard the doorbell, followed by Scott's, "Come on up—remember it's PH." Then, "Wait a sec; I need to key ya up."

Scott's voice grew louder as he approached. "Hola Dreamweaver, people are starting to arrive." Without waiting for Grey's reply, he was off. "The elevator's not registering our floor again. And you call yourself president of the Condo Assoc—" His last comment was cut short by the sweeping of the closing door.

Disregarding the censure, Grey enjoyed his final few minutes of solitude. The water was silent and murky; its movement reflected the final rays of sunset. There was a deadened, shadowy instant as New York shifted into night. It was too brief and unremarkable to be called twilight. It was a slight murmur, almost undetectable, in New York's otherwise vibrant heartbeat. It held no mystery, only transition. Grey was motionless, expectant. The air was warmer in the stillness.

And then it was done. The sun had set behind Hoboken's modest skyline. Every night, as winter took hold, it seemed faster, less reluctant than the night before.

In that instant, as nighttime fell, nature relinquished control. Electric lights buzzed to life, fluorescent, neon and tungsten. Instead of slowing, the city's metabolism sped up, manic, extending consciousness to a sleep-deprived 24-7. Only the Hudson rested. It darkened, descending into a subliminal dream state— purging, cleansing. Transforming.

Scott materialized on Grey's left, handing him a glass of red wine. He was wearing a flapper costume with a beauty-contestant sash that read *Miss Millie Knee-'em*. Scott had come up with his drag persona months before and couldn't wait for their annual Halloween party to try it out. He had prepared a repertoire of knee-isms such as, "*Knee*d anything?" and "Looks like *knee*ther of us girls has a cocktail," which he planned to accentuate with an accompanying and prolonged knee lift to the groin. By the end of the night everyone would be felt up at least once. That is, except for Grey.

Again Scott withdrew as quickly as he appeared; his derision trailed behind him, "If you're not going to wear a costume, at least act like you're having fun." Grey took the glass without turning around, faithful to his role as the anti-social introvert. The buzzer rang a second time. Scott barked one last plea before the first guests arrived. "Grey, could ya get the buzzer—*PUH-LEASE!*"

A light flicked on in the turret of the adjacent hotel. Grey used to wonder about the octagonal room, an oversized widow's walk with large windows on each of its eight sides. Ever since he moved in, it had sat empty, devoid of furniture or human presence. But then, inside the decrepit halls of the Hotel Riverview, the Jane Street Theatre was born from either vision or desperation and this windowed attic was now the dressing room for the actors of *Hedwig and the Angry Inch*.

From his deck, Grey had witnessed the play, or at least its costumes, evolve through six months of rehearsals, and continue to be tweaked on a regular basis almost two years after opening night. He had grown familiar with the small cast.

The buzzer rang again. Scott glared at Grey from the bar and then turned in deference to make the special request cosmos for Brian and Greg, dressed as Judy and Liza, who were faux-apologizing for always being the first to arrive and the last to leave.

"So true," Grey sighed to himself as he pulled shut the door."

13

In blending their respective ideals, Grey and Scott had created the consummate party space with an open floor plan and an enormous roof deck. When Grey bought the condo in '92, his friends told him he was crazy, that it was in the middle of nowhere—a dangerous nowhere at that. And it needed a complete overhaul. His honest excuse was its unobstructed view of the Hudson. So what if he lived next to a crack hotel and had to step over strung-out transsexuals every morning on his way to work.

Grey had moved to Jane Street the summer before he met Scott. His Orion stock had done extremely well in the market and his accountant told him that he needed a tax write-off. He was looking for something small, mid-300's, on the Upper West Side. On paper, a 3,000-square-foot fixer-up in the outer West Village didn't quite fit the bill. During the ride over to see the property, his starched and bowtied realtor, Drake, apologized, saying that he "couldn't im-*AH*-gine what his office was thinking." It didn't matter to Grey; he was enjoying checking out the different neighborhoods and peeking into others' lives.

Until Drake's Miata turned from Greenwich, Grey hadn't recognized the street name. As he stepped out of the car, memories of Miriam and Pete flooded back. "Drake, wait just a sec; let me get a feel for the street." He walked down to the West Side Highway and then retraced his steps of eight years prior. He was transported back in time. His selective memory omitted a few choice details, two of which were the Hotel Riverview on the corner and its cracked-out inhabitants who lined the sidewalk. Not that he minded his memory's selection criteria, especially since it also excluded Tom. He stopped midway down the block, at the point of the sidewalk where the four—in his mind's eye, three—of them had sat and rested. Across the street were the same urns in which the two handsome mid-thirties men had planted geraniums. Now there were roses—an upgrade. Grey took this as a good sign. As he walked over to get a better look, their fragrant bouquet welcomed his notice.

It was a stately building, the most dignified on the block, Federal style with a decorative fanlight over the door and identical rows of shuttered windows on each of its four floors. Grey wondered if the couple still lived there. Of course they were a couple. Back then, he thought they were two friends planting flowers together. He thought about the naïveté of innocence, reminding him of his loss of both; Elba had been only a few weeks after the memories he was now reliving.

Lost in reflection, he was staring at the urns when Drake startled him back. "Hey what's wrong? You just want skip it?"

Grey's voice was distant. "Oh, sorry, I was just daydreaming. No, I think I want to see it. This street has a certain unspoiled charm."

A longtime member of Manhattan's historical society, Drake noted a bronze plaque on the building's façade. "Hey, this must be an historic site. What does that plaque say?"

The bronze was tarnished; Grey had to step past the urns into the building's small courtyard to read it. "It says that the first U.S. Secretary of Treasury, Alexander Hamilton, died here in 1804 after a duel with Aaron Burr." As he turned, he slipped on a discarded syringe and almost toppled one of the urns. Rebalancing himself, Grey commented, "I guess if he thought Jane was a good investment, she can't be that bad." A sudden wind gusted. It was a clear day and the sunlight flickered through overhanging trees. "Let's see what we got across the way."

Realtor and client stood outside at the foot of the stairs, looking up to the *For Sale* sign on the top floor. Unlike Mister Hamilton's abode, the architecture of 111 Jane Street was anything but dignified. "Some '70s abortion," Drake called it before he exclaimed, "What a dump."

Grey was wondering if there was some unwritten rule that every gay man had to impersonate Bette Davis at some point in his lifetime, when a junkie sitting next to the building's stoop interrupted.

"*Aloha.*" He was young, likely in his early twenties, but in his unwashed euphoric state it was hard to tell.

Drake ran up the stairs to the landing. "Grey, I'm really sorry about this." The junkie didn't move a muscle.

Grey smiled at the lifeless greeter, looked past him to the river and inhaled a slow deep breath. "Drake, don't worry. I can tell you now, if it has the view of the river I think it has and we can figure out how to swing the price, then this could be the place."

The next hour, Drake and Grey pieced together an offer. It was tricky because, to build in enough money for the renovation would mean selling Grey's vested options, as well as all of his stock. It was a huge risk but one that would turn out to be the best investment of his life.

"*Ciao*," the junkie called out as they were leaving.

Right before Drake peeled out like a teenager (or a forty-year-old realtor in a midlife crisis), Grey nodded out the window to the junkie. "See ya around." He had no idea just how true his statement would become.

Jane Street gave Grey and Scott a project on which to focus. Grey had heard it said that if a couple could make it through a renovation, they could survive anything. In truth, the renovation years had been when they were at their best. Maybe it was the newness of their relationship and the excitement of unknown possibilities the condo represented or the amount of unaffected alone time they spent with one another, conceiving something together. Or maybe it was something much more basic: that the creation of a beautiful home was one of the few activities that fell within an ever-shrinking overlap of interests. The renovation was not only a metaphor for their relationship; it was the glue. In the three years since its completion, they had become a different couple—the fabulous fags with a fabulous flat in the fabulously trendy meatpacking district. Somewhere along the way *condo* had changed to *flat*.

Grey was at the sink washing the bulbous red wine glasses that didn't fit into the dishwasher. Once the grind of elevator motor signaled that Brian and Greg were out of earshot, Scott spun around in a dramatic pirouette. The beads of his flapper dress fanned out, sounding like sleet against a windshield. Although no longer on stage, Scott still used his dance training to impress his intended audience. His elbows jutted akimbo a good two feet from his body, creating a stick figure effect upon his wiry frame. His black bobbed wig cut into his gaunt face.

"Couldn't you have waited two more minutes to start cleaning? I hate it when you do that."

Grey flashed on a random image of a nagging Olive Oyl as he picked up the next glass from the aligned dirty glasses to the left of the sink. He washed it methodically, rinsed it and placed it in a row of aligned clean glasses upon the uniform grid of dishtowels to the right.

Scott held Olive's stance. "Well?"

Grey grabbed the next dirty glass. "C'mon, Brian and Greg always overstay their welcome. If I didn't start cleaning, they would never leave."

Scott rolled his eyes, threw his hands up and about-faced to the bedroom, slamming the door behind him. He would be asleep by the time Grey got to bed and they wouldn't discuss it in the morning. Scott would begin the day with the silent treatment, demand an apology and then the tension would fade as he started in with a catty postmortem of the party. "Did you see Grant's ass in those tights? Can you believe Doyle's new boyfriend? What trash." By noon they would be preparing for whatever Scott had scheduled that night. The day would pass without a single intimate word; all conversation would be idle gossip or logistics.

Grey surveyed the room as he worked his way through the last row of dirty glasses. It was indeed a beautiful home, perfect for entertaining. They had done a great job. Three quarters of the indoor living area were divided between the living room and the kitchen that, along with the deck, stretched across the condo to take full advantage of the view. All that separated the two rooms was an immense island. On the kitchen side, it served as a sink, dishwasher and counter, but on the living room side was a full-service bar complete with matching bar sinks halfway down each side and an impressive stack of seven fifteen-foot-long floating glass shelves that hung from the ceiling. Because the support wires were translucent, the shelves appeared to float in midair and upon them, all the essentials of a good cocktail: vertical liquor bottles, horizontal wine bottles, assorted glasses of every type and other bar tchotchke including decanters, shakers, linen cocktail napkins, specialty martini olives and a variety of tropical drink umbrellas that made it into almost every drink, tropical or not. Acclimatized mini-fridges terminated each end, one for whites, rosés and mixers and the other for the more expensive reds they wanted to age. Uplighting through the countertop created an illusory effect. The bottom shelf was beveled so that when the columns of light hit it, they splintered, dispersing pinpoint rays up though the other shelves and barware to create a glittering spectacle. The bar was an archetypal combination of almost art-like beauty and efficient functionality that one rarely sees in interior architecture. The rest of the room—Swedish modern ultra suede furniture, a simple glass-topped dining table, blond inlay hardwood floors—was designed to complement this centerpiece.

The only space other than the two bedrooms that did not open into the main area was a smallish study, but even this wasn't closed off, rather it was set apart by a three-quarter height etched glass slab-like wall open above and on both sides like a modern interior henge stone. Its placement and irregular shape afforded sufficient identity to define a separate space but enough inclusion that, during large parties, it became an adjunct lounge.

The wall of windows to the deck was custom-made so that every panel, even the door, could open out like a tent flap. Titanium catches held the panels horizontal from the building so they created broad glass eaves overhanging the deck. For summer parties, when these panels were raised, there was an indoor/outdoor effect more characteristic of West Hollywood than the West Village.

Grey finished wiping down the counters and made his way across the room, turning off lights as he went. One extravagance among many was the additional bar light switch by the master bedroom. Grey had anticipated that he would sometimes want to admire the singly lit bar as the last image before going to bed. This was one of those nights. His clean glasses glittered in homage.

Outside, there was a catcall exchange between two groups of Halloween stragglers. Grey thought back to another Halloween, the day the electrician hooked up the bar lights. They were supposed to have gone to Brian and Greg's *Titanic* party and then *cruise* around the Village. Grey had come home late from work to complete darkness. "Sorry I'm late. Scott, you home?" he called as he walked into the unlit room. Scott stood by the bedroom door and flipped the switch. Grey gasped; even empty and unfinished it was more beautiful than he had imagined. In front of the bar, their mattress was made up with new chocolate brown satin sheets and a matching duvet that transformed their old stained comforter. Beside it, Scott's prized heirloom tablecloth that his grandmother had hand embroidered was spread with all of the ingredients for a romantic indoor picnic. Scott had spent three weeks preparing for this surprise and it was worth every minute.

They laughed and talked of the future they would share in this room. Scott had said, "I'm tired of Brian and Greg's parties. Why don't we take over Halloween?" Grey listened as Scott chatted excitedly about a *Gattaca* theme where everyone would wear sexy sci-fi drag. "And at our party, you're going to *have* to wear a costume. I'll be Uma to your Ethan," Scott said as he pulled Grey on top of him. They made the kind of love where neither knew where his body stopped and the other's started. Grey awoke in darkness, on the bed's edge with Scott beside him, spread prone across the rest of the mattress. For what seemed like hours he lay still and watched Scott breathe, his smooth back rise and fall, as dawn's light began to shimmer on the Hudson. Superimposed upon the river, upon the deck's wall of glass through which Grey peered, was an exact reflection of the bar. They hadn't turned off its lights before drifting off to sleep.

Grey turned off the bar light and slipped into the dark bedroom.

14

The recovery was not as usual. Scott hadn't said a word all morning and when, at noon, asked if Grey was ready for brunch, didn't flinch when Grey reminded him he had to wait for Rothko. Instead, he scoffed on his way to the coat closet, "Remember it's at Randy's, not Christian's," and then left. If this was Scott's stepped-up cold shoulder, Grey preferred it to his holier-than-thou routine. Of course he would never let Scott know this.

No sooner had Scott shut the door than the buzzer sounded. In the electronic eye stood a lanky, baggy-clothed teenager. Grey leaned into the video intercom even though the overpriced system could probably detect a pin drop across the room. "John, I'll be right down." Scott would be certain to pass John in transit but given the morning's state of irreconciliation, Grey was just as certain that Scott would not wait around for Grey to pay John and take Rothko inside. Grey grabbed his threadbare pea coat and took the stairs, a habit that ensured at least some daily exercise.

Unlike the rest of the building, the stairwell had undergone only a modest cosmetic facelift. The scuffed gray linoleum steps were one of the few signs of the building's past. The door echoed as it closed behind him.

In the six years that Grey had lived here, John had grown from a boy into a young man. At times, John's new maturity imbued Grey with nostalgia, the natural result of living somewhere long enough to witness the neighborhood kid grow up. As Grey ran down the six flights, he recalled the first time John rang the doorbell.

It had all the trappings of a typical New York scam—a ten-year-old child with a box of handmade pottery he was trying to sell door-to-door. Grey didn't even open the door but shooed him on his way. A week or two later, when Grey was lugging a toilet seat home from the hardware store, the kid approached again.

"Hey, I'll carry that for ya for a quarter," the boy propositioned.

Again Grey was cautious, but it was broad daylight. Anyway, it was just a cheap make-do to appease Scott until the renovation started.

Dressed in baggy Nike shorts, windowed and colorful Air Jordans and an extra-large NY Jets sweatshirt that swallowed him, John began verbally hemorrhaging as only a cocaine freak, drama queen or irrepressible child can. He was a rare phenomenon—a Manhattan working-class kid. He lived two streets over. His father was a postman and his mother—who now lived in Stamford—was an executive administrator for an investment banking firm in the city. In the five minutes it took to walk back, John detailed personal intimacies of his life including that his parents had lived on Banks Street for twenty-five years and that his adoption was their last attempt to save their marriage. He now spent weekdays and went to school in Connecticut and saw a therapist twice a week. Summers were reversed—weeks in New York, weekends in Stamford. In his hyperactive nonchalance, he conveyed that he did not consider his childhood anything out of the ordinary.

John was a born businessman. During the summer months he went through every childhood moneymaking venture he could devise. He hustled pottery kilned in his Thursday art therapy sessions. He was the neighborhood kid who set up a lemonade stand, but since this was New York, his product line was a mite more eclectic—herbal tea and homemade biscotti. Then he figured out how to make money from urban inconveniences: he was a personal shopper, grocery carrier, soap opera recorder and repairman letter-inner. For a short period, John even convinced his father to let him turn their enviable mudroom into a neighborhood laundromat.

Sometime in the mid-'90s John began to specialize. The yuppification of the neighborhood brought with it canine companions and with them, the ultimate niche opportunity for a non-working-age teenager. The concept of a pampered pooch for which owners would pay for a daily constitutional around the block was an opportunity John seized with his usual entrepreneurial vigor. He could be seen walking up to ten dogs at a time—plastic bags overflowing his low-riding jeans. John's entourage included every shape and size from a pair of Great Danes, one white—Mason, the other black—Dixon, to a family of three pugs, Winkin', Blinkin' and Nod, who were indistinguishable to the untrained eye. Regardless of the size of the pack, he somehow managed an orderly ensemble. Dogs, like people, were drawn to John; charisma was one of his many gifts.

Grey rounded the corner of the final flight of stairs, remembering the day he and Scott had brought Rothko home from the S.P.C.A. They called John over to set up a puppy-sitting and training schedule. Knowing John, the housebreaking process would take less than a week. They had not yet picked a name when John arrived. Scott insisted on Chelsea, arguing that a dog named after the largest gay neighborhood in the country conveyed a flagrant sense of camp. Not a big fan of flagrancy or camp, Grey wanted something subtler, more *J. Crew* or *Abercrombie & Fitch*-ish, like Montana. John, who was bent over, scratching beneath the puppy-tufted chin, interrupted, "How about Rothko?" Grey and Scott stopped mid-bicker and looked down at the puppy teething on John's hand. "I mean, look how his coat gently fades from one hue to another." Rothko whined in bliss. "And orange Rothkos are my favorite."

John and Grey gaped at each other, surprised at this teenager's reference to the famous pioneer of modern art, but more so at his eerie clairvoyance into the very characteristic that made them choose Rothko over the fifty or so other abandoned dogs. He was orange. Not yellow or golden or tawny, orange.

In exploring John's knowledge of Mark Rothko, another anomaly of this average neighborhood kid surfaced. Grey and Scott had often wondered how divorced parents with blue-collar jobs could afford his NYC brownstone, her Stamford three bedroom *cottage* and the cost of raising a teenager that included private education and therapy sessions twice a week. It just so happened that John's parents shared a love that kept them together long after their love for each other had died: modern art.

John told them how in 1952, his seventeen-year-old mother met his eighteen-year-old father in a dingy West Village café known to be frequented by the avant-garde pop artist. They were both voyeurs into a world they admired even though (or maybe because) its intense, aggressive, often drug-induced passions contrasted their respective dull passivity. This shared interest led them down the path of matrimony and sustained them for thirty-two years until each recognized their reflection in the other and began to detest the constant reminder. But at this café they still maintained a standing twice-a-week dinner date—during John's therapy sessions—even after five years of divorce. John joked that at least their mutual love of art would last forever.

Through the years they developed not only a weakness for the emotional extremities of the personalities who represented their vicarious flat-line idolatry but also an unerring eye for the neophyte genius. They purchased early works of Jasper Johns, Robert Rauschenberg, Andy Warhol, Robert Indiana and Keith Haring. John confided that the sale of one of these early purchases, a large Rauschenberg collage that they had rolled up in the basement and had never even displayed because it was too big for any wall in the house, had paid for the divorce and both houses, and would cover John's education through Ivy League doctorate, if he should be so inclined. Even John's name was of this eminent field. His parents were discreet enough not to name him Jasper but found a more subtle way to honor their favorite: John's middle name was the single initial S.

In answering the question, why they still worked, John replied in pitch-perfect therapy lingo that revealed a disquieting depth of emotional insight for a child his age. "Retirement would require they either engage in their lives or completely give themselves over to their obsession. The thought of either immobilizes them."

15

Grey squinted when he opened the door to the bright sunlight. John was talk-ing to Jimmy, a heroin addict who lived in the neighboring hotel but who had established a secondary daytime residence on Grey's stoop. John was decked—cap, shirt, sweats, socks and shoes—in Nike. Underwear, for all Grey knew. His loyalty to Nike was one of the few things about John that had remained the same throughout Grey's six years of knowing him; the swooshes just got larger. Jimmy, on the other hand, wore mismatched charitable contributions and dump-ster acquisitions. He was probably only five or six years John's senior but their drastic differences in physical appearance made them appear at least a generation apart.

John was lecturing Jimmy, "Man, that stuff is gonna kill ya," as Rothko did his full body wag at Grey's arrival.

Rothko was all puppy, brimming with visceral excitement to compensate for each missed moment or in anticipation of every new adventure. Greeting his master outdoors on a clear crisp day after a night away carried with it the promise of both. He was beside himself, barking and writhing with such unfettered joy that he even got a rise out of Jimmy.

"Looks like somebody's goin' for a long walk . . . maybe to the *park.*" One of Jimmy's earpieces was missing so that his Ray-Ban knockoffs were tilted up on the right side of his face. Counterbalanced by the leftwards slump of his body, the glasses were the sole horizontal element of his entire visage.

The *w* word was bad enough but Jimmy had gone and said the *p* word as well, fueling Rothko's frenzy to the point where all four feet were propelled off the ground with each body-wag.

"Thanks Jimmy. I guess now I've pretty much my next hour committed for," Grey said in pretend frustration.

Without twitching a muscle, Jimmy responded, "*No hay problema.*"

After being paid, John moseyed down Jane Street for a game of pick-up. Voicing Grey's exact thoughts, Jimmy said, " Hard to believe how he's grown up."

Grey considered Jimmy's skeletal frame slouched against the wall and wondered how such a fried brain could still function with relative clarity. "What'll it be today—bagel or croissant?"

Somewhere along the line, Grey had developed a relationship with Jimmy that hinged on a self-adopted responsibility to provide Sunday-morning sustenance. With Jimmy, as with John, Grey experienced something he didn't get from Scott, nor their friends, nor his work colleagues. It was a clean relationship, not based on a façade of the flawless couple or the successful business guy or whatever image people had of him. Each Sunday morning he found himself anticipating his and Jimmy's powwow. There had been only a few weekends in three years, not counting inclement weather or times he had been sick or out of town, when this ritual had been broken. And most of those were because Jimmy was too strung-out to make it downstairs. For Grey, their relationship had become a touchstone of sorts that, like an actual touchstone, was smooth and familiar with repetition.

Jimmy stretched his long skinny arms to each side and left them extended as if he needed them to stay aloft. "Anyway we could do a late afternoon sandwich instead?" As with all relationships, theirs had evolved.

"Sure. Hey, you should use some protection." Grey tossed a sample bottle of Kiehl's SPF15 moisturizer into Jimmy's unflinching lap. (Grey rarely left the house without sunscreen.) "Early winter sun can be the worst." Jimmy did not reach for the lotion; his wings remained protracted.

During this exchange, Rothko had been tugging toward the river like a lab toward a felled duck. Only Rothko was no lab and he hated to get his feet wet, much less jump headlong into any body of water. But on a dry day his exuberance for an outdoor adventure would fill him with the energy of even the most spastic of Jack Russells. Sizewise, Rothko was somewhere between a Jack Russell and a lab. He had short coarse hair, not shorthaired-short but more wirehaired terrier medium short, that gradually darkened from his pumpkin nose to his amber belly and then lightened back again all the way to the blond tip of his long rigid tail. With his bearded face and permanent quizzical left ear flopped forward, he resembled a cross between Little Orphan Annie's beloved Sandy and Tramp of Disney fame.

"OK boy, let's go to the park."

Rothko yelped with such excitement that, combined with his running-in-place nails scratching on the sidewalk, it brought motion to the limp body before them. Jimmy lifted his outstretched arms and wrapped them around his head. His emaciated biceps pressed against his ears and his forearms fell, crossing over his eyes and knocking off his sunglasses. His inverted, prodigious hands dangled side by side just below his chin, cupped forward and pleading, not only trying to block out Rothko but all other sensory intrusion disrupting his high.

"Go on, man. *Tempus fugit.*" At last, Rothko's paws got traction.

There wasn't a designated park per se because of the constant construction of the Hudson Riverside Project. It didn't matter, because to Rothko the word *park* probably translated to a longer walk where he didn't have to go back inside immediately after peeing and pooping.

The City had learned from the South Street Seaport development of the '80s that even concrete-loving, high-rise-living New Yorkers are drawn to the water's edge. The Hudson Riverside Project promised to reclaim the Hudson waterfront for a long, thin Chilean promenade from Riverside Park to the tip of the island. Every weekend there was bulldozing and jackhammering around some new fenced-off area, usually an old dilapidated pier or warehouse. Then, out of the blue, a new mini-park would appear and fill with sunbathers, Starbucks drinkers, tai-chi classes, and nighttime cruising (which, rather than a brand new constituency was simply a clientele upscaling from the dilapidated pier days). The immediacy of this transformation, this opening up of ignored dis-use to the flow of humanity, made the Hudson's banks seem more fluid than the river itself.

Of course with each human activity came a wide assortment of dogs, all of with whom Rothko was eager to become acquainted. As Rothko pulled them forward, Grey fantasized skipping the brunch altogether. It was to be an all-afternoon affair—mimosas and Bellinis from ten to twelve, quiche and coffee from twelve to one, and then Christian was to premier songs from his new musical. That would drag on until at least three. Various cliques would then divide, each heading off to a favorite Sunday afternoon watering hole. An abstention could result in six hours to himself—six unscheduled hours. Rather than making a decision right away, Grey decided to walk for a bit, to remind himself what spontaneity felt like.

"Rothko, sit!" Rothko did not yet comprehend the dangers of the West Side Highway. Grey had been struggling to teach him the difference between the safety of sidewalk and the treacherous roadways four inches below. Rothko had learned pretty well except for the one street that blocked him from nirvana. The memory of unleashed dogs, saliva-caked tennis balls and infinite smells negated all training. He saw the Westside Highway not as a life-threatening danger but an entrance fee to a sensory-filled world he got to visit far too infrequently. Grey's biggest paternal fear was that one day Rothko would break from his leash and make a dash for the Hudson's call.

At Grey's fourth *sit*, Rothko, eyes remaining focused on the river, lowered his back haunches but kept the tension in his legs like he was crouching into a starting stance for a race. Upon the safety of the light change, Grey released Rothko's hold. "OK boy, let's go."

Across the highway and five minutes of unkempt sidewalk later they were at a chainlink fence blocking off yet another changeling of the Hudson Riverside Project. Two side-by side old piers, in better shape than most, extended their reach fifty or sixty feet into the river. Rothko ran over as if he knew it held the promise of future adventures and he wanted to determine just how strong that promise was. He added his own personal mark to the groundbreaking.

It was a beautiful day; its reflection shimmered off the water. Ahead was a lush new walkway lined with benches under which lay or sat at least a half-dozen dogs ignored by their Sunday *Times* consumed owners. Instead of pushing forward, the two paused at the fence's corner, each contemplating possibilities unmet rather than the reality of the path in front of them. Grey thought about Jimmy— how could such a bright man lose his way so completely? But then, had he? He always appeared to be perfectly content. And the things he said. At times, he seemed almost prophetic. It was Jimmy who, one Sunday a couple of months back, joked, "You know, today's Assumption Day so I *assume* you're buying me breakfast." Grey hadn't thought of Assumption Day in years. Since Elba.

The riverbank was just a few feet away. There was an audible gurgle testifying constant movement undetectable except when one was this close. When gazed upon from his flat, the river was part of a static landscape. Here, it took on form and life. If he were to get past the fence and wade in deep enough that he could no longer touch the silty bottom, motion would lose relativity and the dream would resurface. He would become one with the water yet again. Grey listened.

Their respective fantasies were broken when a passing greyhound puppy challenged Rothko to a race. She was a beautiful slate gray, two shades darker than a Weimaraner. With her sleek coat, cheetah-like grace and speed, sculptured musculature, she appeared to be a different species than the orange mutt loping far behind. Ten feet ahead was the dog's tall, broad-shouldered owner—also wearing a gray coat, the exact color of his dog. Grey unleashed Rothko so he could give into the chase. Rothko sprinted full speed ahead in his quest. Grey took his time.

It wasn't yet too cold; without any wind, one almost didn't need a jacket. Surprisingly, there were only a few people scattered about. Despite the day's warmth, New York had already begun to adjust to winter. Only one rollerblader, a beginner clad in brightly colored sleeves and tights, braved the trail. She jerked along at a pace much slower than the average weekend stroller.

Grey took a proud parental stance beside the greyhound's owner. They watched the frolicking duo for a couple of minutes without speaking.

"Strange color—your dog, what is he?"

Up close, the cashmere of his overcoat was not slate but charcoal, peppered with white flecks, more like his own hair than his dog's. He had a strong angular jawline that promised a wide Midwestern or Eastern European face. As he turned, Grey was glad to discover the promise unbroken. This was one of those men to whom Grey couldn't have talked except in business or about his dog.

"He's a Summa." Grey flinched, realizing that it was a Scott quip that he had heard so many times it had become ingrained.

"Summa?" His eyes were the deep yellow-green that Grey had only seen in some South Americans, but his jet hair and pale skin were more Black Irish.

Grey dropped Scott's flippancy. "He's a mutt. You know, summa this and summa that."

"Ahhhhhh." The man paused to watch the dogs playing and then looked back at Grey. "Cute."

Grey and Wade talked for a good half-hour about the pros and cons of breeding, Pedigree versus Science Diet, the new stringent enforcement of leash laws, and other dog-related matters, nothing too deep. If Scott or any of their friends had seen them, they wouldn't have believed it—the serious, introverted Grey chatting up a tall, dark stranger. Scott may even have been jealous. That may have even been a good thing.

Wade eased into the personal, following the innocuous, "Where do you groom him?" with, "So do you live around here?"

Grey nodded across the highway. "Yeah, my partner and I have a flat over there on Jane Street, next to that hotel on the corner."

Wade's demeanor shifted from pursuit to honest inquisition. "Next to the Riverview? Have you seen it yet?" A third dog, a spunky black Boston terrier, joined in the play. The three were a picture of doggie diversity.

"What?" Grey asked confused.

"*Hedwig*, I hear it's not t'be missed."

Perhaps he had misread simple friendliness. "No, not yet but occasionally I see the actors prepare from my deck." Grey pointed. "They use that turret as a dressing room; my flat's just on the other side."

Wade reached into his pocket and pulled out three dog biscuits. He squatted and gave one to each dog. "Maybe we should go sometime."

When he stood back up, he was closer than before. His breath was warm and minty. "We could see the whole play unfold from costumes-on to costumes-off. That is, if you don't mind inviting me up before the show." Wade's Bo-Derek-in-*Ten* slow motion head turn was most definitely calculated. "And after." His eyes were almost luminous. "It'd be like *Rear Window*."

The air was colder against his face; Grey turned toward the playing dogs. "Sure, that sounds like a great idea. Let me check with my partner and see what our schedule is like for the next couple of weeks. Do you have a card?"

16

Grey fingered the business card in his pocket. Both he and Rothko were energized, Grey from the flirtation with a stranger and Rothko from some rigorous wrestling. The butterflies in Grey's stomach fluttered with each breath he took, carrying him back to another autumn day years earlier. While the weather had been cooler, the tingly inner warmth was the same.

It had been his first real weekend getaway. In the seven years Grey lived in New York, he had spent all of his holidays in Memphis, and while certainly there had been outings to Coney Island or Park Slope, those didn't count even though Grey still considered any time he crossed a bridge or tunnel a pseudo-vacation. But this was a pack-your-bag-and-take-a-bus kind of trip, all the way to the Berkshires. His friend Gene had talked him into going to see the Boston Pops play in Tanglewood. Gene found a cute bed-and-breakfast and got them tickets for two late season summer stock performances in addition to the symphony. They had just unpacked after moving from the Magnolia Room with the queen-size bed to the Dogwood Room with two twins. Gene was head over heels for Grey, and there was always some happenstance—a third round of cocktails, a cancelled date, the only available room—that could influence a compromise. With each one, Grey would pretend not to notice and sidestep with grace.

"Lucky us; someone cancelled," Grey told Gene when he came back from the reception, "but she said we'd better hurry if we're gonna make the theater on time."

The piece was an austere all-male ballet set to Phillip Glass. Grey was mesmerized. As they walked to the restaurant across from the theater, Grey said, "I've never seen men dance together like that. It was so . . . sensual."

Gene regaled in his mentorship. "If you liked this you'll love the Les Ballets Trockadero. They are fabulous; I can get us tickets the next time they're in town." Although there were a few open tables, Gene wanted to wait for a cozy two-top by the fireplace.

A large raucous group came in behind them. Their envoy tapped Grey on the shoulder. "Excuse me, is there a list?" Grey turned around to the entire ballet troupe that they had just seen perform. The envoy, Scott.

Rothko's attention was soon diverted by yet another frolicking bitch. Grey's wasn't. He spent the next ten blocks ten years in the past. It was nice to be back.

Scott had invited them to sit with the ballet troupe and Gene wasn't fast enough to devise a gracious refusal. One of the more effeminate dancers who chose not to remove his stage makeup cornered Gene while Grey and Scott talked throughout dinner. Gene feigned sick to escape his admirer, and they left before dessert.

Scott clasped Grey's outstretched hand with both of his own, a Southern intimacy one never experienced in New York. "It was great to meet you; I hope this won't be the last time."

When Grey pulled his hand away, Scott palmed him what appeared to be a business card but only had Scott's name and phone number. It was the first personal calling card Grey had ever seen. He rubbed his thumb over the beautiful embossed letters; Aquinas oblique, Scott informed him later.

"What's that?" Gene asked and tried to snatch the card out of Grey's hand. "That twink didn't give you his card, did he?"

"No." Grey pulled the card away from him. "It's just the name of a restaurant he recommended in SoHo."

Back in the bathroom of the bed-and-breakfast, Grey pulled the card out of his pocket. On the back Scott had written the number of the motel where the dance troupe was staying and below it:

> *Maybe we can even get together before you head back.*
> *Scott*

The following day, Gene gave Grey the silent treatment and took off for a massage appointment during which Grey met Scott at the town coffeehouse. They spent the whole day together, Grey quizzing Scott on the life of a dancer, and Scott, Grey about growing up in the South. They got to the Norman Rockwell museum right before closing. Pointing out each brushstroke variation, Scott knew everything about the artist from his idyllic depiction of Roosevelt's Four Essential Freedoms what Scott called his "lesbiana" painting of Rosie the Riveter. Grey was captivated. That night when he returned to the bed-and-breakfast, Gene had already checked out. He and Gene never spoke again.

Colors vibrated around him. A light breeze cut the sun's fragile warmth. Grey was conscious of his leg muscles, their contraction and release propelling him forward. He started to run. The Hudson paralleled them on their left, the midtown skyline on the right buffered by an even stream of traffic coursing down the West Side Highway. The sun above them was centered in a midday sky.

Two hours later the sun had made its way over the river, and Grey and Rothko had made their way up it. They happened upon a cute spot on the river called the Boat Basin Café. Grey vaguely knew that there was an actual basin on the Upper West Side and in fact, now remembered meeting one of Brian and Greg's friends who had tricked with the owner of a houseboat docked there. But he had never heard of this charming café. It was like being on the Cape, sitting in an outdoor café under the stone arches of a bridge, looking out across a harbor. For Rothko it wasn't the cute factor but the scrap factor. He was already scrounging, maximizing the full radius afforded by his leash. They decided it was lunchtime.

Grey ordered a second chilidog after Rothko convinced him to forgo half of his first. After paying, he pulled out the wad of cards he kept below his driver's license. Sure enough, it was there:

Jude Scott Barclay
212.714.8355

The card was beaten up, the embossment scraped away and the message on the back barely readable. But it at least was still intact. *Jude.* Grey smiled. Scott had hated the name until Jude Law appeared on the scene. Now he went so far as to use it when introducing himself to new people whom he would likely not see again. "It *is* my name," Scott replied when Grey questioned him. This thought made Grey smile even wider. Maybe he and Scott could go back to the Berkshires around the holidays. They were supposed to go to Brian and Greg's for the millennium but they could find a time before then, just for a weekend. He would check out some places on the web.

He put the cards back into his wallet and picked up the Arts & Leisure section of the *Times* the previous patron had left on the table.

The lead article was titled, "The Tao of the New Yorker."

> *For the average fast-paced, high stressed New Yorker, a meditative lifestyle is next to impossible. The best most of us can achieve is a healthy coexistence with our mania. Here are twenty-seven tips to help you slow down your life while remaining in the fast lane.*

Grey put down the paper and surveyed the café's clientele. It was far from crowded and everyone seemed calm and relaxed, no one hurrying to power through lunch. Were these the same people who rushed past him every morning at Grand Central Terminal? Or were they from elsewhere, other boroughs, or out and out tourists? One pretty woman with long, straight blonde hair two or three tables over smiled at him. He smiled back but without encouragement.

She reminded him of Miriam. It was apparently going to be a day of memories. She caught his eye and stood up; the two actions may or may not have been related. Below the chin she didn't resemble Miriam in the slightest, standing at least a foot shorter and wider. Grey quickly looked away.

"Hey, boss!" Madge Miner, named after her grandmother, Jan Miner, who played the character Madge in the '60s Palmolive commercials, was Grey's admin. She was a twenty-five-year-old *actor* (Madge once chastised Grey for calling her an actress, indicating that there was no need to underscore an actor's gender) who temped on the side to support her art. That she had temped for the same company for the past three years did not stop her from refusing a full-time position with a substantial raise and health benefits. Most girls her age would have changed such an outdated name or taken on a more age-appropriate nickname. Not Madge. She didn't flaunt her grandmother's fame but she certainly wore her name with pride. "She was one heck of a grandma," Madge once told Grey. This was the first time that he had ever seen her outside work.

She wore bright yellow biking shorts and a sleeved, skin-tight, royal blue spandex shirt covered with names—a memento from some sponsored sporting competition like windsurfing or a triathlon or, true to her kneepads and skated feet, rollerblading.

Grey welcomed her as if he expected her to show up. "Madge, don't you think you're tall enough without those three-inch lifts?"

Rothko sequestered the attention of another woman who was with Madge and whorishly beguiled her to rub his newly exposed belly.

Madge bantered back, "Ha, ha. Who knew you could be funny? I guess it's an outside-the-office kind of thing, huh?"

Giving him no time to defend himself, she sidled over with the awkward rollerblade toe-walk and sat down. "Seriously, it's good t'see you have an alter ego."

The underfed, tattooed, Gen-Y waiter delivered Grey's second chilidog with far more mannered efficiency than the first and mumbled some lispy question to show off his tongue jewelry to the two women.

Madge's eyes widened. "Oh, you even eat unhealthy—I love it!"

The possibility of another half chilidog brought Rothko upright and back to his master's side, acting as though no stomach-rubbing woman could ever turn his head.

Madge reached down and scratched under Rothko's ear, hitting his sweet spot and causing his back leg to gyrate in ecstasy. "Awwww, whadda cutie." This week, Madge's pixie-cut hair was the exact same shade of orange as Rothko's tail, all the way to the blond tips.

"Hey, I read that article this morning." Madge's friend was a little shorter and less flashy but had Madge's same casual, self-assured composure. Her short dark brown hair was cut in what Scott referred to as a Dorothy Hamill modified wedge.

She sat down on the other side of Madge. "He has some good suggestions but without some kind of discipline, the neuroses of this city'll win every time."

In Madge's expert way of always knowing the exact information Grey needed, she jumped in. "Kathe's my yoga teacher."

Before they left, Grey promised he would go to one of Kathe's classes and that they could borrow Rothko anytime.

He intended to follow them south and go back but at the thought of being trapped at Christian's piano singing show tunes, he decided to compose his own West Side story.

17

It was almost four. Grey was sitting on a bench in Riverside Park, Rothko snoozing at his feet on a bed of crispy, muted leaves. Their journey had led them up the Hudson, hugging the river unless forced, by construction or curiosity, to detour inland for a block or two. These tangents opened discoveries. They browsed boutiques and gift shops, and investigated a gallery exhibiting dog art—various artists, various media, but all of dogs (ironically, the only establishment on their tour that prohibited Rothko from entering). If Riverside Church hadn't beckoned, they may have made it all the way to the Cloisters.

In admiration Grey contemplated the church—he had always been in awe of its liberal history. For him, Riverside Church represented the true ideals of Christianity, ideals that were all too rare in his adult life. Grey leaned back into the wooden planks of the bench and imagined what it must have been like during its Depression-era construction. His errant historical placement fashioned Riverside Park full of upper-society top hats and bustles, a Seurat painting or a scene from an Edith Wharton novel.

Scott loved Wharton. The loose sequitur lead Grey to an argument during the first year or two of his and Scott's relationship, when Scott had sat on pins and needles waiting for Grey to finish *The House of Mirth* so they could discuss the tragedy of Lily Bart, born to be a society belle but destined to die an impoverished addict.

"Whaddya mean she could've easily avoided her fate?" Scott had yelled at Grey. "You just can't sympathize with her because she's witty and beautiful and not some poor hag from the wrong side of the tracks." That argument was over four years ago and although it was after their relationship had started to turn, at least then they still discussed things like literature, art and politics. And sex.

Grey wondered if he didn't miss their passionate discussions of sex even more than the act itself. After their Berkshires encounter, they didn't see each other again for a while but instead began an intense email dialogue, exchanging countless messages that started as a discussion of the New York art scene but somehow wound around to a deconstruction of gay sex. From animalistic attraction to social repression, anonymity versus intimacy to anonymous intimacy, strong mothers and absent fathers to the adulation of the untouchable virgin, all the way to Grey's systems theory of gay desire as the Earth's protection against overpopulation; they had gone on and on. Grey slumped back and rested his head on the bench. He smiled, remembering how, when at last they did get together, this sexual discourse had created such expectation they both had to get plastered to make it into the bedroom, where they groped each other in the dark like two teenagers.

The air was cooler in the shade; Grey buttoned up his coat. Light scattered through the remaining dead leaves that dangled tentatively, having for a few extra days escaped their autumnal release. He was a seven-year-old boy staring up through the outstretched limbs of his backyard maple tree. The clouds above were translucent cirrus against a pale sky. His childhood dog, Little Bit, lay curled under his armpit.

The church chimed the hour.

Above the branches rose its gothic tower. He had once read that in the tower's belfry hung the world's largest carillon bell and that its peal was said to cast a musical tone and quality impossible to replicate.

Grey again closed his eyes and listened, transported further back in time, this time to the '60s, to a faint memory of news footage with throngs of silent protesters bursting out of Riverside Church onto the steps, enrapt by Martin Luther King, Jr.'s famous "Beyond Vietnam" speech. This image was reshaped by the second bell toll into a 1968 scene from Grey's suburban Memphis elementary school.

He stood in a classroom, listening to a frantic radio broadcast as competing sirens blanketed the city. A single siren signaled a tornado warning, but Grey knew that their multitude meant something of far greater importance. The frenzy of the sirens and radio was countered by his spellbound teacher, Mrs. Johnson, an austere woman with teased hair and a limp from a childhood case of polio. He watched in awe as tears streamed down her face; he had never before seen an adult cry. As the school scrambled single file into the hallway, he heard the boy behind him say that downtown some king had finally been shot. The ensuing riots shut down Memphis for what seemed like an eternity.

The third toll transported him to Duke Chapel. He sat in a pew beside Miriam and her husband Jim; Pete was at the altar beaming down the aisle as his future wife approached. Miriam leaned into Grey, grabbed his hand and whispered, "Didja ever think this would happen?" When she released her hold, he ached with coming-of-age loss.

With the final toll he was kneeling alone in a small Florentine chapel the Sunday after Elba. Unseen in a room somewhere behind the apse, a chorus of men chanted, deep and resonant. It was the last time he prayed.

Grey opened his eyes; Rothko was still asleep below the bench. His coiled body rhythmically expanded and contracted in time with a slight but audible snore. Grey mumbled to himself, "A dog's life," as he took a small spiral-bound notebook from of his pocket.

For fourteen years Grey had continued to journal although he no longer chronicled events or activities. He had even stopped noting the dates of his entries. Instead he used the journal as a reflection of his constant analysis, his inner dialogue that posed unanswered question after unanswered question. Until a couple of years back he still used larger, more substantial journals like the one Miriam had first given him, but then he started wanting something more portable. He tried a man-purse but never felt comfortable carrying it in public. The only downside to the smaller notebooks he now used was that he went through about two a month. That and the banality of the cardboard and spiral. But the tradeoff was worth it.

He was just about done with this one; he turned to the next to last page and wrote:

> *I want to feel alive again. Somewhere along the way I lost myself. I'm not sure where or when but now I just feel numb. Aren't we supposed to be liberated? My and Scott's relationship is as insipid as my parents. Is this what we've been fighting for?*

I don't want to be like Scott, always wanting more, nothing ever enough. But I do want more. Is this selfish? Then I look at John and Madge and even Jimmy and I think I'm missing something fundamental. Some life force. Did I ever have it? Before Scott? Maybe it's not Scott. Maybe it's the City. Today I feel like there have been times when I was truly happy and none of these times were in New York. Maybe we could move. Maybe to the coast. Just being next to the ocean—its smell, its sound, its touch.

He ran out of paper but he didn't know where it was going anyway. Scott would never move from New York. At least not now that he was finally on a career track. And by the looks of his dot-com job, Scott had the potential with his options to earn more as an office manager than Grey could ever at Orion, even if he were promoted to an executive position. Millions more. Grey thought, *Maybe in a couple of years.*

18

"Huuuuuu-uhhhhhhhh," he exhaled, stretching and twisting lazily toward the river. "Come on, boy." Rothko woke himself up with a Pavlovian yelp. He jumped up in exuberant confusion as if to say, *I just heard my bark so I must be excited. Wait, there I go again; boy, I can't wait to see what I'm excited about.*

They walked home, again skirting the riverfront, exploring the side streets only if Grey saw a cute store or Rothko had a hankering to mark a new territory. At Seventieth they ventured inward. A New York anomaly in its staying power, Café Luxembourg was still a popular restaurant, although Grey had never returned. He tied Rothko up to the awning post and went in. It looked exactly as it had in 1985. There were few patrons as it was early for dinner and so Grey didn't feel too out of place in his casual attire. He sat at the bar and smoothed his hands across the worn shiny zinc. A tuxedo-vested bartender approached, young, with a shaved head and a goatee.

"You wouldn't know how to make a Tom Collins, would you?" Grey asked.

"Tom Collins, wow, I've only heard them ordered in old movies. That's gin, right?" The bartender flipped his bar towel over one hand like he was wrapping his fist for a fight and extended the other toward Grey. "By the way, the name's Mike."

Grey shook his hand. "Grey." Mike reached below the bar and grabbed a shaker. "Since my day feels like an old rerun, a Tom Collins is perfect. It's been a while but gin sounds right and I'm guessin' lemon juice, that is if you don't have Collins mix." Mike raised his eyebrows and with a playful *yea, right* wink. The crunch of scooped ice was drowned out by Rothko's bark from outside.

Grey flinched. "He's mine; I'll be quick."

"No worries," replied Mike as he stretched to get the gin from the shelf behind him.

"I wouldn't say that." Grey rubbed his thumb across the spiral binding of his journal in his pocket. He was sitting not ten feet away from the table where he and Miriam had celebrated *life*. The chain she gave him still hung around his neck.

The last stop was *Alessandro's*, an Italian grocery store on Twenty-fourth Street. Its awning, a replica of the Italian flag, attracted Grey's attention. He thought once again of the small Florentine chapel. Without realizing it, he had been gawking at the outdoor stand of wooden slatted vegetable baskets filled with tomatoes of all shapes, colors and sizes, many varieties he had never seen before.

"You can bring the dog in if you want." The owner, Alessandro, was an Italian man in his fifties. He was of medium build and height but carried himself with a stature far taller and stockier. He wore a coarse, bushy mustache that, like the remainder of his hair, had been died jet-black. Like Wade's. A beardless mustache would have seemed a bit of a '70s throwback if it hadn't come with the Italian swagger as authentic as the awning.

"Just ask if you wanna know about anything," Alessandro said and followed Grey in, returning to his behind-the-counter stool to watch a baseball game. Grey glanced at the TV; he thought baseball season was over but then he could never keep sports seasons straight.

There was an old-world feeling to the store; it smelled of the mingled odors of meat, fish and dirty mop. Grey walked past the narrow aisles to the large deli and examined the hanging pastas of various lengths and thickness. With a hunch he would strike a chord, Grey raised his voice over that of the sports announcer and asked, "Are these any better than packaged pasta?"

"Excuse me?" Alessandro eyed Grey with such astonishment an onlooker not privy to the exchange may have been frightened that Grey had just declared a holdup.

Grey lied, "I was just coming in for some basic spaghetti and wondered if I should try this instead." That was all it took. From that point on, Alessandro never stopped moving or talking. He marched out from behind the counter, spewing disbelief at such an inane question, and filled a large bag with black linguini. He did not politely inquire and influence but rather shadowed Grey through the store, demanding that he buy this and that. Another day Grey might have been offended at his aggressiveness, but it wasn't another day.

Grey taunted him, "Why would I pay this for tomatoes when I could go uptown to Fresh Fields with a much larger selection at about half the cost?" Alessandro recoiled, threw up his hands and ranted that there was no store in Manhattan with tomatoes as fresh as his.

"I grow them myself in my backyard. Here, you eat one and tell me that any store in New York sells tomatoes like this."

Grey popped a cherry tomato into his mouth and after swallowing, pressed Alessandro further. "Wow, tasty. Seriously, where do you get them? You don't expect me to believe that you actually grow them?"

Alessandro thrust his open hands forward into Grey's face, causing Rothko to growl in protection. Up to this point Alessandro's English had been excellent but now his passion started to impact his conjugation. "I close up and you come with me now. I show you my backyard. I show you my garden."

They continued this combative rapport throughout the store as Grey questioned the value of homemade pasta sauce and specialty olive oils. At this Alessandro yelled, "OK, that's it!" and marched back to the front of the store.

He ignored a young couple with a stroller who, as Alessandro passed, turned and smiled at one another. *Regulars*, Grey thought.

Alessandro searched under the counter. "Tonight you make the best meal that you ever eat." Standing back up, he handed Grey a pad of paper and a pen. "Listen and write." He led Grey up and down the aisles, detailing the importance of each ingredient before he placed it in the cart. Grey was enthralled. Alessandro valued olive oils so much that many were kept behind the counter with the fine wines. When Grey challenged a fifteen-dollar, twelve-ounce bottle, Alessandro responded with a ten-minute lecture on the different varietals and the regional variations. He was now more instructional than argumentative. "It's as important to know the maker and year of an olive oil as it is for a wine." With this point he seemed to reach a crux in his argument because he quieted with an abrupt, almost religious reverence as though he had entered a confessional after a hard month of sinning. He climbed a short stepladder to retrieve a hidden treasure from the top shelf. Grey examined the label—Brunello. It was still a young wine, a '97. But it was only thirty-eight dollars.

"Do you have any French wine?" Grey asked with feigned seriousness.

Halfway home Grey was chuckling to himself when some sluggish mathematical synapse fired and he realized something was wrong. The grocery bill seemed low. He pulled the receipt out of the bag, examined it and noticed that Alessandro had thrown the wine in for free.

When he rounded the corner onto Jane, his good mood dampened and he started to regret having dallied. What was he thinking? Scott had certainly made dinner plans; he always did.

19

"Whatcha get for dinner?" Jimmy sat in the same spot where Grey had left him eight hours earlier.

Grey winced. "Oh shit, Jimmy, sorry about lunch but believe me, dinner'll make up for it. I'll be back in a flash."

Grey had just made it through the door when Scott barged in from the study where, until Grey arrived, he was ensconced with a martini and MTV. "Where'n the hell have you been all day? What the fuck do you think you're doing not leaving a message?"

Two feet away, on the living room side of the bar, Scott stood, furious. His breath reeked of gin and his face was so red that his normally undetectable acne scars stood out in mottled pigmentation. His thinning hair lay disheveled, limp against his head—sweat more likely alcohol-infused than anxiety-induced. Like a carnival mirror image, Scott sidestepped to match Grey's movement down the bar as Grey put the groceries on the counter. Grey bent down to remove Rothko's leash and when he came back up, Scott had moved around to the kitchen side. His eyes were filled with anger; he was a teapot on the brink of a shrill whistle. There was an almost comical silence, an outtake too long to be taken seriously.

"Well?" Scott managed with insistent elocution he usually reserved for a different brand of four-letter word.

Grey lunged at him, wrapping his arm around Scott's waist. With his other hand he reached behind Scott's head and pulled it to his own. Their mouths collided, contorted in mutual disgust. Scott struggled but could not match Grey's strength.

"Quid'it!" Scott sputtered through his teeth, his words accompanied by a spattering of Bombay and saliva. He wiggled out of Grey's hold and backed a few steps away. "What the *FUCK* is wrong with you?" His face had gone from red to white in mock fear.

Grey was struck with an eerie clairvoyance that he would remember this moment as the end. It was so intense he had to lean against the counter to regroup.

Scott turned his back, a choreographed *pas-de-deux* rejection, and lowered his voice. "Wherever you've been today, whatever you've done to trigger this . . . *dis-play*," he paused and exaggerated his enunciation on the word *display* for effect, "I don't want to know about it." He walked over to the sink without acknowledging the groceries on the counter. He filled his martini glass with water and chugged it in one gulp. His voice was now calm, in control. "Shower and change; I promised Grant we'd go with him to that new restaurant on Tenth." He put the glass in the dishwasher. "You know, the all-white one with the courtyard." When he looked up at Grey, his complexion had returned. So had the emptiness of his eyes. In passing he whispered as in confidence, "He heard that all of the cute Latin boys go there so he's itching to check it out." Grey finished unpacking the groceries.

Grey stirred the sauce. It had not been difficult to convince Scott to go by himself. As a twosome, Grant would not look like the pathetic third wheel. Scott, empowered by his victory, had been confident enough to agree. He even kissed Grey on the cheek as he left. "Don't wait up; you know Grant."

The room glowed with dimmed halogen and candles. Grey lifted the wooden spoon from the pan to his lips. He smiled, happy again to be alone. In an adjacent pot, Alessandro's inky black linguini boiled. Grey searched his notes to see how long it needed to cook. Alessandro had been thorough. He took a sip of his wine and checked his watch. Though Grey didn't notice that Scott had left without turning off the TV, he swayed back and forth over pot and pan to Madonna's "Justify My Love."

Grey leveled both plates as he opened the door with his hip. This time he took the elevator.

Jimmy was ten or so feet farther down the sidewalk, cross-legged in front of the hotel. Ever since the show had opened, Jimmy had taken to relocating his nightshift so he could milk the generosity of the theater crowd.

"Man, this's good," Jimmy said, spinning the linguini around his fork. It reminded Grey of the childhood habit he'd abandoned at the simultaneous emergence of both Scott and the formal business dinner into his life.

As Jimmy was taking his third or fourth bite—more than Grey had ever seen him eat in one sitting—Grey reacquainted himself with the pleasure of spun spaghetti. "Jimmy, can I ask you a question?"

Jimmy took another bite and started his response with a full mouth, "Chure man, bu ca-it like, ait 'ill u'orrow; the show's out in fibe an if you're ere, well . . . " He swallowed. "Let's just say that ya may impact my brand identity."

Grey put Jimmy's plate into the dishwasher and heaped a huge second helping onto his own. Rothko was in the corner, asleep on his Donghia dog bed, snoring as usual. Grey walked out onto the deck. It was cold; he wouldn't be able to stay for long. The sauce steamed in defiance to the frigid air.

The show was over and Jimmy was selling his shtick six stories below. Across the roof, the actors were changing back into their street clothes. Grey wondered about the lead actor. Every night this boy would stare into a small Victorian vanity mirror centered on a battered '50s city-issue office desk. He would remain transfixed until an hour later when he put on his costume. The full contrast would always strike Grey—the smooth pale boyish body with the elaborate face of a painted lady, a severe transvestite donning platinum Farrah Fawcett hair. Grey knew every outfit, every wig. At the end of the night, after the show was done, the actor returned to the room with a masculine intensity that belied both his boyish frame and the feminine persona he had worked so hard to create.

While he had heard that *Hedwig and the Angry Inch* had become a surprise hit, Grey chose to neither read nor listen to anything about the play, instead letting his imagination craft and recraft his own interpretation of this actor's nightly transformation from boy to woman to man.

The turret stood prominently against the dark Hudson. It was now deserted except for the young actor who was always both first to arrive and the last to leave. He was as meticulous removing his makeup as he was applying it. A half-hour after the show, after everyone else had gone, he would be left staring into the mirror, once again a young, pretty, androgynous boy.

No matter how many times Grey witnessed this scene, he was mesmerized, even though the boy, unlike the other actors, had never once looked out of the turret window across the twenty yards to Grey's deck. Never once had they locked eyes.

No longer steaming, the half-eaten linguini succumbed to the cold.

20

Grey's eyes snapped open to the light upon his eyelids. The alarm clock read five-thirty. He wondered if the electricity had gone out but then realized that both he and Scott had forgotten to close the blinds. He slipped out from under the covers and grabbed his robe from the hook beside the bed before the morning air could raise a chill on his bare flesh. Across the river the morning sky was orange and rose. The days were already waning; before too long he would be rising to darkness. Grey felt a pang of dread for the onset of winter workdays when he would only see sunlight in suburbia from inside his glass-walled office.

Scott lay on top of the covers, naked, on his stomach, legs and arms stretched at his side—a facedown balding Da Vinci anatomy study. Grey used to find this such a turn-on that he would sometimes climb back into bed to arouse Scott for a session of morning lovemaking. He sat back down on the edge of the bed and placed his hand at the base of Scott's spine, rubbing his fingers across the raised bottom vertebrae he always thought so sexy. Scott didn't stir. The strap of his sleep mask cut a line across the back of his head, matting his oily hair. To his left, in the middle of the depression that marked where Grey had slept, lay a waxy blue earplug that had fallen out of one of Scott's ears. Without disturbing him, Grey slipped out of his robe and went to take a shower.

John was waiting by the time Grey made it out the door at seven-ten. Grey had just walked a delighted Rothko around the block. The normal routine was that Scott, since he slept in two hours later than Grey, walked Rothko in the mornings. It was the only Rothko chore to which Scott had begrudgingly agreed. But fresh from the magic of the previous day's journey, Grey aimed to prolong the effect.

"C'mon man, you're late," John yelled out the window, exhaling visible gusts of breath in the cold morning air like the tailpipe exhaust from his sky blue vintage Camaro. Grey sat down in his white leather bucket seat and was greeted by a warm blast from the dashboard heating vent and John's standard eye-opening screeching from the radio.

"Let me guess, Smashing Pumpkins?"

John was gunning the car before Grey had even closed the door. He flashed a sideways glance, "Not taking the bait," and turned onto the West Side Highway. "One grunge band's not like all others. Unlike that bubblegum '80s crap that you listen to."

"Not taking it either." Grey unfolded his paper. He and John had an ongoing debate about music. Grey thought every screaming Kirk Cobain was pretty much the same while John combated with his theory that the gay male's acute artistic sensibility was normalized by the glaring omission of musical discretion. He joked about a gay genetic defect that rendered the average gay man's musical ear to that of a twelve-year-old girl. In truth, Grey did prefer Madonna to Billie and musicals to opera but he would never admit it. And so they bantered. Without looking up, Grey turned to the Arts & Leisure section to read part two of the Tao article as he retorted, "If this shit is musical appreciation, then it's just one more reason that I'm glad to be gay."

John responded by turning up the volume. "Listen to that intensity, that depth of conviction—how can it not move you?"

"Easy." Grey stopped short of punctuating the word with intended disdain when a below-the-fold headline stopped him cold.

Off Off OFF Broadway Show an Unforgettable Experience.

The young actor's face stared at Grey for the first time. "John, have you seen that show playing next to me?"

John lowered the volume. "Did I hear you right? Grey Tigrett asking about a non-pop music experience?" He pantomimed surprise as he turned onto Eighteenth Street. "Oh yeah, I guess it is musical theater of sorts."

"Ha, ha."

They stopped at Eighteenth and Tenth. Beyond the passenger window, a typical Chelsea street scene: two rough-looking musclemen with shaved heads, one clad in leather, the other in army fatigues. In another part of town they may have caused a pause for consideration, possibly triggered a surreptitious hand movement toward the automatic lock button. Here, holding hands, they were as conspicuous as blue-suited bankers on Wall Street.

John didn't even glance at them, focusing instead on the traffic light ahead. "It's supposed t'be the rebirth of the rock musical, as if the paltry two or three rock musicals of the '70s denote enough of a genre to warrant the term *rebirth.*" John raced the engine, impatient for the light to change. On foot he took his time, but a car was a different matter. "I hear it's amazing but I just can't imagine any transvestite rock musical topping *Rocky Horror.*" John paused in uncharacteristic awkwardness and then added, "I mean, it's sorta weird that outta a handful of rock musicals, two are about transvestites."

Ten minutes later Grey was at Grand Central Terminal. He was in line to buy his monthly pass that he had once again forgotten to renew by mail. It was 7:25. The teller had just informed the man in front of him that his credit card had been denied. While the man spewed vitriol, Grey surveyed the recently completed celestial ceiling. He was still in awe of the renovation. As he searched for Taurus, his attention narrowed to a small rectangular patch of sky, on the south side, darker than the rest, which appeared to be left intentionally unrestored.

"Hey, Dreamweaver, are ya interested in say, hmmmmmm, movin' the fuck along." Shocked by the uncomfortable familiarity of the nickname, Grey tripped and barely missed hitting his head on the counter. His heckler stepped around him to the ticket window before Grey had a chance to regain his composure. Grey sheepishly slipped back in line behind him.

21

"I see we missed the seven-thirty. Extended your Sunday-on-the-town a little too long, huh?" Madge said with her usual cheerfulness. She got up, walked around the desk and pecked him on the check. "Good for you." She looked back over her shoulder as she headed toward the break room. "Don't worry, I smoothed it over; he's back on at four-thirty. Single or double this morning?"

"Double."

Grey watched Madge saunter off. She wore a Pucci miniskirt over pumpkin-colored tights and '70s-style hoop earrings that looped down way below her pixie hairline, almost to her shoulders. Madge was the only woman Grey knew who embraced her femininity with such uncompromising assurance of equality that she could, one minute, kiss her boss on the cheek and get him coffee while the next, insist on the term *actor* over *actress*.

"Dontcha think you should be directing those eyes at our numbers or haven't you listened to your voicemail yet?" Jane was Grey's top rep. She was aware of her femininity as well but standing five-foot-three to Madge's five eleven, Donna Karan to Madge's Pucci, and thirty-seven-year-old wizened professional to Madge's twenty-three-year-old ingénue actor were merely the tip of the differential iceberg.

"I see you haven't." Jane lifted her right hand in a pose that evoked Rodin's Thinker but with far more attitude and supposition. "Late morning?" She followed his attention to the break room. "Anyone I know?"

Halfway down the hall to her office, she added, loud enough for the entire office to hear, "Wouldn't be the first time in this Peyton Place of a company." Jane stopped at her door. "Listen to your messages and let's tackle this together.

I'll run the numbers. You do the begging."

Grey hung his coat on the rack by his office door, wondering whether he had just been dissed, railroaded or offered genuine assistance—most likely all three. His ordered functional office was a study in corporate monotony. He picked up the phone and dialed four numbers that, if asked, he wouldn't be able to recall unless he watched his hand mimic the dialing sequence and mentally mapped his finger movements to the numeric telephone grid. A soothing voice answered, a voice more intimate than any other in his life. "Press the asterisk key to enter your mailbox."

Twelve hours later Grey was on his fourth double espresso of the day. The previous day's *joie de vivre* was a distant memory. Bob, the head of sales, had left a voicemail indicating that he wanted the quarterly numbers cross-referenced by industry and put in an urgent request to close an additional million by the end of the day.

Grey hung up from his last sales call where he secured another $250K order, ending the day at $875K. He pushed the phone back into its nighttime resting place. In his managerial climb Grey had learned that a manager's desk must always be neat—to reflect control and completion. The only giveaway of work undone was the phone's voicemail light that shone red, but then it always did. In Orion's voicemail-obsessed culture, the light had become more of an aesthetic than a feature.

Grey sat back in his chair and tilted his head from side to side. His neck cracked louder than usual. It relieved some of the tension, the result of stress, bad posture and his ill-designed office chair. His senses were dulled but not negatively so; they were more impartial. At some point long ago in his career, he would have been perturbed by falling $125K short but tonight's state of mind had more to do with the burnout of continuous firefighting and embarrassment from forever manipulating customers into buying equipment they didn't want.

Thumbing through his briefcase, he stopped at the folder that Madge had dropped on his desk on her way out. It was labeled, *Annual Sales Conference* and sealed with her signature Hello Kitty sticker. Madge sealed every folder she gave him; it was her way of marking completion.

"Wanna ride to the station?" Jane wore a Burberry overcoat and carried a custom Louis Vuitton computer case. Jane liked visible labels.

"Sure, give me a sec." Grey put the folder back in his briefcase and shut down his computer.

Jane stayed in the doorway. "How'd ya do?"

He stood up and pushed his chair back under the desk. "Eight-seventy-five."

Jane responded with a mixture of disbelief and respect, "Without extra discounts? From who?" She handed him a folder with the revised spreadsheet. He put it in his briefcase in front of Hello Kitty.

Grey's office was beyond neat; it was sterile. There was no personal item such as a frame or a trade show gadget to indicate any sign of inhabitance. It looked either vacated or refurbished for a new employee. From outside the building's one-way mirrored walls, it was an isolated square that shone a soft metallic glow against a bank of darkened panels. Grey and Jane began down the hallway. They didn't turn off the lights; there wasn't a need—the electric eye would soon detect no motion.

"AT&T booked 500K." A waft of Jane's perfume emanated from her neckline. It smelled both expensive and freshly applied. Grey inched away. "I promised to get them their Q2 orders by the end of the month."

Jane's expression changed from awe to cynicism. "Good luck on that commitment." It was a preface to the usual diatribe. "I am so sick of this hockey-stick crap. It was one thing when they gave us some discounting room but now . . . Especially when they don't ship our backlog. What're we supposed to say, 'Please buy more. I swear we'll ship the stuff you've already paid for . . . eventually?'"

Grey and Jane slipped into their roles, the game they played and would continue to play no matter what management said. It served them well. They both had excelled because they were good at it. Yet everyone complained; it was the scripted dialogue of their repeat performances. Grey opened the door for Jane and they stepped out into the humid warmth, a far cry from the morning's chill. The only sound was the fluorescent buzz of a parking lot streetlight about to go on the fritz. New York City seemed a thousand miles away.

Jane escorted Grey to the passenger side even though her electric key unlocked all doors. She had not yet finished her lines as she opened his door. "I don't know which is worse, the refusal to hire a third manufacturing shift—at least for the last week of the quarter—or their intentional nonshipment of backlog to balance the numbers."

Grey studied Jane as she strutted around the front of her Jeep Cherokee. Her long straight platinum hair bounced against her back. Again he contrasted her with Madge, their different ways of balancing femininity with masculinity were almost reverse images of each other. She got in and unbuttoned her fitted suit coat with the manner of a man but the intent of a woman. "What's with the heat; we had frost this morning. Whatever, I hope it keeps up."

Jane glanced at her image in the rearview mirror before starting the car. "So c'mon, you're doin' Madge, right?"

"No, Jane, I swear I'm not doing Madge." Grey hadn't engaged in such frat house talk in a long time.

Jane revved the engine. "Then who are you dating? You're so obviously a catch."

As Jane shifted the Jeep into reverse, Grey interjected with managerial authority, "Let's change the channel; how're Jack and the kids?"

22

Grey was exhausted. Once again, he decided to go straight home and skip the gym. Even though working out was his only personal respite, it was always the first to be sacrificed. He took the sealed conference folder from his briefcase and ripped through Hello Kitty's face.

Bob had scheduled the conference smack-dab over the Thanksgiving holidays. For Grey this was fine; it meant one less evening with Brian and Greg, but he hated having to ask his employees to forgive another of Bob's oversights. Grey scanned the itinerary. It was spectacular—a cruise up the Italian Riviera to Monte Carlo. While he dreaded the mingling and posturing, these things were always first-class, and unlike usual, it looked like they had scheduled in plenty of free time. Grey sighed as he thought, *I'm sure Bob will fix that.* He put the folder back in his briefcase and looped the shoulder strap around his arm for security. Clutching it in his lap, he leaned his head back against the seat.

The woman across from him similarly strapped and clutched her plastic grocery bags. She was a young mother with two toddlers, a boy and a girl, who sat on either side of her. She wore a tight red sleeveless shirt that was far more fashion than sport. Its big blue Nike swoosh cupped her left breast. Her eyes were shut but she was not asleep. She was mouthing the words to the song blaring through her Discman headphones. The music was so loud Grey could hear it three feet away. It was gospel of some sort. Grey was pretty sure she didn't know her lips were moving. He wondered what facial expressions he himself made behind closed eyes. As he was being rocked to a light sleep by the train's narcotic percussion, he thought how good it would be to get away.

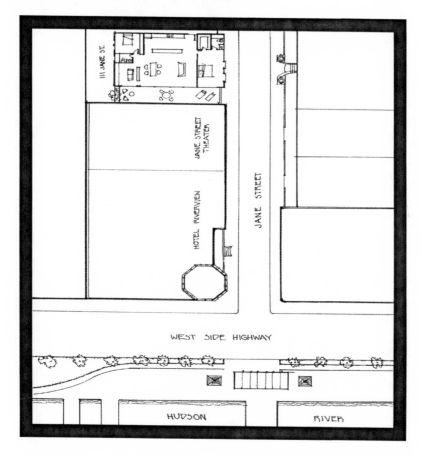

23

Grey slipped out of the meeting under the pretense of reviewing his slides. There was no one in the hallway—Orion had reserved the entire deck. Even the stairwell was empty. He climbed from beige indistinction to the colorful main level. Here there were at least the sounds of non-Orion life; the clinking of silver and dishware from the central cafeteria contended with the clanging of slot machines from the portside casino. This was not Grey's preferred ambiance but relative to the sterility below, there was no contest. When he opened the cabin door, the gust of cold air invigorated him. He was heading to the ship's small top deck, three flights above the main level, where few others ventured since it was only reachable by an exposed outdoor stairway. In the short time they had been aboard, it had become his personal getaway. At the second-level landing, the Mediterranean opened into full view. It was choppy but the waves were not capping. It teemed with motion. He watched the V of the boat's wake overtake the asymmetry of the sea. The small cruise ship cut through the rough water, unaffected. Two levels below, on the windowless subaquatic deck, the lack of sensory stimulation was so numbing it was easy to forget you were not in some drab landlocked Marriott.

But above, the sea was everywhere. The gentle lists of the ship, imperceptible below, here were magnified against the water's disharmony. The sky moved as well. The clouds had been thickening since they boarded and the sky was now almost as dark as the water. The massive orange sails beat against their masts. Grey wanted to savor what little time he had. They had been afloat for four days and in meetings a good part of the time. He craved the sea air. Since he had stepped on the boat, his desire to be outside was like an addiction. So much so he had begun smoking, a vice with which he had only flirted in college, as a mannered excuse to escape. Outside, he, like the boat, could drift.

It was 4 A.M.; Grey and Miriam lay in bed unable to get to sleep. They had spent most of the day flying back from Europe and were jetlagged. She spooned up to him and whispered, "Whaddya say we move to New York?" When he laughed, she rolled over and didn't speak to him until three days later when he brought up the subject again.

"Would you really consider moving to New York?"

Miriam looked up from her cereal to gauge his sincerity and then started in slowly. "Well, I was thinking I could see if my agency'll put me in touch with someone at Ford or Wilhelmina." Miriam had gone on about it for weeks. She had even sent a portfolio to Wilhelmina but then she stopped talking about it. Grey couldn't remember if this was sudden, caused by Wilhelmina's response, or more insidious, the waning idealism of post-collegiate life that forced her to accept reality—a reality that included the deterioration of their relationship.

Two months afterwards, in the interview with Orion, the recruiter asked him, "Would you move?"

Grey was expecting this question to test his eagerness. His response should show both flexibility and backbone. "It depends—to where?"

The recruiter fumbled through her papers; she couldn't have been much older than he was. Three years after Grey had taken the job, he had run into her on one of his trips to Corporate. They were at a Friday beer bust and, a bit tipsy, she admitted that it had been only her second college recruiting trip and she had been distracted by how attractive he was. She quickly added that it didn't influence her recommendation.

"Well, most of our open reqs are in California. We do have a few sales positions in the Research Triangle office." She flipped to the next page, "Oh, and one in the New York office."

Grey had just learned the maintain-eye-contact lesson in his interviewing class. He managed to hold hers long enough to force her attention back to her list and was emboldened by his success. "New York would be great."

A month later, when he got the job offer, Miriam sat across from him at a table in the student union coffee shop and cried. "For joy," she said. He knew better. Outside, after he and Miriam parted, Grey pulled out the pack of cigarettes he kept hidden in his backpack. He had promised her that he would quit, and for all she knew, he had. It wasn't like he was addicted; he would give it up eventually. There were three cigarettes left. He crumpled the pack and threw it in the first trash bin he passed.

"Hello." The voice surprised him. Grey jerked around too fast, resulting in momentary vertigo. Jane was reclining on a deck chair with a lime green windbreaker thrown over her like a blanket.

"What are you doing out here?"

"Smoking," she responded in monotone.

He sat down on the edge of her chair and took a pack of Marlboro Lights from his coat pocket. Jane pulled her legs farther into herself to make room. He tapped the box on his palm, ejecting a cigarette that he did not offer to her. "You don't smoke." He took the cigarette in his mouth.

She watched as, with cupped hands, he ducked and twisted to several different positions trying to light a match. At each angle the wind extinguished the flame. She reached over and took both cigarette and matches from him. "Neither did you before this trip."

Jane lifted her coat over her head and a second later pulled it down again, handing him the lit cigarette. Their hands touched as she passed the cigarette from her fingers to his. Grey eluded her eyes.

"What's up?" Jane asked. "I've never seen you so jittery."

Grey looked back at her, curled up in her cocoon. On the hem of the hood was a small tasteful swoosh woven in a green just darker than the coat; even Jane wore Nike. For no apparent reason the boat droned its dull, passive horn.

"I don't know. I was thinking of my first trip to Europe. You know, the whole after-college backpacking thing."

Jane sat up and crossed her legs yoga-style in her deck chair. "No, I don't know. I couldn't really afford to travel back then, and besides, I went straight to law school."

Grey took a drag of his cigarette and turned away from her to exhale. "Law school, I didn't know that."

Her voice hardened into sales rep aggression, "Not so fast mister, we were talking about you."

Grey's cigarette hung from his mouth; its smoke was undetectable, dispersed by the wind. It bobbed up and down as he talked. "There's not much to know— friends bummin' around Europe together."

Jane straightened her back; her entire body language shifted. She went into full sales pitch mode. "Then why so intense? C'mon, pony up."

They both turned toward the clang of someone coming up the metal steps.

24

"Well, well, well, sometimes I hate being right." Grey stood, again too fast. This time his dizziness got the best of him and he immediately sat back down.

"Don't worry—all rules are off on the open water."

Bob was undoubtedly the handsomest man at Orion. By any means or measure. He was six-two with the ideal swimmer's build that comes from either a lifetime of training or genetics. His was the latter. Bob, AKA Roberto Dias, was a Brazilian who lived up to the breathtaking ideal of the *Experience Rio* vacation ads. His skin was the color of toffee and his hair, a Michelangelo cap of tight brown curls tipped with just a dash of amber, too perfect not to be store-bought. His eyes dominated his narrow face not due to their size but rather their setting and unique color. Grey's mother had always referred to eyes like Bob's as bedroom eyes, almond shaped and angled downward at the outer edges, giving them a sleepy, sensual quality. They were rimmed by mascara-black, quarter-inch-long eyelashes that, because of their lack of curl, were not noticeable until you saw them in profile. They caught you off guard like a hidden scar or unexpected accent. As for their remarkable color, that was the subject of much office speculation. They were violet and, as with the numerous recountings of Elizabeth Taylor's, they did entrance their subject. They were rumored to be contacts. Still, it was difficult to deny Bob anything.

Bob's promotion to head of sales had been big news in Silicon Valley. While other computer manufacturers had not been able to break the Latin America sales code, Bob managed a twenty-five percent market share—twice Orion's share in any other non-US geography. From a societal standpoint, Roberto Dias was the highest paid Latino in an industry centered in a fast-growing Latin community.

Roberto was now Bob and lived on a sprawling ranch in Woodside. His English was impeccable but he still used his accent when it was to his advantage.

"Jane, if you don't mind, I am going to steal Grey for the presentation that he was supposed to have started ten minutes ago." He e·nun·ci·at·ed ev·ery word ful·ly.

As they headed down the stairs, Bob threw a brotherly arm around Grey's shoulder. "You dog," Bob whispered in his ear, elongating each vowel in Portuguese effect. Bob's eyes shifted downward, misinterpreting cause and effect. "You be careful with that; she's a married woman." He punctuated the cama-raderie with one of his signature winks. The lavender of his eyes darkened from the light shades near the pupil to the darker hues at the edge of the iris. Like a Rothko.

Grey stood behind the podium and although his erection had subsided, he was still discombobulated. He could not attain his usual composure and stared over the audience to the back of the room where Jane and Bob stood side by side. Bob leaned over and whispered in her ear. Grey smoothed back his hair as he adjusted the microphone.

He cleared his throat. "Sorry I'm late but I was having a little chat with Bob." He redirected his attention to the front row. He was nervous but kept his voice from cracking. He resorted to an age-old Toastmasters trick of imagining the audience in their underwear. This worked and he began to relax until he glanced back again at Bob. The podium served as both power and shield behind which he now allowed his body's natural reaction to go unsuppressed. Like the Mediterranean above, the unrestrained intensity inspirited him. Gripping the podium's edge, he remained focused on Bob.

"I wanted to make sure he'd stick to his promise of entering the *new* millen-nium with a *new* set of rules."

Bob tilted his head and gave a questioning smirk, a challenge that redoubled Grey's passion, both oratorically as well as physically.

"I wanted to make sure that he'd meet his commitment of . . ." Grey leaned into the podium for effect. " . . . increased discounting flexibility . . . " The energy of the crowd shifted.

" . . . full shipment of backlog at the beginning of every quarter . . . "

Applause shot through the room. Bob folded his arms beneath his chest, accentuating his V-shaped frame. Grey thought of the ship's powerful wake; he was so hard it hurt.

"... and no more last-minute urgent off-plan bookings requests."

The room sprung to a standing ovation. Bob's smile broadened either in admiration or defiance.

25

The water was surprisingly warm and clear, and alive—a panorama of color swaying to a silent orchestra. The world above ceased to exist except as autonomic life support to which he was only dependent as an air supply. Grey's melodic breathing through the snorkel was a backbeat against which the sea danced. Flecks of color glinted from myriad fish encircling him. When he reached into their midst, the fish grouped and scattered. The sea's color bled away, leaving a vast expanse of deep blues and greens. Stillness replaced the dance. His breath throbbed in his ears. The sea's floor wasn't the natural purity he had imagined but was littered with man-made debris. He could not judge its depth; the clarity was too distorting. As he swam ahead to find everyone, the landscape became more filthy and lifeless. Amidst unrecognizable rust there was a half-buried computer monitor next to a porcelain toilet. He reversed his arm motion and hovered in place to get a better look. It was off to his left.

The monitor, if unearthed, would have been of comparable size to the toilet, a testament to its antiquity. Its screen was broken to the darkness within; he was not close enough to see its innards. The toilet gleamed white, not a barnacle on it. It was in mint condition with its seat upright as if left there by a neglectful husband. Grey was certain it was new because it was the same model as the one in his master bathroom—the one Scott had badgered him to buy, with its European style that set them back five times that of any American toilet—the one that within a year of its installation had a mal-fitting O-ring that had to be replaced at a specialty import cost of seventy-five dollars. It shined against the dullness of its surroundings. The limited edition two-hundred-dollar handle had snagged a wayward net that trailed behind. It flared out and enjoined with another thick mass of nets so immense he could not see beyond it. It didn't sway with the water but was motionless, an ominous web. When Grey looked back, the monitor and toilet had vanished; he had floated past them. The sea began to darken. To the left, the tangle of nets had grown in size and density like approaching storm clouds. He rolled over to check on the boat. Blackness engulfed him. Frantic with confusion, he realized that he had somehow drifted beneath the surface but had no idea how deep. Holding his breath to conserve the remaining pocket of air in the snorkel, he searched for the others. From the corner of his eye, a vibration disrupted the stagnant water.

It was a dim glow. He assumed it was the ship's hull bobbing upon the sea's wavy surface above. He rushed toward it but as he approached, saw that it was not the ship but a cage on the sea floor. An enormous crab clutched the wire mesh that imprisoned it. The scratching of the crab's desperate claws against the metal pierced the depths, breaking the reticent silence, reminding Grey that he was holding his breath. He stopped swimming and floated in front of the cage. The crab, in reaction to the presence of a perceived predator or a savior, ceased his struggle and sat paralyzed in the corner of the cage, claws still clamped around the rusty wire. For an instant they were frozen in mutual awareness. And then Grey's vision dimmed and both cage and crab dissolved. He no longer felt the water against his skin. In this sensory deprivation it was now his slowing heartbeat that took over, ringing in his ears. Each beat amplified louder, each one a longer interval than the one before. He heard not his heart but the final notes of a languid sonata; he saw not the claws of a crab but the pianist's fingers slowing, connecting one by one with the last few keystrokes. Grey's fear subsided and his disparate thoughts dissipated into blankness. He surrendered. The boundaries between his body and mind and the water ceased to exist. He became one with the sea. As before, sensuality befell him.

The crab began to shake the cage with such violence that it tipped over, breaking Grey's trance. Grey grabbed the anchoring rope and climbed, hand over hand through the murky water. The perspective before him, the static line's distant convergence with the surface, revealed just how deep he had gone. He ripped the mask from his face. The rush of water intensified his will to live but its bitter salinity blinded him. Racing against fading consciousness, he pulled himself upward. He fought the instinct to inhale, instead expelling from his lungs what little breath remained. A single thin column of bubbles trailed his ascent. Grey broke the surface to an empty lifeboat. Strengthened by the adrenaline coursing through his veins, he managed to climb in.

When he awoke, it was nighttime. Somehow his ordeal had taken him through late afternoon and twilight. He searched the horizon for the ship; it wasn't far ahead. He couldn't tell whether it was moving toward him or away. In his exhaustion, he didn't care. They would find him either tonight or in the morning. Before passing out he lay in the bottom of the raft, the lull of the sea beneath him, a sea of stars above. Orion was centered in the sky with his sword raised high. All the other stars capitulated to his dominance.

It was morning—puffs of clouds drifted overhead. He shivered. A shard of sunlight blinded him. When it passed, its source, the twin towers, proudly announced the New York skyline. Grey was embarrassed. His little pre-commute fishing jaunt had turned into an expedition. Now he felt ridiculous, sitting in a small rowboat dressed in a business suit, in the middle of the Hudson. His shoulders strained with the tautness of the line. Whatever he had hooked had pulled him out into the river and had now looped around and was towing him back to shore. In the turnabout Grey couldn't get the boat around and pointed toward land; it remained parallel with the flow of the river, its full length resisting the water's crosscurrent thus making the tension on the line all the worse. Scott would be waking up soon and he would be pissed at Grey's foolishness. Grey glanced up at the skyline and found their flat but it was still lifeless as far as he could tell.

His arms ached. Instead of a fish, it was as though he were dragging the isle of Manhattan toward him. The gap between water and land finally began to close. Sweat dripped from his forehead, stinging and blurring his eyes. His shirt would be ruined; he would have to go back and change. Sweat became rain falling from a clear sky. *Where's the rainbow?* he wondered.

He was drenched and his entire body shook with fatigue. The shore was now only fifty feet away. He again searched for their flat. He couldn't see it; he was too close. The hotel now blocked it from view. Framed in the turret's front window was the young androgynous actor. He was staring out to the river. From the river the turret appeared much larger and the actor much younger than Grey remembered. He was just a boy.

Storm clouds obliterated the sun and it began to pour. Grey was overcome. The scene around him muted like a kaleidoscope, the dark purple and green beads displacing the orange and yellow ones. Concentrating wholly on the boy, Grey sent a psychic siren for help. It was now raining so hard that the boat was half full of water. Grey screamed with his eyes. The boy began to turn his gaze downward. Grey held on, sustained more by anticipation than fear. His attention was diverted when the strain in his arms lessened and his line began to surface. The shore was now within reach, the catch lodged in the shallows of the bank but when Grey looked down into the five-foot gap between boat and land, it appeared as deep and impassable as ever. His boat, its rim now level with the river, exhausted its final buoyancy. As an image surfaced at the end of the line, water overtook him. A pair of reflective green eyes burned into his.

26

Grey opened his eyes to the darkness of his cabin. He reeked of alcohol. The ship listed hard to one side, splashing against the porthole. His arms were numb, a result of passing out face down with them trapped beneath him. His head throbbed and his eyes burned from dehydration. Yes, he was truly awake; this was not another dreamy transition.

His cabin was on the lowest passenger deck with the ship's waterline was just below its portholes. In the morning's turbulent water, indistinguishable blackness of sea and sky traded his porthole's view. For a moment they shared it, the sea foam marking the jagged edge of delineation. But only a moment. It was as disorienting as his dreams and much worse on his stomach. Still, he remained a few minutes longer, staring into the hypnotic turbulence, reconstructing the previous evening.

He lay back down to avoid throwing up.

After his presentation Grey had become back-slapping popular in the competitive crowd of his contemporaries. He was the big-man-on-campus he had never been and was surprised at the ease with which superficial reflexes came to him. He laughed at the right times, nodded sympathetically in condemnation of Orion's cronyism and even flirted with a couple of the event coordinators. Female, of course. When the boat docked in Monaco, he had groupies.

"Where ya been all night?" Grey was already three sheets to the wind when Jane sidled up to him in the casino.

The wine had flowed at *Le Saint Benoit*. Bob had bribed the chef to prepare a traditional American Thanksgiving dinner. As the Orion crowd got louder and louder, Grey drank more and more to assuage his embarrassment, until his behavior fell rank and file in with his colleagues.

Jane swirled the ice in her glass. "Your entourage has been a little difficult to work one's way through." She motioned with her glass, the ice clinking against the side, toward Grey's craps companion who, nipples-to-hips in white Lycra, had been rolling his dice. "Especially the booth babes."

When Grey turned back around after his next roll, Bob was at Jane's side, shaking his head. Lips pursed in faux-concern, he reprimanded Grey with three fraternal "tsks" as he put his arm around Jane. He pulled her to him, closer than he would have in the office. "I hope he's not exerting undue influence. Remember Grey, you are her boss."

Jane's smile was directed, at first, to Grey. The metallic clanging and congratulatory cheers for someone's nearby slotted victory almost drowned her out. "The winner takes it all." Then, to Bob, "Will you accompany me while I replenish?"

Too impaired to catch Jane's innuendo, Grey returned to his solicitous gambling partner.

The boat's motion got the best of him. Grey banged his shoulder against the narrow bathroom door, making it just in time. He retched until he was throwing up bile. After two rounds of dry heaves, he remained crouched on his knees in front of the toilet. Spread across the cold porcelain rim of the bowl, his folded arms cradled his head.

He had only a mottled recollection of the events that followed except for one interaction that stood out with visceral clarity. His fragile stomach tightened in humiliation, causing him to throw up one last time. When he lifted his head, he shuddered to recall the final conversation of the evening.

At three in the morning the casino had shut its door to the obnoxious contention, even booing, of Orion's most predictable rabble-rousers. Among them, more subdued but no less drunk, was their newest inductee, Grey. On their way out, Grey slurred to the doorman, "This's'sssertainly no Vegas."

To which the young man replied, "No monsieur, it certainly isn't."

Back on board, Bob woke up the captain and insisted that he reopen the ship's casino. Sleepy-eyed, in his bathrobe, the captain was more befuddled than reluctant. Bob pulled out a thick wad of bills from his pocket and threatened, "Look, you will get half of this now and I am certain to lose the other half in far less time than it would take for me to call your CEO to register a complaint."

Some indeterminable amount of time later Grey was once again alone at the ship's rail. The cold air began to sober him. It was dark but there was enough light to make out the profile of the sea, more so because the waters were rough. The storm that had followed them for their entire trip had still not broken. From nowhere, Bob materialized next to him.

"Don't jump," he said between cigarette drags. Bob had given up smoking upon his promotion; it was a trip for taking up old habits. He flicked the cigarette into the water. "If you jump, I'll not only lose a great sales manager, I'll lose a bet."

"Huh." It was less of a question than a bemused sigh. Bob had taken off his tie and unbuttoned the two top buttons of his shirt. His collarbones protruded, framing his chest and beneath them, a light coat of fine, black hair, even more distracting than his eyes. Grey retreated to the sea.

"Jane and I have this little bet." Bob turned toward Grey; he was so close that his belt buckle snagged a belt loop on Grey's pants.

Grey kept his stance, outward against the rail. Again, even with the alcohol in his system, his body responded to Bob's proximity.

Bob's warm breath was distilled from the cool sea air. "You see, I think you're straight and Jane thinks you're gay."

Now Grey was sober. He felt his pulse beat through the palms of his hands as he tightened his grip around the cold painted metal of the rail. He looked over again, this time into Bob's eyes. They were deep brown—so the rumors were true.

"If I win," Bob paused, his smirk as obvious as his allusion, "well, that's really up to me and Jane." Grey held his stare. "If you jump, we'll never know."

Grey's voice was calm and articulate. "And if you lose?"

Bob inched forward, eliminating the little space that separated them, and whispered in his exact enunciation, "Then I get an experience that I have fantasized about for quite some time." Any doubt of his intimation was contradicted by the insistent contours of his body. Other rumors were true as well. "You see, I don't make bets I can't win."

Grey turned and pressed his body into Bob so that Bob could feel his losing victory "Do you wanna fuck or get fucked?"

27

At last Grey had finished with the bathroom. He was spent. A faint light shone through the porthole. The view of sea and air was now intermediated by a third: land. It didn't appear to be too far away. Grey suspected they would dock in less than twenty minutes.

He shut the porthole cap, yet in the ambient light he saw motion every-where. He lay back down but the room continued to spin, as did the previous night's images he had summoned forth.

Grey's challenge to Bob was a frozen moment after which the lucidity of his memory shattered, like a glass thrown against a wall, leaving scattered fragments unified only through the intensity of the emotion that lingered. Bob's face floated, that of an unbeatable victor stunned by an unimaginable upset. There was Jane's laughter, the nervous laughter of complicity. And then he was alone, standing in front of his cabin door.

The spinning slowed. Grey reached under his cot, grabbed his Dopp kit and rummaged through its contents looking for the bottle of Valium he had picked up at the last minute. After popping two into his mouth, he sank into a deep dreamless sleep, waking up six hours later to Jane's relentless pounding on his door. He was a little wobbly but otherwise fine, excellent compared to his earlier state. But he must have felt better than he looked because when he opened the door, a fresh-faced Jane reacted as if she had smelled something rotten. "Shit, not a good night, huh?"

She had on a pink cotton skirt—much shorter than he had ever seen her wear—and a gray, loose cashmere sweater that accentuated more through texture than fit. A small, casual Burberry bag hung at her side. She looked no worse for wear; on the contrary, she looked better.

"Everybody's heading out. A tour's been organized."

Grey yawned. "To-ur?"

Jane smiled at his sleepiness and rumpled clothes, unchanged from the night before. "Yep—ten minutes; we're settin' out at two." She consulted her watch. "You probably slept through the announcement. We had to detour last night due to rough waters. Hurry up, time's a-wastin'."

"Awwww—anks," Grey responded through a second yawn. He started to close the door and then stopped. "Wait." Jane spun around. "Where are we?"

Jane shrugged her shoulders. "Some island called Elba. They say it's where Napoleon bit it. There's some supposedly impregnable fortress we're gonna poke about in."

Her words splashed over him like a bucket of cold water yet he responded as though it meant nothing. "You go ahead; I'll catch up in a few."

Jane shrugged. "Whatever suits you." As she rounded the corner she twirled back around; her silky blond hair swished in the model perfection of a shampoo commercial. She was far too perky. "Just so you know, the tour's only an hour." With a final tilt of her head and a wink, she added, "The fresh air'll be good for what ails you."

Grey shut the door. The bright midday sun encircled the closed porthole like an eclipse. He opened the cap to a hillside that rose above a harbor filled with boats.

Within fifteen minutes he was showered and off the boat. Nothing looked familiar. On the hill Grey had seen from his porthole was the walled fortress. There was a group of his colleagues halfway up the slope. He spotted Jane and she, him; she waved for him to come up. He nodded and quickened his pace to indicate that he would join them but instead of turning at the ticket gate, bypassed it and walked around the fort's coastal edge. On the other side was another harbor, with a picturesque boardwalk of ochre and red buildings. Still no recognition. He stopped at a tourist office and picked up a number of brochures. One included an aerial photo of Elba annotated by historical points of interest. It had a ferry timetable and detailed maps of the two largest cities, Portoferraio and Porto Azzurro. Behind the counter was an attractive middle-aged woman with her black hair pulled back into a tight bun. She wore a mauve blouse accessorized with a large salmon and white cameo broach that secured its collar. Grey noticed that her exact painted eyebrows were devoid of hair.

"English?" he asked.

"A little." Her voice was deep and throaty.

Grey was conscious of speaking in simple sentences. "What city is this?"

"Portoferraio," she said smiling either at the familiarity or the stupidity of the question.

Grey assumed the former and smiled in return. "*Grazie.*" He searched the timetable. Portoferraio was the only direct ferry from Piombino. The memory of his first visit to Elba was indelible; he was certain there had been no second stop. Putting the brochure into his pocket, he nodded at the clerk. He ingratiated himself with a final "*Grazie,*" as he opened the door to leave.

He continued down the boardwalk. Though the water had calmed, the sky above remained gray. There were hardly any people on the street. As he passed two older women, one whispered something to the other. They laughed. Lost in thought, he didn't notice.

28

At the center of the harbor a restaurant called Café Roma caught his eye. It was a small place split by an expansive bar that connected the front of the café to the back. The bar appeared to be the café's social backbone, where four or five older Italian men were chatting with one another. The bartender, a young handsome kid, manned an industrial-size cappuccino machine that seemed overkill for the tiny café, even in Italy. He had one hand leaning on the handle of one of the six espresso slots and with the other doled out four demitasse plates to the group of men before him. He tossed them on the counter with the precision of a hustler in a high-stakes poker came. Dealing the spoons with similar efficiency, he spun them, angling and aligning their handles in a neat row, each pointed toward its intended recipient. He turned to the espresso machine as if to hasten its task but then jerked his head back around in response to something one of the men had said.

He threw his hands in the air. "*Non è vero!, Lei non lo farebbe mai. Vecchio uomo non spettegolare nel mio caffè.*" The shortest of the men, wearing a houndstooth touring cap that made him look more Irish than Italian, retorted some response which the bartender again rebuked as he snatched the four cups from the machine tray and dealt them in identical sequence, handles to the right, beside the spoons. "*Conosco Danielle da sempre.*"

Grey squeezed past to the other end of the bar toward the rear of the café. The bartender made his way over but kept his attention focused toward the conversation in which he had become involved. "*Danielle non penserebbe mai di mollarlo.*" He turned abruptly toward Grey. "*Prego.*"

Grey was intimidated at the thought of speaking Italian, even for such a simple request. His tongue was sluggish in his mouth. "*Un cappuccino, per favore.*"

The young man returned to his espresso machine, "*Lei ama Alfredo con tutta sè stessa.*" He grabbed the men's empty espresso cups one at a time and threw them into the sink with a back-snap of his wrist. They slammed into an existing pile with a crash that seemed to Grey would shatter the lot. Grey opened one of the brochures to the map of Portoferraio. He studied it. Nothing was familiar— not the double harbors, the street names, nor the names of the various beaches surrounding the town.

The bartender sat a foamless cappuccino down in front of Grey but remained faced away. "*Su via, non mi faccia buttarla fuori dal mio caffè.*" Without looking, he reached behind him and pushed to Grey a plastic sugar bowl that contained an equal proportion of sugar cubes and little blue packets of their artificial alternative. With exactitude guided by the bartender's intimate spatial awareness, the bowl stopped an inch from Grey's right hand.

"*Grazie,*" Grey responded with more assurance.

Grey lifted the cup to his mouth and turned the page of the brochure. A small advertisement caught his eye. *The Crystal Hotel—A Taste of Sophistication on an Island Paradise.*

When Grey looked up from his pamphlet, the bartender was now to his left, talking to two men who had entered from the back of the café. He was studying the wall behind the bar on which hung a colorful poster of ice cream cones, the same poster that Grey had seen in every café and trattoria in Monaco. He grabbed a pen from the cash register and started tapping various ice cream images, announcing a number with each tap. "*Un, tre, quattro, due . . . no tre.*" After he had ordered five or six different types, he stuck the pen into his mouth and continued to deliberate.

The older of the two men leaned into the younger, a master to an apprentice, winked and then challenged the pensive café owner. "*Che ne dici di questi? Vanno alla grande al Café Isla.*"

The bartender didn't turn around but stayed fixated on the poster. "*I ragazzetti vanno da Luigi; non vengono qui.*" With a last pen-tapping order of, "*Tre di questi e quattro di questi altri,*" he terminated the transaction, ignored the salesmen who were finishing their paperwork, and turned back to Grey.

"*Nient'altro?*"

He had thick wavy curls and deep brown eyes. Grey flashed on his previous night's confrontation with Bob, his face flushing red as he asked, "*Parlate inglese?*"

"Yes, whaddya want?" He spoke English with self-assurance and no discernable accent.

Grey pointed to the advertisement. "Do you know the Crystal Hotel?"

Pulling it closer, the bartender spun the brochure toward him and flipped back a page to the city map. "It's here." He marked an X on the map. "Close to the other side of town."

Grey contemplated the upside-down map. The other side of town, yet a third harbor, appeared to be only a few blocks away. "Walkable?" Grey asked.

"Sure." He traced a path as he gave directions. "If you go down the board-walk and take a right on the second street after the fort, it'll take you to the other side. Take a left when you get to Via Cairoli and the Crystal'll be on your left, midway down the block." He slid the pamphlet back to Grey. "Fifteen minutes tops."

Ten minutes later Grey was in front of the hotel. The name painted on the draped plate glass window was newish, as was the green awning that jutted over the door. Everything was different. He would have walked right past if he had not been given explicit directions. The street was paved, he remembered sand; the facade was humble, he remembered grand.

29

The bench to the left of the hotel's door sparked a reflection that magnified as soon as he entered the lobby. The unexpected interior of dark wood and marble, while far less elegant than he remembered, evoked his distant first impression. His memory incorporated the revisions of both exaggeration and renovation. The young woman who approached from behind the registration desk became the receptionist of fourteen years prior. Instead of stopping, she opened a door and disappeared into a back room. From the other side of the twenty-foot counter, an older gentleman leaned over but did not walk down to meet Grey. A carved wooden cane rested against the wall behind him.

"Can I 'elp you?' he asked.

"No, *grazie*." At Grey's refusal, the gentleman propped his elbows on the counter and continued to read a newspaper. His large muscular forearms were covered with gray hair. Grey studied his profile and wondered if this could be the man from whom he, as an impatient American college student, had demanded a room.

Outside, Grey sat on the bench and tried to conjure up that long-ago day. He shut his eyes and imagined the warm sun upon his face. Relaxing his shoulders, he thought about the encounter that he had so many times tried to expunge. In the end, time had taken its course. He could no longer remember the details, even while sitting at the origin of its inception. The images, words, even the emotions were all locked away.

He opened his eyes. The sky was still gray and cloudy. A cold wind blew down the street; he wrapped his arms around his chest to keep from shivering. Beside him, the old man leaned on his cane. On closer inspection Grey was certain that this short stocky geriatric was the hotel's manager who had seemed so powerful and intimidating. "*Scusi*, are you O.K?"

"*Sì, sì*, just a bad night."

The old man chuckled, "I weesh I am young enough to 'ave a bad night." He turned and walked back inside; his left leg jerked with each step. "Eef you need something, I am 'ere."

Grey reached the end of the street and glanced down at his watch. It was two forty-five. A trail of people wound its way down the hill, his colleagues heading back to the boat. He turned left, away from the port. In front of him a tall lean man stood facing away, talking to a woman. She held a sleeping baby at her breast; a yellow blanket was thrown over her shoulder, blocking its face. She was rocking her hips side to side. At first Grey thought she was breastfeeding, but on closer inspection, the baby seemed to be asleep. The man's right hand was on his hip and the left waved in front of the woman as though he were consecrating the sleeping child. Its powerful arcs pierced the air, abrupt but fluid, masculine but feminine.

Grey stopped in the middle of the street. A car swerved to avoid him. For the first time it occurred to him that Antonio might still live on the island. The enormity of the thought struck him so hard his knees buckled. The clouds broke and light fractured, slowing, erasing the present. The mother and child disappeared; there was just the father, his tight cap of grey curls bound against his head. A shard of light glinted from the man's ring finger as his hand swirled in front of him, rising higher and higher into the air. Grey's mind fractured as well. The road was now his Hudson, the man, both actor and catch, enveloped by an aura of color. *At last, the rainbow.*

Another car honked as it passed. "*Togliti dalla strada, imbecille!*"

Antonio began to turn. The colors that encircled him intensified and melded into pure white. Grey exhausted his last few moments of buoyancy.

"*Stai bene?*" The trio hovered above him. The baby was now awake and stared down, cooing her support for the poor American who had fainted in the middle of the street.

Of the three faces, the man's was the only one Grey would remember. It was drawn and taught, sun-leathered skin stretched over its angularity. Small dull eyes were eclipsed by an enormous nose that hooked over his thin upper lip. There were no curls, only a loose nest of gray on his balding, spotted head. He was not Antonio.

"Yes, I just forgot breakfast this morning." Only after his promise to eat something did they leave.

Grey again stood alone. From this vantage point he could now see the Mediterranean over the rooftops to his right. Myopia guided him as he continued his search. Grey had never imagined the aged Antonio; every fantasy had ignored the progression of time. His stomach tightened. He drifted down the sidewalk, slowing with each considered question. Would an older Antonio render the dream impotent? Might he live in the same house? What about Maria? If Antonio and Maria were still happily married, if he faced this reality, could he at long last come to terms with all that it implied?

He passed the hill's peak and began to descend. Three blocks away the street forked; one tine stretched to the right, toward the beach, and the other cut inland. He stopped to get his bearings. Although the foreground was altered with a few more buildings, it was indeed that of his memory. He followed the shoreline left past the short pier to a pillar where two or three rowboats were tied. Farther down was the path where he and Antonio had walked silently to and from the sea. It was the same, more true to memory than anything else he'd seen. This was his last chance to turn back. Nothing would be lost, nothing gained. As he began to retrace his steps, time melted away.

Kids scampered in the same yard where they had scampered before. He stopped two doors down from Antonio's house. His weakened stomach ached; he felt like he needed to throw up again. He grabbed his hips and bent over until the cramping passed. It wasn't worth it; he decided to go back. He tried to turn around but he was unable to move. Paralyzed with indecision, he couldn't take his eyes from the house. Then he noticed the sign affixed to door: *AFFITTASI.*

No one answered his initial knock. He knocked again and looked back toward the beach. The rose bushes that edged the sandy yard had been recently pruned. He peered into the front window. Contrary to the Crystal Hotel, the inside was much less familiar than the exterior.

Grey walked around to the back of the house. The olive grove was still there, its stone wall jagged from stones dislodged over what looked like years of neglect. The trees were much the same as he remembered but as it was November, their branches hung dormant, the ground free of netting. Grey turned to see the faucet, small against the brick of the house. Like the branches, it too was denuded, hoseless. Its rusted handle turned easily. Into Grey's cupped hands the brown water bled clear.

Grey lay on the ground. The olive trees grew in perspective and filtered light through their tangled limbs. His hazel eyes flickered—with the light, green, with its absence, brown. He had missed a haircut appointment before his trip and his bangs fell long into his eyes. Grey lay perfectly still and listened to the water spill to the ground behind him. He stared past the lifeless trees to the gray sky above.

30

"Would you like me to hang your coat?" The flight attendant was in her fifties yet had the body of a woman half her age. Her blond hair spanned a wide spectrum of yellows and golds in an overall effect that incorporated her natural gray. Instead of masking her age, it cushioned the transition. It was long and straight, pulled back into a ponytail, revealing a strong widow's peak.

Grey thought of his mother, who had been so proud of her widow's peak that she eschewed more popular hairstyles of the times for ones that showcased it. "Supposedly it's a sign of great intelligence but God knows what happened t'me," she always said whenever someone commented on it. Without realizing it, Grey pushed his hair back, revealing his own.

"Sure." He twisted in his seat as she helped him take off his jacket.
"And you, ma'am, would you like me to take your purse or would you like to keep it with you?" Her Southern accent further reminded Grey of his mother.

Jane looked down at the red Kate Spade handbag in her lap, trying to decide whether she needed it or not. Her long blond hair was also clipped back in a ponytail but whereas the flight attendant's was casually held in place by a cloth scrunchie, Jane's was more expensively secured by a large tortoiseshell clasp. And no widow's peak.

Jane zipped her purse closed. "Sure, why not."

As the flight attendant leaned over him, Grey read the nametag pinned to her left breast: *JANE.* Jane, Grey's colleague, didn't, nor would she during the entire flight, notice the coincidence.

Jane took a sip of pre-takeoff champagne. Grey was reading *Napoleon: The Myth of the Savior*, a book he had picked up on Elba. Jane rested her chin on the edge of the glass, smiling over at him. "Grey, thanks again for the upgrade."

Grey didn't look up from his book. "My pleasure."

The Monte Carlo gods had shined on Grey as he continued to ride the wave of his sudden popularity. Over the forty-eight hours since Grey's presentation, his company persona had mushroomed. His usual introversion that had always been interpreted as standoffishness was now magnetic self-confidence. But it was his run at the roulette wheel that solidified the transformation.

Grey had been the last person to return to the boat after the Elba tour. No one knew where he was. Bob was agitated when he called everyone to the conference room to tell them that the ship's captain had agreed to delay their departure in order to search for Grey. At the end of the announcement, when he asked if anyone had any idea where he was, an unassuming Grey raised a glass of champagne from the back of the room. "The prodigal son has returned." The crowd turned to him. Grey's eyes were now the only ones on Bob; Bob's were two of the hundreds on Grey. Grey swept his arm over the crowd. "Drinks at the *Outrigger* on me."

The storm drifted south, forcing the ship to return to Monaco where Grey had again strayed. While everyone else grouped together at the slot machines or the blackjack tables, Grey took his chance at the roulette wheel. He played alone until his fourth spin when Jane and Jeff, the other sale rep from the New York office who'd made President's Club and got to stay on after the conference, joined him, one on either side. The croupier pushed about thirty red chips to Grey. Over the course of the next four games, the crowd grew in direct proportion to Grey's winnings. At first there were the other sales reps from Grey's region, then more Orion folk and finally strangers. At one point, the crowd began to cheer after each spin. At the end of the ninth game, Grey had amassed a sizable mound of red and green chips, even a small stack of black ones. The croupier was replaced by an older gentleman who looked like he had mastered the wheel from a tenure extending back to the Monaco's glamour days, when Grace Kelly's marriage to Prince Rainier had captured the world's imagination.

In the time it had taken for the shift change, the crowd had doubled. It wasn't that Grey's winnings were significant by Monte Carlo standards; there were tables with minimum bets higher that the ten thousand or so dollars stacked in front of him. But the gradual gathering of Grey's colleagues had been infectious.

The new croupier announced, "Place your bets." Everyone waited. Grey had been the only one playing for the last nine spins. The crowd respected his streak; no one else placed a bet. Grey overlooked his following. He saw Bob approach with Jackson, Grey's West Coast Regional Director counterpart.

For the thirteen years Grey had been at Orion, he had not climbed the ladder; he had tripped up it. He had never applied for any new position, but through the sheer staying power of his sales numbers, he had been recognized. Many at Orion thought it was Grey who should be V.P. of Sales, but that Bob had cajoled, some say blackmailed, the CEO. Grey didn't believe those rumors; the international market was Orion's future and Bob knew international far better than Grey. But it *was* odd that at every Christmas party, Bob and the CEO's wife shared more than a couple of dances. With Orion's move into Asia, the sales structure had expanded: Bob was promoted to Executive V.P. and would in turn promote three new V.P.s—Americas, Europe and Asia. Instead of the usual corporate bashing, all gossip at the conference was speculation on who was in the running for these positions and how they were going to woo Bob. While Grey was smoking and gazing out to sea above deck, Jackson and others were schmoozing and gazing into Bob's eyes below. After the previous evening's finale, Grey had further avoided Bob's attention, except for the prodigal son comment, which won him no points. But then Grey was certain he had lost that game and had moved on to another.

"Bob," Grey called out over the crowd. Bob jerked his head up, decidedly caught off guard. He did not reply. "How much did you say our new Q4 quota is?"

Bob, regaining his composure, this time took Grey's challenge. "Twenty-seven million." Grey turned back to the croupier. Until this bet, he had only chosen red or black rather than a specific number.

"Twenty-seven red." The crowd gasped; Grey took advantage of its pause. "All of it."

Filmed, the spin would have resembled the cliché hyper-anticipatory, slow motion roulette scene from many a movie. The ball rolls and rolls. Splice in crowd and presumed love interest Jane—all eyes wide, all mouths open. Ball pops in and out of a couple of nearby numbers, teeters on the brink of one and then finally lands. The croupier: "Twenty-two black." It takes two rakes for him to collect all of Grey's chips. Cut.

Before the gasps turned to conciliatory remarks, Grey again forced Bob's regard. He shrugged his shoulders and winked. "If you only wouldn't've raised our quota." The crowd parted as Grey walked over, stopping just in front of Bob, confronting him face-to-face. He waited just long enough for the murmur to silence before he grabbed Bob's elbow and added, "Again." To be forgettable, the gesture required an immediate release or follow-up comment. Grey did neither. Non-Orion members of the crowd began to nervously disperse. A mixture of awe and concern shone on the faces of those who remained. Even Bob's. On this fourth confrontation of the trip, just how far would Grey push it?

"Grey." Jackson reached over in protection but Grey had already slid his arm around Bob's shoulder and started walking him through the crowd, toward the bar. It was a borderline unprofessional intimacy they had all seen Bob initiate many times before but never on this side of the equation.

"Ya win some; ya lose some." Grey's response to Jane was so casual, it sounded almost jaded.

Jane pushed off her shoes and rubbed her stocking feet together. "But you lost all of that money." She pinched her left Achilles tendon between her right big and second toes, massaging it up and down. "You know, Bob's not gonna let you expense this." She took another sip of champagne.

Using his ticket stub to mark his place, Grey closed his book and placed it in his lap. "Actually, I did pretty well last night. I ended up about nine hundred ahead." Before Jane could protest again, he added, "Anyway, I used miles. Don't worry, it truly is my pleasure."

Jane, the flight attendant, returned. "We're about to take off; could you fasten your seat belt?"

Jane scooched back into her seat and began to search for the half of the belt nearest to Grey. One hand pressed against his thigh as she struggled to pull it free with the other. "Sorry, it seems to be stuck."

The empty champagne glass passed from one Jane to the other. "Would you like another glass after we take off?"

Jane crossed her legs, adjusting the belt to a more spacious fit. "As soon as humanly possible." Both smiled in feminine camaraderie.

Jane bent the wing of her headrest so she could lean her head to the side. *A good sign*, Grey thought. But after testing its comfort, she continued her line of questioning. "So then, tell me, why'd you bet it all on one number?"

Grey tilted his head. "I don't know; it was a game, I guess. It didn't feel real."

The other Jane was two rows in front of them, demonstrating how to use the oxygen masks in case of an emergency. They both ignored her. Grey continued, "You can't lose what you never had."

"Huh?" Jane loosened her seatbelt and resumed her original position facing Grey. "I don't get that, but then I'm not a gambler."

Bracing for a longer conversation, Grey put his book in the elastic pouch on the back of the seat in front of him. "I'm not either."

Jane smirked. "You coulda fooled me." She looked down and inspected her manicured nails; they were unblemished. Her voice was barely audible due to its projection into her lap. "You certainly gambled with Bob."

Grey stiffened.

"You showed him up twice—I've never seen him so on edge." Jane raised her head, clasping her hands in front of her in exclamation. "I've definitely never seen Bob speechless." Her fisted hands sliced through the air for emphasis. "When you put your arm around him, I actually thought he was gonna blush."

The engines revved beneath them; flight attendant Jane buckled herself into her fold-down chair. Jane continued, uninterrupted. "I would love to see Bob blush."

"Haven't you?" If Grey's eyebrows weren't raised, his intonation was.

Jane's smile vanished. "No, I haven't."

31

Grey apologized, "I didn't mean—"

Jane interrupted. "Yes you did and if I were you, I'd probably think the same thing."

There was an awkward silence. Jane looked out the window and Grey across at Jeff, whom he had also upgraded to first class. The woman he was talking with, a coiffed brunette in her fifties, was laughing at something he said. She glanced over in Grey's direction. Grey's return smile was strained. He leaned his head back against his headrest, tempted by the seduction of the engines' rumble, but after having been so rude, thought that nodding off would just make things worse. Five uncomfortable minutes later he was just about to reach for his book when Jane spoke. "I bet it'll surprise you that I'm deeply in love with my husband. And that underneath, when it comes to matters of the heart, I'm pretty old-fashioned."

Her arms released and unfolded; she placed her palms down onto her thighs. On her left hand was a simple unremarkable wedding band accompanied by another of simply remarkable diamonds. Anticipating his judgment, she clasped her hands together, concealing the rings from view.

"Look, I can play the game with the best of them. I've learned the rules along the way and I walk the line, a line which—I might add—is far thinner and riskier for a woman."

Grey looked up. Jane was as vulnerable, and subsequently as beautiful, as he had ever seen her.

"We have to look just so but not so much, our hair needs to be done but not overdone, our faces painted but not too painted, our skirts tight but not too tight."

Jane tried to remain relaxed; her voice was calm and unwavering, but there was a slight protrusion of the veins in her neck. "We must navigate the ever-changing rules of female professionalism and all that entails while remaining alluring and leaving a strong hint of availability." She raised her eyebrows with a matter-of-fact shrug. "A very strong hint. And then we have to work twice as hard, doing our own faxing and flight arrangements—because, you see, your competitive, flirty secretaries are not nearly as responsive to us as they are to you—and then deliver at least twice as much as our male counterparts, while all the time the rumor grows that the secret to our success is either A) we're whores who've slept our way to the top or B) we're obsessive, cold, overly-ambitious bitches who don't have lives."

She concluded her monologue without any hint of emotion, as if she had been reading a script. But at the very end, she lowered her head to shield her face from Grey's view.

Grey was speechless.

Jane looked back up. Her expression had hardened into a Cheshire grin. "But there is the satisfaction that comes with mastering complexity." She reached back and freed her hair from its tortoiseshell bond, but when she leaned over, she realized that she had checked her purse. Clasp in mouth, she again pulled back her hair.

"Don't get me wong," she mumbled and then clipped a ponytail in the same manner as before. "You guys have your own game." On her face was genuine intrigue. "Which, by the way, my dear boss, you often seem oblivious to."

The cabin shook violently as the plane accelerated down the runway.

A seasoned flyer, Jane kept talking without concern. "A trait I simultaneously admire, pity and envy."

Grey keyed on *pity*. The plane lifted off; the wheels ground beneath them, receding into their housing. "Whaddya mean?"

Jane thought for a second and, for the first time in her portrait of the corporate woman, an element of sentiment swelled in her voice. It wasn't the pity but the envy that prompted her response, "You get by because you're so damned smart and good looking." Followed by the admiration. "And honest."

In Grey's peripheral vision, her window was a rectangle of blank white; they had just begun ascending through the clouds. "Well—"

Jane clipped his confession. "I don't mean about your personal life—that's nobody's business. I mean your no-holds-barred integrity." Grey flinched but Jane continued without acknowledging it. "Look, it's a modus operandi that's impossible for a woman in business and very difficult for a man. And you appear to do it not from a self-inflicted code of ethics but almost like it's . . . normal." In a pause of consternation, she rolled her eyes to the ceiling, reflecting on the ambiguity of her last statement. "I don't know how to say it but it's different. To top it off, you're never self-righteous in the least; you're more naïve, like you really don't see any other option."

Jane—the flight attendant—interrupted with not two glasses, but a full bottle of Cristal. She handed it to them with a wink, not at Grey, but at Jane. Jane had indeed mastered the game.

After taking a sip of the expensive champagne and a moment to savor it, she continued, "But while your oblivion is admirable, it's also frustrating as hell. Both you and your employees could go a lot further if you simply paid attention." Since the night Grey had blacked out, he had sworn off alcohol; it was now time to renege. While he was pouring his glass, Jane reassured him. "Wipe that hung-dog look off your face. I didn't mean to criticize you; you're a great boss. But it might behoove you to come down to earth and take a look around every now and then so you can at least understand how the game is played. Although I obviously no longer need to tell you this, because this last week you played it with the best of them. Overnight, you seem to have gone from naïve to expert, to the surprise of everybody, especially Bob. If you don't get one of those V.P. jobs now, everyone'll be shocked."

Whether it was her insight or her candor, something clicked; he opened up to Jane like the best friend he didn't have—never had—not when he was a kid and definitely not since he had been with Scott. Maybe Miriam or Pete but he had screwed up both of those relationships. After so many years, it felt good to confide in someone other than his journal. He told her why he was drawn to technology, how in his childhood he was always taking things apart and trying to rebuild them, how his mother would call on him to untangle her jewelry, how he had built intricate forts inside the bushes that edged the backyard. Jane listened. She cringed when he told her of the poison sumac that, unbeknownst to anyone in his family, had covered his backyard bushes and, after his fort-building escapade, his entire body as well. She nodded in understanding with his decision to abandon his lifelong dream of architecture the second week into his first computer course. "It was the similarities of logic and perspective that drew me to technology." While Jane had heard of Grey's unusual career path from engineer to pre-sales to sales, she was surprised to discover Grey's insecurity with management. He missed technology; he missed solving problems; he missed feeling like he made some sort of difference.

Somehow, over the course of two hours, his disillusion with corporate politics led to his disillusion with Scott. And in this singular acknowledgement, Grey began to disassemble the divisions of the social compartmentalization he had spent years constructing. When this discussion led to the broader topic of his homosexuality, Grey became almost chatty, talking faster than normal, not from his usual dissociation from the subject but nervous excitement brought on by the unfamiliar freedom from restraint. He chose not to tell Jane about Bob and that, given his performance or lack thereof, he would likely not be offered one of the V.P. positions. Rather he attributed his momentary corporate agility to luck, an accident resulting from his spontaneous reactions to the three unrelated thrusts into the collegial limelight. Nor did he ask about her winnings. He knew there was no bet or collusion; her performance was just a finesse of the game she played so well. At some point, Jane moved her arm onto their shared armrest and placed her hand on top of his.

As their conversation wound to a close, she asked him, "Why'd your parents name you Grey?"

"Some family name. Why?"

Jane yawned. "I don't know. It's weird. My religious nut of a mom named me Jane after some martyr, Jane Grey. She was queen of England for nine days before Bloody Mary cut her head off, so of course my mother christened me Mary Jane after both of them . . . thanks, Mom." Jane shifted toward the window. "This is the first time I've ever heard the name since—either first or last." She curled away from him, rolling onto her shoulder. "I mean, except for Dorian and everybody knows how that turned out."

Grey tried but did not sleep the entire flight. Renewed possibility invigorated him. He gave up, opened his eyes and waited for them to adjust to the dark. The cabin illuminated, dimly lit by a few cracked window shades, an overhead light three rows behind him pinpointing a lone reader, and the pulsating screen of flying toasters across a laptop computer that sat untouched in the seat ahead of him while its owner wheezed asthmatically in his sleep.

He looked over to Jane wearing a Burberry tartan sleep mask. She maintained her composure even in slumber. Her hands sat in her lap clasped right over left, still concealing her rings. An orange earplug protruded from her ear and a thin band of hair had loosened itself, falling over her face and crossing the bridge of her aquiline nose. Grey was reminded of Scott, masked and plugged, stretched out naked across their bed.

When he closed his eyes, the water from the faucet of Antonio's house splashed against his face as a prism of sunlight streamed through the overhanging olive trees.

32

Mr. Grey Tigrett. John was holding the only sign among the ten or fifteen people waiting outside the gate, his other hand thrust deep into his pants' baggy pocket. You couldn't see the earphones hidden beneath his long hair but knew they were there because his head bounced to a silent beat. Next to him was Jane's husband, Jack wearing a blue blazer over a starched white shirt. Other than the sign, John looked like a teenager trying to maintain cool independence from an embarrassing Docker'ed and Polo'ed father.

"My, aren't you the one." Jane nudged him with her elbow.

As he wound his earphones into their case, John explained his presence which, had it not been for Grey's in-flight discussion with Jane, could have been awkward. "Scott sent me." He folded the sign under his arm. "He said I need t'get you home ASAP."

Grey introduced John to Jane and Jack. After an abridged but congenial exchange, the four walked together to the parking garage. John's Camaro announced itself as soon as they stepped out of the elevator, doggie ESP instigating Rothko's yelping even though he was blocked from their view, a good two or three rows of SUVs away.

"So I'm gonna say goodbye here 'cause that's my little siren alerting everyone to our presence." Grey put his suitcase and laptop down and stood back up empty-handed. "Jane, thanks for listening." Their prolonged embrace was only possible with their respective certainty that Jane would tell Jack everything. In that moment, as Rothko howled, as John looked away, as Jack straddled perplexity and inactionable jealousy, Grey and Jane cemented a new friendship that would last the rest of their lives. It would prevail long after Rothko's last bark,

John's emergence as one of America's leading documentary filmmakers, and Jack's excruciating death from stomach cancer.

They opened the car door to a frenzied tongue-lashing. Grey grabbed the leash as Rothko jumped out of the car and marked both of Grey's bags.

"I guess he missed you," John said, opening the trunk. In settling in, Rothko nestled into Grey's lap, head out the window, full of anticipation for the road, while Grey tried to extricate the seatbelt buckle from under Rothko's butt. Without being prompted, John answered the unasked question. "Scott said you'd've forgotten about the HRC dinner." The engine turned; the familiarity of the grunge music and the car's erratic piston fires helped mitigate the news.

"You've gotta be kidding." Grey twisted around to the back seat to get his wallet out of his coat pocket.

At first John said nothing but as they pulled up to the toll both, he turned to Grey. "I don't know how you do it."

The ride was uneventful. There was less traffic than usual on the Manhattan Bridge and even getting across town was a breeze. When Grey flippantly generalized "it's Europe's Vegas" to John's question about Monte Carlo, John came back with a dissertation on the political symbolism of the new Dale Chihuly fountain, the edge on which Grey had sat after the roulette incident. He had wandered outside the casino to the enormous fountain in the middle of which stood a twenty-foot high tarp-covered centerpiece. Grey chuckled to himself, *A Monte Carlo Christo*, but then read about the glass sculpture's millennium unveiling on a plaque that also gave detailed background on the artist. That night, as he sat in the fresh air and reflected on his experiences with Bob, he thought that this bound, unexposed, prickly fountain was a perfect symbol for the entire trip. He had even purchased a disposable camera to take a picture of it. Of course John knew the artist.

"Good luck," John said as he stepped back into the car. Grey looked at his watch—it was just before six—and then up to the windows of his flat.

"*Bien Venue*." Jimmy was wearing the fur-lined parka that he had worn every winter day for the past three years.

Leaving his bags on the curb, Grey led Rothko over to the front of the hotel. "So the iceman's hereth. Don't tell me it's already winter." Grey pushed the button, shortening the retractable leash to protect Jimmy from Rothko's irrepressible tongue. "Why over here? You're a couple a hours early for the theatre crowd."

"Banished, shunned, exiled." Jimmy pulled the hood closer around his face. Every year Grey had the same recurring thought—that a parka was not the best attire to convince even the most liberal of New York's limousine liberals to spare a dime.

"Huh?" Grey was still thinking about the coat and didn't register Jimmy's response.

Scott's voice fell from above like a rock. "Do you think that I paid for a personal car service so you could sit outside and dally?" Its tone was both playful and whiny. "Come on—cocktails start at six-thirty."

"Ask him." Jimmy's fur-lined face tilted, looking past the open window from which Scott had protruded to the open cloudless sky.

33

Scott was aflutter with pre-party adrenaline. "Hey, honey, your tux is on the bed. I hate to hurry you but Brian and Greg'll be here in twenty." Scott yelled from the bathroom, where he was in front of the mirror, trimming his nose hair. Grey set his bags outside the bedroom and unleashed Rothko, who made a dash for his water bowl.

Laid upon the bed were Grey's tux, shirt, cummerbund, tie and cuff links. The pants legs folded over the bed's foot, each pointing downward to its respective shoe stuffed with its respective sock. It was a phantom image of a well-dressed man who had lain in perfect symmetry atop a perfectly made bed and had disintegrated without the opportunity to so much as crease his pants.

Scott shot by him into the kitchen, kissing him on the cheek as he passed. "Fifteen minutes and counting." He slid across the floor in his sock feet to the bar where he pulled four hanging wine glasses from their perches.

Slumped forward in the shower, Grey enjoyed the water's warm spray. Miriam's silver chain hung from his neck. At the base of his hairline was a thin white scar, so trivial even Scott had never noticed it. From the chain, his childhood medallion dangled freely, creating a conduit down which the water streamed to the floor, across the Italian glass mosaic tiles and swirled down the drain between his feet.

Grey drifted through the evening as he had done at so many similar events, always thankful for the distraction of the silent auction. He sauntered through the items, reading the descriptions word for word. In the Restaurant & Travel section he stopped at one in particular:

ROMAN HOLIDAY
*One-week vacation in a private two-bedroom home (courtesy of Jason
Jeffries and Aaron Katz) overlooking the Spanish Steps. Roundtrip
airfare courtesy of American Airlines. Retail Value: 10K.
Minimum bid: 3K.*

From previous auctions Grey had purchased haircuts, lithographs, and
dinners, but he had never spent more than two hundred dollars. He picked up
the pen that dangled from the clipboard and wrote, 3K. It was a whim. Since he
had been with Orion and Scott, he had never once decided on a vacation; all travel
was either for business or some gay group event. Why couldn't just he and Scott
go on a vacation alone for once? To someplace that didn't draw half the boys in
Chelsea. It would be great for them to get away. They needed to get away. Grey
decided to suggest this later, when they got home. Scott could even choose the
destination as long as it was just the two of them.

Between the entrée and the dessert, while the third speaker of the evening
was being introduced, as the waiter poured a third glass of wine, Grey attempted
to strike up a conversation.

"So anything happen while I was away?"

Scott, who had spent the previous half-hour discussing with Brian how
brave it was to serve veal without a vegetarian option, replied without taking his
eyes from the podium where HRC's executive director Elizabeth Birch was
introducing Congressman Barney Frank. "You know, the usual."

Grey took another sip. He had heard Elizabeth many times before; she was
a dynamic speaker, fighting the good fight, not the usual populist in need of liberal
media mention. She was saying something about the Supreme Court shunning the
issue of gay marriage. Her words triggered Grey's memory. He turned back to
Scott. "Hey, Jimmy said he'd been exiled from our stoop and told me to ask you
about it. Did he have another one of his visions?"

Scott looked at Grey; his angular face was tempered. "Promise me you
won't pull your egalitarian shit?"

"Huh?" Grey furrowed his brow, confused.

Scott crossed his legs and leaned in. His whisper was audible to no one but

Grey. "Well, I was having brunch last Sunday and the first guest mentioned that Jimmy made her uncomfortable."

Grey's attention was no longer split. He glared at Scott, certain of his manipulation: Scott would never invite a woman to one of his brunches. With hushed restraint, Scott defended himself. "What? I simply asked the cop if he could request that Jimmy sit a little farther away from our steps."

Grey held his anger in check, knowing how Scott would use a public scene to his advantage. "Whaddya mean, cop? If you were so concerned, why didn't you ask him yourself?"

Scott rolled his eyes. "He's your charity case, not mine."

Grey tried to respond but Scott cut him off. "Can we finish this later; we're being rude."

Three long politicking speeches later the dinner came to a close. None of their table stayed for the feeble dancing that only drew those for whom these events were an opportunity for nostalgic voyeurism. Instead they headed for Brian and Greg's rented limo to be chauffeured on an all-night barhopping tour scheduled to end up at Twilo at 4:00 A.M. Everyone's club clothes were packed in the limo's trunk.

On the way to the car, it was Scott who suggested that Grey must be tired and should take a cab home. Grey was about to insist that Scott come as well when Brian stopped them. "Well, well, well. We only got the scarf and the cappuccino maker, while you boys get to jet off to Rome."

"WHAT?" Scott belted out, a response misinterpreted by Brian as surprise at being the highest bidder rather than his ignorance of Grey's bid.

Brian, who was wrapping the Hermes scarf around his neck, continued, "I can't believe that you got it for 3K. I've seen pictures of Jason's place—it's fabulous. It has a grapevine-covered terrace that looks right out on the steps. You can practically touch all those beautiful Italian boys who sit there reading their poetry books." He threw the fringed end of the scarf over his shoulder and pursed his lips to imitate a French accent. "Eend muhbe you h'will."

Brian continued talking as they started toward the door. "C'mon; we can go. They're delivering the cappuccino machine, and since yours is a vacation package, they'll call ya tomorrow to confirm." Scott glared straight ahead, holding his tongue; his fury was palpable. Brian tried again. "Seriously, his apartment's to die for. Not only d'ya look down over the steps but also you're high enough to look across the city's rooftops. You can even see the river."

"Good, so Grey can gawk at the water in Rome." A hush fell over the group, but a couple of minutes later Scott turned the tables and began bragging about the trip to the envy of everyone within earshot.

As they piled into the limo, the conversation turned to the remainder of the evening. Scott dared everyone to change clothes in the car, windows down, while they rode down Eighth Street. Grey waited until everyone else was inside and then leaned in. "Guys, I'm beat. I'll just catch a cab home. Besides, it'll give y'all a little more leg room."

Scott leaned across three laps to give Grey a lingering kiss. "Bye, babe. Get some sleep 'cause I'm gonna be horny when I get home." The group erupted in a high-pitched, gay-locker-room bravado that only died out as the limo rounded the corner.

34

"Some fancy shindig, huh? Looks like a good time." The cab driver had a Caribbean accent; his shoulder-length dreads were tied up in a green and black cloth that looked like it could be a miniature Jamaican flag.

Grey shut the door and exhaled the tightness that had been building in his chest since Scott told him about Jimmy. "I'd take your night any day."

It was a little after midnight; Grey hadn't slept in over twenty-four hours. He stared out the window as the cab sped down the East Side. When they passed Rockefeller Center, he noticed the yellow construction crane against the building. It clutched the tip of an immense pine tree, presumably just torn from the wilds and transported a great distance to grace the city as one of the country's most visited yuletide sights. He muttered under his breath, "I can't believe it's Christmas already," rested his head against the seat and closed his eyes.

It was Christmas morning—midmorning. Grey was twelve. A few years before, the thrill of Christmas had faded. This year he didn't awake in predawn darkness to sneak, heart pounding, into the living room to be the first one to see the presents their parents had stayed up half the night wrapping. His father hadn't slept on the couch as a sentinel against his poaching. Rather he was there because, at some point, the couch went from his Christmas Eve watchpost to his occasional late-night falling-asleep-in-front-of-the-TV spot to his permanent bed. This year, Grey, as everyone else, showed up in his own time. He had been awake for a couple of hours but stayed in bed reading *Stranger in a Strange Land*. It was way above Grey's head but Dale had gone on and on about it. When Grey had asked what it was about, Dale just laughed and said, "Don't bother; you don't got the brains for it." Grey was determined to get through it whether he understood it or not. Steve was at their desk, reading as well. This would be the last Christmas Grey and Steve would share a bedroom; next year Dale would be ousted from the house to move in with his girlfriend, and Steve would get Dale's room. When Grey heard sufficient rustling he put away his book and wandered out into the hall. His father was showering in the boys' bathroom he now used with the same constancy as he slept on the couch. Dale was in the den on the phone with his girlfriend, and his mother was in the kitchen cooking breakfast.

His mom's home-cooked breakfast was a Christmas tradition that, unlike his father's sleeping arrangement, never increased in frequency; it came once a year and once only. Grey walked into the living room and glanced over at the tree. It was still a fresh-cut tree because Grey had pitched a fit four years earlier when his mother had suggested they get a plastic one instead. Each year at least one string of lights burned out and was not replaced, fewer ornaments made it from storage, and more and more presents remained unwrapped. Grey turned his attention to the TV in the opposite corner. Until the others arrived, he sat on the couch, dull-eyed, watching *It's a Wonderful Life* which, for twenty-four hours from eight o'clock on Christmas Eve to eight on Christmas Day, looped nonstop on Channel Thirteen.

One by one everyone drifted in. No one said anything until Grey's mother turned off the stove, the last to join. Unmemorable words were exchanged, indicating that it was time. The smell of sausage overpowered the pine of the tree. There was no excited anticipation; the mood was less celebratory than it was obligatory. Grey, the youngest, faithful to his role as family catalyst, sat on the floor in front of the tree and handed out presents. Each person played his or her part, displaying a modicum of emotion, surprise or thankfulness, whatever was warranted by the present at hand. There were strained smiles and stilted exchanges as well as some genuine familial unity that was so rare even if it was suffused with awkwardness and discomfort. After all the presents had been distributed Grey's mother said with a slight trill in her voice, "Grey, did ya miss one?"

Grey looked over and saw her grab his father's thigh. Such a touch between them was incomprehensible; Grey ignored her words. His father got up, walked behind the tree and retrieved a large box that had been hidden beneath the white bed sheet that served as a tree skirt. It was wrapped.

The cab turned from Eighth onto Jane.

Grey's memory was so clear he could almost feel the paper beneath his fingers. The first tear revealed enough of the image that he could tell it was the metal detector that he had begged for since he was six.

35

Grey awoke to the sensory deprivation of winter. The black predawn skies redoubled the seclusion of his bedroom, magnifying the sounds of solitude. As he slid his legs across the empty bed, he remembered that Scott had left for Provincetown the previous morning. In the month since the HRC dinner, Grey and Scott had been estranged, speaking only when necessary and touching only when unavoidable; the vacated sheets were a welcomed reprieve.

Grey inhaled into a yawn, stretching as far he could reach. Only at the point when his old shoulder injury began to hurt did he relax. Exhaling with the same conscious slowness, he languished in the unburdened expanse of the king-size bed. He lay quiet and enjoyed the natural awakening of his mind and body, unfettered by either external or internal alarms.

The minutiae of the new day began to invade morning's idyll. The erratic noises of distant traffic that penetrated the soundproof windows were exacerbated by Rothko's rhythmic snoring seeping in from beneath the bedroom door. Grey rolled onto his stomach and dropped one leg to the floor. First he spread his toes, fanning them out against the wood and then stretched his foot's arch into another deep yawn. This morning he would take his time.

It was Christmas Eve.

When Grey opened the bedroom door, Rothko greeted him with his usual morning exuberance. He had been trained not to bark inside and so instead Rothko invested the excess energy in an intensified body spasm forceful enough to leave bruises. Grey bent down and scooped him into his arms. Rothko allowed it, liking the attention more than he minded being held. Grey carried him over to the window to see if the predicted snow had whitened the city.

The clear skies revealed that the storm had passed. There was a light glaze covering the deck furniture, but the snow was too frail to accumulate on anything with residual life: recently-driven cars, rooftops, concrete—anything that radiated the heat of the city. Inanimate objects like their deck furniture, and on the sidewalk below, the frame of an abandoned bicycle chained to a parking sign, held the only evidence of the storm's abated flurries.

Rothko reached his limit of containment and began to squirm. Grey set him down and they both scampered across the cold wood to the warmth of the kitchen's slate floor heated by the hot water pipes that ran underneath. Each sought out his morning sustenance—Rothko, his water bowl and Grey, his Krups. Grey reset the machine to manual and pressed *On*. Inky droplets splashed into the empty carafe and then quickened into a stream as the coffeemaker bubbled to life. It was a little past five when he stepped out his front door onto a street that, from ground level, felt even darker and more deserted.

Grey gave himself two hours to walk to Grand Central Terminal. He had lived in New York for twelve years and had never wandered New York's Christmastime wonderland of consumerism. Not only did he feel uncomfortable in crowds, he also exhibited a genetic defect that, if not kept in check, could be ruinous to the male homosexual. He detested shopping. Every year, Grey would schedule one morning in early December when he would make a big pot of coffee, shuffle five CDs of Christmas music and sit in his home office with a pile of catalogs. He would flip through each one, circling selected items and cross-referencing them to a list of recipients. He would then refill his coffee cup, plug a headset into his cordless phone, and for the next two hours or so, pace back and forth through the flat, chatting with appreciative telesalesmen and women. Within the two weeks that followed, all of Grey's family and close friends would receive generically wrapped packages of completely predictable presents. This year proved no different, except that Grey had traded the phone for the Internet. There was no need to talk to anyone.

Eighth Street had only errant signs of life, but as he made his way out of Chelsea and toward Midtown, he discovered other early risers walking to and fro the avenues. Their pace was slower, less desperate. Grey wondered whether it was the *namasté* space he was in or if these people were a different breed of New Yorker who had an appreciation and the discipline to carve out time for a commute less rushed. Either the season or the hour had availed a reprise from the New York' frenetic intensity. And so he ambled, examining every window display he passed.

At some point in the mid-'80s, NYC retail window design had evolved from generic marketing to a highly competitive art form, and while this was becoming the case all year-round, the Christmas season showcased the masters. Stores would bid out for famous designers, and some windows even displayed signature placards to credit the artist. Grey was more impressed with some of the mom-and-pop windows than the bigger department stores. Many of these were homespun and heartfelt. Others were wildly creative and fanciful. And to his surprise, some were even more elaborate than their larger, better-financed competitors. He stopped at a small flower shop where Santa's workshop had been recreated in assorted flowers, decorative branches and bamboo shoots. Santa and his elves were glued together using thousands of different sized and colored stones smoothed by rivers, oceans, man-made tumblers or from wherever else they had been harvested. The detail was astounding.

When he got to Macy's he was disappointed with the all-American family sitting immobile around a dark fireplace, staring into its obscurity, waiting for the miracle of Christmas. Although the wires were hidden, there was certain to be an electric component to the scene—a pretend fire, Santa perpetually popping out from the hearth to the repeated delight of the hovering children, or maybe a rotation from father to mother with a special gift reflecting his eternal love. But it was too early; there was no warm glow, no movement of any kind. The family sat in their frozen world, hopeful, expectant.

Grey tried to feign delight as he tore the paper from the box. He fooled his father but his mother knew him too well.

"Isn't it the one?" She pulled her hand away from his father's leg.

Grey attempted shock when excitement would have been a better play. "Wow—I just can't believe it."

As Grey was opening the box, his father offered, "Son, ya need any help?"—paternal interest as disorienting as his parents' affection toward one another.

Grey replied without looking up, "No thanks, it seems pretty straightforward."

"Well, I hope ya find us some buried treasure." His father reached down and patted him on the shoulder.

The house closed in on him. The sausage spattered, its odor turning rancid while the chubby jocular angel, Clarence, squealed from the outmoded Zenith console. Grey grabbed the metal detector and ran past his parents, out the back door. He stopped a few steps from the house and bowed his head to shield his face from exposure. Standing in his sock feet on the frozen dew-covered grass, Grey shivered, his cotton pajamas providing no protection. He examined the stick-like contraption in his hands; it looked like a giant prehistoric insect with its long thin body and a huge round proboscis for detecting its prey. The metal felt like ice.

When he was six Grey had begged his parents for a metal detector. They had been on their annual vacation at Wrightsville Beach and Grey had met a boy his age combing the dunes across from Newell's where Grey's mom always set up camp on their one beach-day outing.

The two of them spent about an hour digging up fishhooks and bottle caps. The boy, Randy, said the day before he had found a watch. Grey was in awe as Randy flaunted the adult-size Timex and demonstrated how his father taught him to set it. A young couple walked up to them. Hip and perky, they could have been cast in an Elvis Presley or Frankie Avalon movie. The man squatted in the sand, and the woman, who wore dark round sunglasses, reapplied her lipstick in a gold compact mirror. Grey eyed Randy's father. His swimming suit was tighter and shorter than he had ever seen on a grown man. The hair at the bottom of his legs thinned until there was none. They were as smooth as a girl's at the top. His knees were parted and, between them, the red stretchy material of his suit bulged.

"Well, Randy, I see you found a friend. Did you boys find any buried treasure today?"

Five or so minutes later, after they had escorted Grey back to his mother asleep on her towel, Grey watched the family walk away hand-in-hand to the Trolley Stop for an *All American* hotdog "with all the fixin's."

But that was six years ago—before his mother had gained her weight, before she got third degree burns while sleeping under a sunlamp and stopped sunbathing altogether, before his father moved to the couch. They had told him Santa couldn't afford it but, after two years of Grey whining, Dale had spilled the beans about both Santa and their parents' financial situation so that Grey would "shut the fuck up." Now he couldn't even remember what it felt like to want it so bad he cried himself to sleep every night for two weeks.

The bitter cold dried his tears. It was well below freezing with a Mississippi Delta humidity that made the wind chill far more invasive. Grey's lungs were so constricted he could hardly breathe. With limited mobility in his fingers, he flipped the switch. It hummed to life. His teeth began to chatter as he moved the base of the machine over the ground. The hum wavered and then locked for an instant on a high beep and then wavered again.

His father smiled from the kitchen window. His mother stared into the frying pan and continued to stir the eggs.

With either the automatic or manual determinant of the half-hour, the Macy's window scene came to life. Lights twinkled and motors whirred. The father clamped his rail and off he went but instead of stopping at the mother or the children, he glided past and disappeared behind the scrim backdrop. From the other side Santa emerged, the father transformed, fat and jolly, toting a bag full of gifts.

36

It was seven-thirty—Grey had missed his train. He turned from the Macy's window without waiting for the big surprise, the first of many throughout the iterative cycle of the miniature family's day until an early closing, when the switch was again flipped and they, like most Christian families, slept in wait of Christmas morning.

The city's bell had tolled and New York was now fully awake. The Macy's family was not alone in their scurry. Those around him no longer enjoyed the luxury of an early morning reprieve. Instead, most were racing to their jobs to which, either through necessity, conviction or obsession, they must go even on Christmas Eve. Grey was among them, yet his mind trailed behind, resisting—a resistance that evaporated as he approached Grand Central and the swarms of commuters thickened and crammed into each other, vying for easement on the narrow sidewalks, the most impatient risking the street to pass.

Grey just caught the eight o'clock. As he ran down the stairs to the platform, he tripped to sidestep a young child who had, without warning, stopped and bent over to retrieve something he had dropped. Grey caught the railing, avoiding a nasty fall but not the scorn from the wealthy East Side mother who didn't understand the concept of rush hour. She picked her frightened son up in her cashmered arms, coddling his tears and whispering to him he would never grow up to be as rude and insensitive as the bad man who selfishly pushed through crowds and scared little children. Literally adding insult to injury, someone, in an attempt to step around him, kicked his sprained ankle. Grey limped to the train, barely making it through the closing doors. It became just another New York workday.

Crammed into a middle seat, he took off his shoe and crossed his foot on top of his knee to examine the damage. The businessman sitting to his left gave a quick disdainful glare over his reading glasses and then, with equal disdain, loudly creased his *Wall Street Journal* as he turned to the next page.

Grey's father, who never read anything, much less the newspaper, folded the *Commercial Appeal* to the sports section. Sitting around the table, waiting for breakfast, they looked like a normal every-Christmas-day family.

After five Antarctic minutes of futile metal detecting, Grey was waved in by his mother. She had made her (and by edict, everybody else's) favorite—scrambled eggs with sausage and grits pooling with butter. And Hungry Jack buttermilk biscuits, the ones with flecks of butter in the batter. Dale and Steve kidded Grey about being a momma's boy as he copied her style of pouring the grits over the eggs and biscuits and mixing it all together into a mash. It was his father, not his mother, who spoke up to defend him.

That morning they more than looked like, they were, a normal family. They ate and talked together and remained at the table until his mom suggested that someone make another batch of biscuits. His brothers laughed when Grey volunteered to pop the can but it was in jest, not meant to hurt. It was the first meal in years where there was no laced silence or arguing. When they were finished, Dale even offered to wash the dishes. Steve and Grey looked at each other, mouths agape, as though a body snatcher had invaded their brother.

While Dale and Steve ran around the block to check on what their friends in the neighborhood got for Christmas, Grey decided he would rekindle his childhood affection for his metal detector. He changed and went outside to scour the backyard inch by inch. As the giant proboscis moved back and forth, Grey tried to envision the gold nuggets or locked chest he would find but his imagination failed him. It was monotonous. And regardless of his coat, it was still too cold. After almost cutting his finger on an old soda can tab, he lost what little interest he had mustered. He was about to go in when the now-familiar signal sounded. Laying the metal detector on the ground, he dug with his gloved fingers. There was nothing. He picked up the metal detector again and zeroed in on the exact location of the signal. It was a little off to the left but not much. He should have at least scraped the object. Yet still he saw nothing. He locked his eye on the identified spot and again, gently laid down the instrument like he was tracking a wild animal. He pulled off his glove for greater dexterity. With his bare finger he searched the hole and felt metal. An unbroken section of a thin chain was impressed into a small cavity; it had taken on the same red color as the clay soil. *Mississippi mud*, his mother always called it. Excitement mounted as he dug it out. He yanked off his other glove and loosened the dirt above the chain. It came free. He lifted a small necklace with a dime-size medallion caked in mud. Someone had lost this long ago in his backyard, long before it was his backyard. Once he cleared the mud he could make out a human figure central to the medallion's design. Renewed fantasies of *Treasure Island* and *Swiss Family Robinson* infused him. He left his gloves and metal detector on the ground and sprinted toward the house.

Madge was behind her desk staring at her computer when Grey arrived. He was surprised and although he was looking forward to being the only one in the office, he was gladdened by her presence. Her outfit was more conservative than usual: a red and green tartan skirt that came just above the knees matched her red silk blouse adorned with a very '80s-gal-trying-to-get-ahead-in-business bow at the neck. But of course Madge had complemented this professionalism with two short pigtails that jutted out from the sides of her head like Pippi Longstocking. As Grey neared her desk he noticed the Rudolph-the-Red-Nosed-Reindeer and Hermey-the-Wannabe-Dentist-Elf earrings that hung from the bottommost holes in her lobes. Without looking up from her computer, she said, "Get your coffee in a sec; I'm trying to see if I can get this flight."

"No hurry." Grey stepped into his office, the lights blinking to life at his presence.

Madge yelled, "One or two today?"

Grey yelled back, "Madge, make it a double."

Madge's sideways, cross-eyed face popped into his doorway and then disappeared as she skipped down the hall. It was a good two minutes later, right before she came back with his coffee, that Grey figured out she was mimicking the capricious facial expression Elizabeth Montgomery donned whenever she had to tell Darrin that, whoops, she'd used her witchcraft again without his permission.

Madge handed Grey his NCSU coffee cup with a perfect head of foam and grabbed the headrest of the customer chair in front of his desk. He didn't pay attention to how hot the cup was and burnt his lip when he lifted it to his mouth without looking. *"Ow!"* With his attention now unsplit, he asked her, "How do you know *Bewitched*? That's my generation."

She crossed her eyes again. "Oh, puuuh-leasse, ever heard of *Nick at Nite?*" She twirled around, giving his customer chair a spin, and continued to talk over her shoulder as she left. "Don't forget our eleven-o'clock lunch. And don't think your getting in late is gonna push it out; it's the only thing on your calendar all day."

Back at her desk, she added, "Except, of course, your eight-thirty flight. And remember, you've got to get there a half-hour early. It's the last flight out." The spinning chair slowed and then stopped, facing him as if an invisible customer had just sat down for a one-on-one chat.

After what seemed like far less than two hours, Madge again stood in the doorway, this time with her serious, finish-what-you're-doing-it's-meeting-time posture. "Ready?"

"Sure, give me a second to send this e-mail." Grey had spent the previous ten minutes debating various electronic Christmas cards. Most were Flash animations evoking holiday cheer but he chose a traditional *Peanuts* one, a still of Charlie Brown in front of an empty mailbox. A melancholy Charlie, Santa hat askew, stared blankly from computer screen with a speech bubble floating above his head. It said, *Getting something in your e-mail box is better than getting nothing at all.* In the *To:* field he typed, *friends.family.all.*

A few minutes later he was in front of her desk with his coat on, ready to go. "So, did you get the ticket?"

"Not yet, but I've got another bid in." Madge rolled back in her chair to the filing cabinet where she kept her purse. Her desk was spotless, swept clean of Hello Kitty paraphernalia.

Uh-oh, Grey thought.

Madge looped her arm through his as they walked toward the door. It was then he realized that, although Madge was his logistical lifeline at work, he had never once treated her to lunch. Maybe it was because he knew there would be a day like this when she would up and leave.

"Let me guess, you've got some news for me?"

"Kinda—yeah." More demure than usual, Madge let Grey hold the door open for her.

Grey was on the three o'clock train home; his three-hour lunch with Madge had left him in a bad mood. Her news that she was not quitting but, on the contrary, finally accepting his offer of a permanent position had caused a strange reaction that he hoped was imperceptible. As validation of his enthusiasm, he went a little overboard on a second bottle of champagne. Madge's joining as a full-time employee would lower his administrative expense and provide him with the additional security of a contractual commitment, yet he felt an overriding sadness to her caving in to the pressures of the mundane. On bottle two Madge scooped her udon onto her spoon and talked of returning to Bennington to get her teaching credentials. As they discussed the cost of private versus public tuition and the challenges of the New York acting scene, Grey became certain that Madge would never go back and that this decision would destine an irreversible fork in her life.

37

The train was close to empty and there was no one else in Grey's cabin. He took off his shoes and stretched his legs across to the facing seat. His ankle, while it didn't hurt, was swollen from the morning's fall. He removed his sock to see a large bruise covering the entire bridge of his foot. It reminded him of an injury long past inflicted.

Pain shot up his leg when Grey kicked the door jam that had never been removed after they tore down the wall between the kitchen and den. There, in front of the Christmas tree, his parents were one, their bodies intertwined. They were kissing. Upon hearing him, they pulled apart. Grey didn't stop but continued to run past as though he were racing to make it to the bathroom. Suddenly he was. As he rounded the corner into the bathroom, he threw up.

His mother yelled from the living room, "Grey, are you okay?" The bathmat and surrounding floor were covered with his undigested breakfast; he could still make out the sausage bits. She hurried down the hall, followed by his father. "Grey?" Both of their faces appeared in the doorway, hers contorted, his confused. "Oh my God, Grey are you OK?" was quickly followed by, "Dammit, John, get a mop for God's sake." When she leaned over him, he smelled the alcohol on her breath. Grey felt better; his world began to adjust. He shoved the chain into his pocket before she could see it.

The next day they took down the tree. Everyone maintained distance, both physical and emotional. The familiar oppressiveness of the household had returned. Grey's bruised foot throbbed but he told no one of his injury. Making his subterfuge more difficult was Grey's post-holiday chore: climbing the rickety attic ladder to pack away the boxes of ornaments and lights until the next year. In spite of the pain, he made one more trip than necessary. He scouted to see if anyone was around and then went to his room and grabbed the reboxed metal detector. Grey limped up the seven rungs, wincing with each step. In the attic he hopped past the small, floored area to the back of the roofline and tucked the box down into the insulation, between two studs where no one could see it. For the next two weeks he dodged questions about its location until everyone forgot that it ever existed. Years later when they moved, Grey was charged with packing the attic. It took an hour to carry down all the boxes through the small hatch door. On his last trip he looked across to the empty A-framed space. He remembered thinking that it appeared smaller without any boxes.

For all he knew the metal detector still lay in the attic, buried away, undiscovered by the elderly couple who now lived there. But his foot remained a periodic reminder. Whenever there was a dramatic change in the weather, it ached from the old wound.

He was in luck; *Alessandro's* was still open with Alessandro, true to form, behind the counter watching some football game.

Since Grey first happened upon it, he had dropped by *Alessandro's* at least once a week. They had grown accustomed to seeing one another.

"Wow, I didn't expect you to be open on Christmas Eve."

Alessandro didn't turn from his TV but spoke over his back without acknowledging Grey's entrance. "Then why'd you stop by?"

Grey walked behind the counter and set his briefcase down. "Well, I was *hoping* you'd be open but didn't *think* you'd be open. There's a difference." He grabbed the remote from under the counter and changed the channel.

"*Heyyyyyy*, whaddya doing?"

"Trying to get your attention, whaddya think?" Grey reached into his suitcase and pulled out a finger-size present wrapped in two Brunello labels taped together.

"Is that for me?"

"No, I just thought I'd show it to you—of course it's for you." To avoid any awkward gratuity, Grey walked out from behind the counter as soon as Alessandro took the gift. "It's nothing, just a promotional giveaway with my company's logo on it. It's a wine opener; you can never have too many." Alessandro stared at the gift as if he had never received one before. Midway down the aisle, Grey yelled, "Hey, I'm in a hurry tonight. Do you have anything I can heat up in the microwave? I'm serious—no homemade *niente*.

Alessandro laid the gift on the counter and picked up the remote. "It wouldn't take ya too long to—"

Grey cut him off. "I know, I know, but this time I mean it. I've a plane to catch; I need something fast."

The incessant hollow voices of sports commentary joined their conversation. "One aisle over, at the back, there's a section of canned imports. There's some soups and stews there."

Grey walked around the corner and began scanning the cans. He stopped on one in particular and said to himself, "You've gotta be kidding."

"Alessandro, have you ever tried this?" The label read, *Albonetti's Traditional Elbanian Gurguglione.*"

This time he turned from the TV on his own. "Come on, you know I try everything before I let it to go on my shelves. It's a good hearty stew—zesty, but then I've never had the real thing."

On the label was an aerial graphic of Elba. "I think I have, but it was a long time ago."

As Alessandro was bagging the wine, Grey asked, "So what time are you closing shop? It *is* a holiday."

"Ever since the wife died, I never liked being at home on Christmas Eve— it was her birthday. Kids are all in Jersey; they'll drop by tomorrow."

Grey pulled the bottle back out of the bag. "On second thought, why don't you open that present and get us a couple-a-glasses."

Alessandro filled both glasses with a heavy pour. Grey lifted his in toast. "To Christmas past."

38

Grey answered the door, cosmo in hand. He was buzzed after the champagne with Madge and the bottle of wine with Alessandro. But he was a trouper and kept going; he thought, what the hell, 'twas the season.

John was wearing a vintage shawl collar tuxedo, his hair cut short and gelled back. He went to the bar to pick up the bag of doggie necessities while Rothko assaulted his shins. "Hey man, sorry I can't take ya to the airport."

Grey glanced down at John's shoes expecting black Nikes only to find a beautiful pair of Kenneth Cole updated wingtips that Grey had himself purchased the month before.

"Good God man, isn't it a little early for the prom?" Grey joked.

Ignoring Grey's parental ogling, John shooed Rothko from jumping on him. "Not tonight, boy," John said, grabbing Rothko's front paws and putting them back onto the floor.

"I told you; it's our Holiday Dance."

Grey went back out on the deck where we had just finished eating. The light flashed on in the turret. Grey ignored the young actor sitting at his vanity, his hair banded from his face, motionless, staring into the mirror. Instead he looked out across the Hudson. "Ahhh, that's right, not *Christmas* but *Holiday*. Who'd ya finally choose—Gina or Kristin?"

"Man, you know I asked Kristin; Gina was just, ya know, a diversion."

John joined Grey on the deck. "You sure ya don't need me to do anything else while you're gone?" He tried to get Grey to look at him but Grey remained staring at the river.

Grey nodded to his bedroom where on the bed were several neat piles of clothes. "Help me pack; I can't seem to actually put my clothes in the suitcase."

John put his hand on Grey's shoulder. "Man, I've never seen you so down. I mean, come on, it's Christmas."

Grey turned around. The person in front of him showed no remnants of the neighborhood boy who went door to door selling homemade pottery. It wasn't just his clothes or the adultness of the situation; even his face had broadened into manhood. "I know this may sound weird, but I'm proud of you."

John threw his arms around him. They were no longer lanky but had grown muscular from all of the sports he played. They were far more manly than Grey's. It was now Grey who felt like the adolescent, cradled in John's embrace, comforted by the syncopated beating of their hearts, one indiscernible from the other. When they pulled apart, Grey's eyes brimmed red; John's smiled. "Actually it doesn't sound weird; it sounds really cool."

Grey was washing his dishes when the buzzer rang. It was seven-fifteen. He shook his head as he went to the intercom thinking Madge must have asked the car service to come early just in case.

39

A young police officer appeared on the video unit. Grey pressed the talk button with a queasy suspicion that this was a joke of some sort. "Is there something wrong?"

"Are you Grey Tigrett?" The handsome officer stared into the camera. He looked like he was in his early twenties.

Grey's voice warbled with nervousness. "Yes, why?"

"Would you mind coming down; this is an emergency." The officer held up his badge, obscuring his face and filling the video screen.

As Grey ran down the stairs his mind raced through a thousand emergencies, plausible and implausible, that might precipitate such a visit. The officer looked even younger in person, possibly less than twenty, a teenage boy dressed up like a man. Like John. He was short with skin so white it was pink, that of a baby or someone from a place perpetually deprived of sun. He had the clipped Eastern European accent of a Kristen Bjorn actor. Maybe it was a prank after all.

"Follow me."

Grey sobered instantly. As they turned into the Hotel Riverview, he wondered if he should ask to examine the officer's badge. "What is it? What happened?"

The officer headed straight for the stairs. "Do you know a James Owen who lives in 205?"

They rounded the first landing. Grey's anxiety worsened; he hung back a couple of steps. "No, I don't know anyone who lives here."

"He says you're his closest kin."

Grey trailed behind even farther, far enough so that when the door was opened, he could make a run for it before the supposed officer and whoever was behind the door could collect themselves. It didn't help that the Riverview's hallways were even more dingy than Grey had imagined—peeling paint, exposed light bulbs—straight out of COPS or some other seedy reality show. Sweat dripped from his armpits down the sides of his ribs.

When the police officer rounded the doorway, there was something about his profile that told Grey that this was no setup. Grey stopped and peered in. As his heart and mind slowed, an outline emerged. First he noticed the dank humid smell; he assumed it was his own sweat. There were three other people in the room. Grey didn't recognize Jimmy because only the crown of his downcast head was visible. Next to him, a short, pear-shaped, female officer stood over a man who was, like Jimmy, ageless from abuse. In his filth and dishevelment, the second man sat cross-legged in a lotus position, his hands cuffed behind him, his head also bowed. His long stringy hair fell into his lap like a washbasin, hiding most of his face from view. He was sobbing, his entire body shaking with each breath. Grey was able to make out, "He told me to do it," before his focus shifted and all sounds dissolved in a sensory surge when he realized the horror of the situation. The general outline vanished, replaced by magnified details that obliterated the whole.

Jimmy's body hung on the wall, suspended two feet in the air as if held in place by the centrifugal force of a macabre carnival ride. Four thin vertical red lines stretched from his prostrate limbs to the floor below. They started as three but the one from his left hand separated midway down the wall, an errant fork caused by an irregularity in the plaster, like raindrops on a window. The blood pooled at the baseboard and then trickled again, following the uneven slope of the floor to the back of the room.

Grey's first thought was the carpet would need to be replaced. Yet there was no carpet, only the soft wood sub-flooring. At some point long ago, someone had painted it battleship gray, but it was now so scuffed and stained that it looked like the mottled industrial carpet so common in buildings of this era.

Jimmy lifted his head. His face was drained to a chalky white. "*Feliz Navidad.*"

Grey turned from him, unable to respond. His mind clouded, erased the present, and then with precise clarity, conjured an image from a few months back of Jimmy sitting the on the stoop with outstretched arms hovering at his side.

The worst part of the next half-hour was the sound of the nails being extracted from the wall. In his shock, Grey questioned the irrelevant. Where did they find the bungee cord and why bind his feet? There had to be some planning involved because someone had thought of supports for his armpits and between his legs, otherwise the nails would have ripped through his hands. There was also the exact spacing required. He imagined the two, tweaked out of their minds, beating on the wall to locate the studs. Why, on Christmas Eve, wouldn't someone have complained about the hammering? Did Jimmy want someone to complain? Did he want to be saved? The question of intentionality would plague Grey for the next decade or so until he had buried Jimmy's memory to such a depth that it rarely surfaced.

Toward the end Jimmy began to sober. He could feel the nails being withdrawn; of this Grey was sure. He moaned and his eyes rolled back into his head. At one point it appeared as if he fainted but it was only for a few seconds. Either the intensity of the pain or a desire to experience its undiluted fury brought him back. Or maybe he was simply grasping for the final moments he knew were slipping from him. But for the most part he didn't enter true consciousness, trading his heroin-induced delirium for one of blood loss. There was a point near the end, as the paramedics were transferring him from the bed to the stretcher, when he began to recite the Hail Mary, his bloody hands on his chest silently fingering an imaginary rosary. No one interrupted or calmed him; everyone was perfunctory, continuing his or her respective task. Grey couldn't look at him. He stood with his back to the bed, staring at the wall, at the three holes from which spilled the streaks of blood, insignificant scars against the squalid nature of the room. If you had entered the room five minutes later, you may not have noticed these markings, or if you did, you would have never guessed them to be the site of a crucifixion. From the room's small window, across the dark band of the river, thousands of Christmas lights twinkled amidst the Hoboken skyline.

As they lifted Jimmy from the bed, he sat up and cried out, "Oh God," and then his body just seemed to deflate like a pierced blowup doll, crumpling onto itself. He was dead before they reached the door.

Carrying the stretcher, the paramedics led the procession down the stairs. Grey was not questioned further nor did either officer indicate he would be. The only sound from the group was the whimpering of Jimmy's accomplice, who never once raised his head. His garbled mumbling that he'd "only forgotten some—" dissipated as they descended the last two flights and the voices and sounds of the theater ascended from below. The crowd in the lobby quieted and parted for their passage. Someone asked if this was part of the show. Grey stopped in their midst. Here, there was warmth and excitement. Here, he was just another Christmas Eve theatergoer momentarily distracted by an unexplained tragedy. Outside, the handsome cop opened the ambulance doors. Through the fortified glass of the hotel's door, the wire mesh X'd across Jimmy's sheet-covered body. No siren sounded as the ambulance drove away.

40

It was seven-fifty—Grey had missed his car service. He remained in the crowd, transfixed by its gaiety. He tried to let the smiling faces, laughter, and intimate exchanges of a Christmas Eve outing wash over him and purge the emptiness he felt.

His awareness floated over the crowd, lighting on whatever seemed most distracting—a shrill laugh, a gaudy tie, a Christmas kiss. Someone caught his eye. He didn't allow time to see whether it was a friend, acquaintance, or neither; instead he turned around like he was looking at the picture on the wall behind him. It was an old photograph of a group of people standing at the hotel's grand reception desk, a far cry from the Plexiglas closet it had become. There were about twenty people spanning one end to the other. Below it was a framed newspaper article from April 16, 1912. The headline read:

HOTEL RIVERVIEW *offers free rooms to the surviving crew of the Titanic.*

Grey tried to imagine the frivolity Brian and Greg's '97 Titanic Halloween party, the crowd full of his and Scott's friends. For some reason they hadn't gone that year and Grey's dulled imagination was unable to recast their presence. As the theater doors opened and the lobby began to empty, Grey stood alone trapped in the present.

Ten minutes later he was at the back of the theater. He didn't remember seeing an usher or being asked for a ticket. He could have slipped by as part of group or maybe someone had read his face and understood that Grey needed to escape reality, if only for a couple of hours.

Hedwig came out on stage wearing his first outfit, a sequined American Flag cape that Grey had seen him change into so many nights over the past two years. While Grey had imagined a multitude of permutations for the play, he was not prepared for such an intense emotional experience—a story of love, loss and redemption.

Every scene, outfit and song was imbued with meaning. At one point in the first act, Hedwig started singing a ballad called, "Wicked Little Town." For this number, Hedwig wore a full-length fur with a large stain of fake blood that he joked was "adulation" from an angry animal rights activist who had accosted him before the show.

He mocked his supposed admirer. "What poor unfortunate creature had to die for you to wear that?"

Hedwig's reply, "My Aunt Trudy," filled the theater with laughter. Again, Grey had seen the coat many times so it was no surprise but when Hedwig turned his back so the audience could see the fake blood-matted fur, the laughter turned to moaning. Grey saw Jimmy's splayed body against the wall, the four thin lines of blood pooling onto the mottled floor below. He heard the high-pitched squeak of the nails being pulled from the studs. Through the window he remembered no Christmas lights, only the dark flow of the Hudson.

Grey started convulsing uncontrollably. He thought he was going to collapse. But as the song started, his shaking stopped.

Hedwig came down the stairs and began to work his way down the aisle to Grey. Any other night Grey would have been repelled by the attention or laughed at the MTV-moment of it all. Instead he cried, releasing the tears he had been holding back all day. The tears that first had welled at the compromise of life, the loss of youth, the unstoppable churn and self-destruction, now finally released at the antithesis of this inevitability—a botched transsexual's will to make it work, to fight against all odds for whatever happiness one could muster.

When Hedwig reached Grey, he brushed the back of his hand against Grey's wet cheek and sang, *"There's nothing you can find that cannot be found. 'Cause with all the changes you've been through, it seems the stranger's always you, alone again in some new, wicked, little town."*

Grey was one of the last to leave the theatre. He followed an elderly woman in a red sweatshirt with a sequined reindeer on the front. Her companion, a trendy teen with green hair and low-riding Diesels, lent her his elbow for support as they crept slowly down the aisle. They must have been sitting close to the stage because her sweatshirt and his retro Howdy Doody T-shirt were splattered with roughage from the closing scene.

"He certainly had a lotta energy," she said as they all three walked out into the lobby where there were a few cliques scattered about, waiting for autographs. Grey bummed a cigarette from a group of three women, none of whom could have been more than twenty-five. The one in the middle lit it for him with a Bic lighter adorned with a rippling American flag. She was pretty but with eyes so heavily rimmed with eyeliner it accentuated the wide distance between them.

He inhaled the sweet smoke, surprised that someone so young smoked menthol. Aromatic wisps punctuated his words. "Thank you."

"Any time." She had a slow, lazy blink. The dark slate blue eye shadow didn't help matters.

The cold night air infused with the menthol, the resulting iciness tingling his lungs. Grey stopped at the stoop where Jimmy always sat. The Sunday before Grey's sales conference trip, Jimmy had asked for low fat cream cheese on his bagel. They had laughed about weight loss and Jimmy joked that he had means other than dietetic food to keep his heroin chic figure. "Heroin." After they both stopped laughing, Jimmy had said in complete seriousness, "Actually, I just like it better." It reminded Grey of a line from some existentialist short story he had read in high school but he couldn't recall either the title or author.

Grey pulled a long drag from the cigarette. He hadn't smoked since the sales conference and it was stronger than he was used to. It made him dizzy and nauseous. Upon a closer examination, he discovered that it was not menthol but a clove. He threw it to the ground without bothering to stamp it out.

41

His suitcase had fallen over. Grey forced the door open, dragging it across the floor. Other than it and the dishes in the sink, the room was immaculate, with no sign of life except the answering machine blinking four messages. Grey pressed *Play*.

"Honey, this is Mom. Merry Christmas. We're all here . . . well, except you of course. I just got your card—Dale showed me how to pull it up. Now that I'm finally using that computer you got for me, you'll have to give me some lessons the next time you come home."

Her voice lowered as she whispered into the receiver, "On that note, your brothers and I talked. We agreed that your friend could come home with you— he can have Steve's old room. He and Jules now always want to stay at the Peabody anyway. I know it's too late for this year but next year, okay?"

The television set blared in the background. Grey caught a familiar line, smiling with the realization that Channel Thirteen still ran its holiday loop of *It's a Wonderful Life*.

"Anyway, have a wonderful Christmas. I know you're probably jetting off somewhere exotic like you always do."

"Oh . . . is this thing still on? You'll never guess who called. Miriam. She wanted your number. I gave her your e-mail address too. She sounded a little sad; I hope everything's okay. I know we had our differences but she's really a sweet girl. Call her—I know she'd love to see you again. Okay, I think that's it. Bye now and again, Merry Christmas."

The second message was Madge, reminding him that if he hadn't left yet, he should do so within ten minutes. "And have a great Christmas and pre-millennium

New Year. Remember, next year's the *real* millennium."

The third was Scott.

"Grey, we're at the airport. Your plane just landed and no you. Is anything wrong?"

Brian's voice was almost as loud as Scott's. Grey could picture him screaming over Scott's shoulder. "Tell him if he doesn't make it tonight that you two get downgraded to the pink room."

Greg was farther from the receiver. His, "That suits them anyway," was followed by the laughter of at least two others.

"Honey, call as soon as you get this message. Everybody's worried."

The final message was also from Scott.

"Grey, this is so fucking embarrassing. I look like a fucking idiot whose boyfriend doesn't give a flying fuck about being with him on Christmas Eve or at least letting me know where the goddamned hell he is. And did you think about how inconsiderate this is to Brian and Greg? They've spent months planning this and now tonight's shot with everyone wondering where you are."

It sounded like Scott put his hand over the receiver to muffle his voice as he yelled, "Coming."

He resumed in full vitriol, "I almost hope something did happen so that I'm wrong in my assumption that you just missed the plane because you stayed late at work or went to the wrong airport or some other absentminded fuck-up."

Again his voice was muted. "No, he's not there; give me a sec." There was an interlude of silence followed by an exasperated sigh but then Scott began to speak slower with a tenderness that Grey hadn't heard in a long time. "Obviously I didn't mean that; I'm just upset. Grey look—just call me; I'm really worried. I love you."

Grey picked up the receiver. He opened the drawer beneath the phone and pulled out his contact list. As he flipped through it, he walked to the window. The actors in the turret were throwing a Christmas party. The cast was still there and a few other people had joined them, including the wide-eyed clove smoker. On Hedwig's vanity was a little two-foot drugstore Christmas tree. It was one of those pre-decorated ones with little miniature lights and ornaments.

Grey located Greg and Brian's Provincetown number. Mid-dial, he looked up from the printout. Hedwig was at the turret window. Grey's fingers froze as the young actor lifted his champagne glass in toast. An automated voice was telling him his call could not be completed. Grey lifted the receiver above his head as if he were returning the toast. Hedwig smiled and turned back to his party.

While Grey waited on hold he went back into the kitchen and finished washing the dishes. The gurguglione was good but nothing like he remembered. Of course it was from a can and his fourteen-year-old memory was probably embellished by fantasy. He pulled the empty can out of the recycling bin. The graphic of Elba was generic. It could have been any island.

"Yes, do you have any flights to Florence tonight or tomorrow?"

ELBA 2000

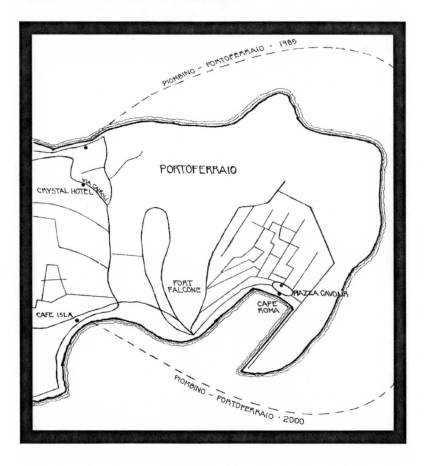

42

"What time are our reservations?" Grey tightened his arms around his chest, easing his grip on the glass so that he wouldn't spill his wine. He took a sip and winced at its sweetness, surprised at how his tastes had changed over the years.

"Honey, don't worry; let's just enjoy our time together. They'll come get us if we're late." As she turned, the wind blew her short fine hair across her face. At some point during the last few years she had stopped coloring it and Grey thought that, with the natural gray against her olive complexion, she was as beautiful as he had ever seen her, as beautiful as her wedding picture. She reached over and cupped her hand behind his neck. "We don't have many times like this anymore."

His eyes began to sting. He faced into the wind so that he wouldn't cry; he was too old for that.

Their shadows stretched and disappeared into the surf. The wind blew harder than he remembered. His tears dried. He glanced down at his watch—it was only five-thirty.

"I'm sorry you don't wanna talk about this but it's important."

Grey dropped his head. His legs disappeared into the sand where he had subconsciously buried his feet.

"Honey, nobody likes to talk about this kind of thing but believe me, it'll be better to decide everything now so I don't have to worry about it later."

He looked up into her eyes that looked so much like his own. They were sincere. This was not one of her manipulations of self-pity.

"It'll take you boys less than a day to decide who gets what and then we never have to talk about it again. Don't worry; I'm not going anywhere for a long,

long time. But you know me; I'm a planner—better to get this all down on paper so there's no mess later."

Grey nodded. "Can we walk a bit?"

"Sure." She reached for his hand. Her soft palms rubbed into his as they interlocked their fingers.

The coastline had narrowed over the years, even with the expensive attempts to bolster it by pumping sand down all the way from Virginia Beach. In his childhood the stretch of sea grass between the sand and the lot lines was as far away as the end of each summer day. Now at high tide it was less than fifty feet from the surf's reach. Ahead in the distance the unmanned lifeguard stand marked their usual turnaround point.

"Mom, it's not the will thing I don't want to discuss."

Facing him meant full exposure to the wind and she couldn't withstand its severity. It was his Southern nature to switch places with her, but he didn't. He didn't want to see her initial reaction.

"It's the kid thing. I don't know if I'll ever have kids." She had allowed Grey to set the pace; he kept it slow but steady. The stand was still a good football field away.

"Honey, I know you and Miriam are havin' some problems, and as you probably know, most of the family's glad about that." Unlike her usual attack, the bite was unintended. Unlike his usual response, he didn't care.

"But of course you'll eventually have children. I know you can't see that right now because you're still young. But I can. I've always known. I can tell you that I've never been sure about Dale or Steve, but with you, it's so easy to see your future. You are going to make some woman very, very happy." Her paisley skirt ballooned out like a spinnaker, outlining her shapely legs, a remnant of her youthful allure.

Gusting wind interrupted them and drowned out all sounds including the crashing waves. When it abated they did not resume their conversation but strolled the last stretch in silence.

"Let's get back," Grey said and dropped her hand to turn around. A red flag fluttered its caution from the top of the empty stand. He hung back for just an instant to look out across the ocean. Stormy darkness rested on the distant horizon, erasing the edge between water and sky.

Out in the ocean, a streak of lightning terminated into the water, marking the delineation. Grey was now upwind; he would see her reaction. This time it was he who reached for her hand. He squeezed it tight and stared straight ahead. "Mom, I won't make some woman happy and I won't have kids, because I'm gay."

She stopped. As her hand went limp, he tightened his grip. Standing still, unprotected, the wind was colder.

43

He awoke shivering. His coat had fallen from his body at some point during the night and lay on the ground beside him. It took a couple of seconds to get his bearings. He sat up and put the coat back on; it too was cold from the concrete. Images began to emerge: the subdued yellow of the streetlight through the sycamore trees, the warm sepia of the building upon which it shone.

Grey had arrived at the train station at 5 A.M. and since it didn't open until seven, had lain down using his suitcase as a pillow. Between the discomfort of his middle-seat accommodations and trying to piece together some rationale to justify his actions, he hadn't slept at all during the nineteen hours of the three-leg flight. Though the hard uneven sidewalk was far less comfortable than his airplane seat, exhaustion took over. His consciousness wakened to the stiffness in his back and an exquisite need to urinate. He blinked the morning blur from his eyes and looked around. The station was no longer desolate; there were a few others, mostly backpacking students, but also some suited and skirted types. They clustered near the gates that Grey guessed someone would soon come to open.

His spine cracked as he arched forward and twisted. When he pulled against his propped-up leg for more leverage, he noticed his left wrist was bare. He first thought he had left his watch in New York but had a sinking feeling that was confirmed as he checked the pockets of his coat.

Twelve hours later Grey caught the last ferry out. The entire morning had been spent on a public phone in the Florence train station. Fortunately, he knew his Orion AT&T account by heart. He had left Scott a voicemail and an e-mail from JFK but the theft of his wallet forced a direct conversation that ended with,

"I don't give a fuck about your being stranded—you made this insensitive self-absorbed bed for assholes, now wallow in it!" followed by the abrupt click of the phone's flip top—the closest cellular equivalent to slamming down the receiver.

Jane was more helpful. She listened, interjecting every now and then with emotive support like "Omigod!" and "I'm so sorry" and "You must be exhausted," before they moved on to the financial logistics. Jane lent Jack as a temporary replacement for Scott, someone who would pretend to be Grey and take care of essential cancellations and reissues. Jane also offered Grey an extension of her credit card so he could manage in the interim.

"Jane, I don't know what to say." His appreciation was evident even though it was almost drowned out by the announcement for a train departing for Milan.

"Think nothing of it," Jane replied. "Now, do I get to run the office while you're away?" It would have sounded gratuitous if they both hadn't known she was the most senior rep to whom the responsibility would fall, and that it was far more responsibility than reward. It was just a comfortable way to avoid an awkward ending to a conversation neither of them knew how to end. It allowed him to switch into work mode and her to respond in-kind.

At the conversation's close, Jane's voice softened into a soothing maternal lilt. "Grey, there's one more thing and I'm only going to tell you because I don't want you to hear it from someone else. Jack just pushed the paper in front of me and Jimmy's suicide is in the headlines. Only they're not calling it suicide. They're saying his father murdered him."

Grey walked out to the ferry's deck. With the fading sunlight, it was bitter cold—a wet cold that cut to the bone. He zipped his coat all the way up and buried his hands in his pockets. He exhaled through pursed lips. His breath was invisible, for a brief moment resisting its evaporation into the sea air. A large craggy land mass dominated the horizon. He didn't remember passing another island. He pulled the boarding pass from his inside coat pocket. His fingers were clumsy, stiffened by the cold; the ticket fluttered out of his hand. For an instant the wind held it immobile in front of him, just within his reach. But then it dipped and caught an undercurrent that lifted it into the air. It danced, twirling and turning over on itself, going higher and higher, but during a blink, it disappeared from Grey's view. He didn't see it lose the wind's hold and fall, floating, a white rectangle against the water's deepening blue, and then sink beneath the surface. Nor did he worry—if he had boarded the wrong boat, he would deal with that later. Grey stared at the island, the bow centered on its breadth. Lights shimmered on its dark mass.

"His only begotten son." The whisper dissolved into the rush of wind and sea.

A half-hour later he was on Elba. He did not need to ask anyone; even in the dark he recognized the stretch of buildings where he had walked a little over a month ago. Grey rolled his suitcase down the boarding plank. Instead of planning the days ahead, he drifted toward the Crystal Hotel, second-guessing assumptions long unchallenged. Fourteen years earlier he had witnessed an insignificant speck of land slowly emerge into view. It was a far greater distance crossed by a much longer voyage. Throughout all that would happen over the next month and the rest of his life, Grey never could make sense of the disconnect between his memory and the reality that unfolded.

44

Sunlight imprinted the floor with a slanted image of the window through which it shone. Grey's journal lay open on the bedside table; he had written a short entry before going to sleep.

> *I have no idea what I'm doing here. All I know is that I had to come. I feel like I left a piece of myself on this island, a peace I need to reclaim. But how will I find it? Will he lead me there? Maybe I just need time, time to reflect, face the past so that I can be freed from its clutch.*

As morning advanced toward noon, the panes of light angled and stretched up and over the bed. A thick shard cut across Grey's waist. He did not wake. Instead his dream world incorporated the slow migration of resulting warmth upon his body. On his feet it was summer. He ran barefoot through Sheep Meadow, his eyes focused on an overhead Frisbee that was lifted by an updraft of wind. It rose higher and higher into the sky. He continued to chase after it even as it disappeared into the clouds. Still, he ran until he was again still, quiescent, his legs warmed by the artificial incandescence of the tanning booth in which he lay. Burning white light encased his body, transforming his olive skin into a pasty gray. Death gray. His body, naked except for a small towel over his genitals, beaded with sweat. It pooled where his skin touched the bed's slippery surfaces and in the hollow undersides of his knees. He couldn't roll over; the bed was too small. Instead he rotated his legs outward against the heat, opening his pelvis until his kneecaps pressed against the clear glass of the bed's cover. Warmth continued to climb the freshly exposed skin of his inner legs. The light vibrated to the rhythm of Grey's heartbeat. He floated upon its gentle waves. His breathing slowed into a counter beat. Grey relaxed into it; he almost let go. But as he tried, he became aware of an electric buzz. It was almost imperceptible, its origin outside the bed.

Fluorescence turned to radiation, the cool, smooth walls of the tanning bed to those of an MRI scanner. The towel became a metal loincloth that some unseen operator had instructed was to safeguard his future progeny. There was the antiseptic smell of a hospital. Covering his eyes, a pair of reflective orange shades had survived the dreamy transition. The claustrophobic tube was oppressive. He had never had an MRI and his dream availed of this ignorance. Radiation sliced across Grey's spread thighs, inching upward, taking picture upon picture, until it reached the lower edge of the protective metal. The proximity and heat aroused him. He strained to control his embarrassing reaction, knowing if he couldn't, the light would extinguish, the test halted, and he would never know its results. His abdomen tightened, pressing against his kidneys. He couldn't contain it. He squeezed harder but instead of diminishing, the pressure triggered a pulsation in his groin. The laser hummed in his ear. He knew at any minute he would be found out. And then darkness, quiet. It was not an altogether unpleasant thought. He stopped straining against it. Tightness dissipated but the pulsating continued unabated. It too was not unpleasant. It flooded over him. He drifted once more as the laser shifted to natural light and the sulfuric odor to the salty brine of seawater.

It was almost noon. Grey lay on his back, limbs spread outward across a large mahogany four-poster bed. Sometime in the middle of the night he had kicked aside the down comforter. It hung off the foot of the bed from the post nearest the window, gathering in folds upon the blood crimson Oriental rug that carpeted three quarters of the room's dark wood floor. His pale skin and blond hair upon the white sheets contradicted the surrounding darkness of the Victorian room. The thin top sheet covered the lower half of his body from just below the navel. Beneath it, every contour was outlined, every movement magnified. Facing the bed was a marble-top Empire dresser beside which a small radiator hissed. Above the dresser, the large attached mirror swiveled downward. The positioning was not intentional but a result of loose joints and the gap between footing and wall, forced by floor molding that was thickened by years of layered paint. The tilt caused a distortion in its reflection. Grey's body shortened; the shard of light was disproportioned, exaggerating further the movement of Grey's hips.

Light rippled across the folds of cotton, like water. In Grey's dream the smooth cylindrical walls roughened to hewn wood. He lay wet in the hull of a small rowboat, sea-drenched underwear clinging to his bare body. The sea hissed beneath them. Above him knelt Antonio, naked, erect—reflected orange in the two glass lenses that obscured Grey's eyes.

Grey didn't bother tucking the sheet under the mattress. He spot-cleaned it in the shower and hung it inside the room below the open window. He took his time unpacking; when he finished, it was dry. In making the bed he noticed a faint water stain but nothing that would draw attention. He surveyed the room before leaving. His empty suitcases sat on top of the wardrobe. The only clothes not put away were two pairs of shoes neatly aligned under the bed. Next to his journal on the bedside table, his leather-cased travel alarm clock was opened, a decorative complement to the room's permanent furnishings. It looked as though he had been there for far longer than one night. Or that he was planning to be.

45

The same young bartender was at the café and addressed him with familiarity. "What's up? Cappuccino, yes?"

Grey stood at the end of bar, in the exact place he had over a month before. "Yeah—good memory."

There were no other customers so this time the bartender did not divide his attention. "We don't get many Americans here." With his back to Grey, he pumped the espresso into its sieve. "Or requests for nonfat milk." He leveled the mound of espresso with the back of his hand and pressed it down with a small metal pistol; it was an old machine. "Given the dark rings under your eyes, I'm guessin' you want two shots."

Smiling at his blatancy, Grey replied, "You're guessin' right." After a slight pause, he added, "If you don't mind my asking, where'd you study English?"

The bartender was twisting both sieves into place and answered without looking around, "New York City—I grew up there."

"Really, that's where I'm from. Wow, how'd you end up here? I mean, I can't imagine that many New Yorkers move to Elba."

At this the bartender turned around. His long curly hair was pulled back in a ponytail, revealing the full expanse of his face. He was more handsome than Grey remembered. And a little older, maybe late twenties. For a second he stood there, silent, as if waiting for Grey to speak again. Grey held off, fearing his pre-coffee blurt came across as snobby. It was an uneasy moment until the bartender smiled and stuck out his hand.

"Paolo."

Grey shook it. "Grey."

"Gray like the color?" Paolo slid open the cooler that ran half the length of the bar. He reached far into the back and pulled out a small half-pint carton, spinning it around to find the expiration date.

Grey hadn't been asked this question in a long time. A childhood rhyme sprung from its subconscious recess, *Watch out, here comes Grey day to ruin our play day.*

"Not really—it's spelled G-R-E-Y."

Paolo poured the milk into a little silver pitcher and put it under the steamer. He turned back to Grey. "Isn't that how they spell the color?"

"Not in America." Grey was looking at the fingernails on his right hand. With his thumb, he was picking the cuticle of his middle finger. It was a habit he had developed over the past year. "At least not where I grew up."

"Which was where?" Paolo grabbed a large bag of espresso beans and poured them into the unwieldy grinder that looked big enough to tackle a side of beef. In pulling the bag away he spilled a few.

An hour later there was still no one else in the café. The two had talked the entire time. Grey discovered that Paolo had moved from Elba to New York as a child, after his father had died in a boating accident. He, with his mother and sister, had grown up on Mulberry Street in Little Italy when it truly was an Italian neighborhood. So much so that over half the kids in his grade school were first-generation Italians. He went away to college, to UC Berkeley, and it was there, after getting his BA in cognitive psychology, that he decided to come back to Elba.

"San Francisco's not like New York. Even though it's not an island, you feel the water around you; it's part of your daily gig. I can't explain it, but it sorta triggered something, something I had to . . . rediscover."

"And have you?"

In the dimming light, Paolo's eyes matched the deep brown of his hair. The colorful ice cream poster hung on the wall behind him. He walked from behind the bar to peer out the front door. The sky was darkening with rain clouds and the boats in the harbor rocked in the wind. It looked like a storm was about to break.

"That, my new friend, is not an easy question to answer. For that we must shift from coffee to wine and from biscotti to dinner."

Two hours later the two sat at a table—two candles, two glasses and a half-empty bottle of wine between them. Paolo had pulled surprise after surprise from the cooler, whipping up a full steak, pasta and salad dinner. Conversation continued uninterrupted as pots boiled and pans fried, while Paolo sliced and Grey grated, through dinner and cleanup, and now midway through a bottle of dessert wine. They talked mostly of wanderlust. Coming to Elba, Paolo had gotten bit by the travel bug but had not yet had the opportunity to scratch its itch. He wanted to know everywhere Grey had been, which places he liked and which he didn't. When Grey told him about his first time on Elba, Paolo was curious.

"So it drew you back as well."

Grey poured himself another glass of wine. "Yeah, I guess . . . hey, this wine, what's it called again? Do you think I can get a case to take back?"

"Ansonica—they call it a *passito* wine because it's made from raisins and not grapes. Sure, my distributor can get you a case. At my price."

The label had a picture of the fort that Jane and his other Orion colleagues had visited. "But aren't raisins just dried grapes?"

Paolo's eyes were magnified through his glass of wine. He was holding it in front of his face, studying it as if searching for any discernible difference that could distinguish it as a raisin wine.

He replied, "Yeah, but it's something about having the grapes dry in the sun a certain amount of time before distilling the wine." He set his glass back down. "Wait, you avoided my question—what drew you back to Elba and what have you been doin' the last month? How come I haven't seen you around?"

"Actually, I haven't been here a month. I just arrived last night."

Grey gave few details—a friend had died and he needed to get away. He chose Elba because his brief two-hour visit had reminded him of his first time, and yes, he was drawn back.

Paolo yawned. "You should be the tired one. Aren't you jetlagged?"

Grey's eyelids were leaden with exhaustion but he was enjoying the evening so much he forced himself to stay awake. "Not too bad—I slept for twelve hours last night."

Paolo got up and grabbed the empty glasses and bottle. "Where ya staying?"

"The Crystal Hotel." Paolo carried the dishes behind the bar; Grey followed and resumed his original seat in front.

"Donovan's place. Didn't you ask about the Crystal when you were here in November?"

"Yep."

Paolo looked up from the sink. "I guess you liked it, huh?"

"Yeah, especially this time of year—it's warm and inviting. I don't know if I'd want to stay there during the summer."

Paolo tilted his head. "I'm surprised Donovan gave you a room—I thought he closed up in winter, except for his regulars."

"I guess he felt sorry for me; I sorta called at the last minute and he remembered who I was."

"Well, you're pretty memorable." Paolo was wringing out a rag he had just wet. In the quiet of the café, its dripping resounded from the sink's stainless steel basin. The comment caught Grey off guard. He was pretty certain that he was blushing but intent on his task at hand, Paolo didn't notice.

"As I said, we don't get many Americans here, much less twice during the rainy season." He finished wiping down the counters and threw his rag into the sink. "Ready?"

Grey noticed a computer in the corner. "Does that thing work?" he asked.

"Yeah, most of the time." Paolo started turning off the lights. "I just leave it on because it usually crashes when I shut it down."

"Can I get on real quick to check e-mail?" Grey asked.

"Sure, take your time; I'm in no hurry." Paolo walked over with him.

"It'll only take a minute." Grey sat down and logged onto his e-mail account. Paolo went to the bathroom just behind the table where the computer was. Through the wall Grey could hear him peeing. Grey scanned the message headers. There were five or six, mostly replies to his Christmas card.

The final one was from Scott. The subject line was blank.

> grey,
> i wanted to put this down in writing because it seems we're not able to talk anymore. i'm tired. i'm tired of constantly being judged by u. i'm tired of ur moral superiority. and I'm tire of being the bad guy. look, i love u. u probably don't believe that because u think i'm incapable of love. i feel it every time u look at me. i feel unworthy. yes—i like being silly and caddy. i like having people laugh at my jokes and i like

treating our friends with the respect that u seem to reserve only for strangers. should i apologize for that. or for not being as deep as u. for being happy to walk though the day and not analyze the implications of every second, of every word. i'm not going to apologize for being who i am and i'm tired of being made to feel bad about myself.

certainly u'll over-dramatize this as a dear john e-mail and maybe that is what it is but . . . look, i want us to work but i can't see the way. in order to salvage our relationship we're both going to need to take some drastic measures and i'm not certain either of us are up for that. i've talked to shelly, our in-house counsel, and she's put me in touch with a mediator who specializes in gay divorce. i went this route because i don't want any of our friends to know about this til we settle everything.

i'm truly sorry about jimmy but dammit its not my fault. and i don't think it justifies how inconsiderately u've treated brian and greg. or me. an apology is not that hard even in the direst of circumstances. but i do know u need this time away and i don't want to rush ur return. take ur time. john and i have worked out an arrangement for rothko.

figure it out grey. maybe this is what we both need. u always talk about how u recreated urself in college. maybe u should do it again. all i know is that i want to be happy and i don't think i can be while were together. and i don't think u can either. but i do, and probably always will, love u.
-scott

Grey logged out.

"Anything important?" Paolo asked, shutting the bathroom door.

"Not really."

They exited the backside of the café into the small piazza. Paolo pulled a pack of cigarettes from his shirt pocket and offered Grey one. The pack was half full and the lighter had been shoved between the cellophane and the carton, crushing the empty half. The sea blue lighter with an image of an American flag triggered a recent memory Grey couldn't place. Cupping the fire to shield the wind, Paolo lit Grey's cigarette and in doing so, brushed his hand against Grey's cheek. Grey raised his eyes for just an instant and caught Paolo staring over the lighter at him. He returned his attention to his cigarette, puffing on it to catch the flame.

"I'd walk ya back but my place is right across the way." Putting the pack back into his pocket, Paolo pointed with his chin and exhaled a steady stream of smoke toward the third story of one of the buildings encircling the piazza.

"That's OK—maybe next time." Grey didn't turn to leave.

"Maybe." Paolo put his cigarette to his mouth and stuck out his right hand with a directness that revealed his New York upbringing.

Grey clasped his hand but did not shake it. Paolo's skin was rough and cracked, older than his years. They hesitated, neither consummating the incomplete gesture. Grey couldn't remember who pulled away first.

Before going their separate ways, Paolo asked, "Are ya still around for New Year's?"

Grey nodded. "Looks like it."

46

For the next three days, it rained nonstop. Grey stayed in his room. He slept and journaled and only left to venture downstairs to the small hotel restaurant. The other guests were indeed regulars, an elderly group of widowers who ate together and played *Scopa* while gossiping about various Italian personalities. When Grey asked about Antonio's house, Donovan told him the family had moved from Portoferraio. When he added, "They keeps it nice," Grey got the distinct impression that they didn't live too far away. He hadn't the chance to inquire further because the rain had aggravated Donovan's limp and so he hadn't come by the hotel for the last two days. Rather than anxious to know more, Grey was somehow relieved. Maybe he would just let it be.

On New Year's Eve the storm abated. Grey planned on going to Paolo's party but he dallied. First he took a walk down the beach and then attempted a different route across town. It took about a half-hour longer than it should have because he lost his way. He didn't mind; he was in no hurry and it gave him a chance to see more of the city.

Paolo's building was unremarkable among the fifteen or so others that bordered the small piazza. Or rather, it stood apart because of its modesty. Most of the others had converted the bottom floor into a café or boutique or if not, had added distinctive awnings and geranium-filled window boxes. His was one of only three or four whose façade remained plain, unaltered from its original design. It was a typical sienna-washed Mediterranean edifice with green metal shutters upon each of its four second- and third-story windows. On the top floor, the one to which Paolo had pointed, the shutters had been thrown open. From it was cast that special kind of winter party light that implied warmth and conviviality, compelling attention from those who passed below. Through it, Grey could hear the faint lyrics of Madonna's latest CD. Some things were truly universal.

The doorbell was nowhere to be seen. At first he didn't know what to do. He looked around the deserted piazza and then up to the window and thought how Tennessee Williams the situation was. But Grey was no Stanley Kowalski nor could he even remember the last time he raised his voice, much less yelled. He tried the handle and fortunately, the door was unlocked. From the small communal foyer the staircase wound around a central atrium. It looked original, or if renovated, it was done pre-twentieth century, or nineteenth or eighteenth for that matter. Grey never ceased to be awed by the weight of such a past. A bright green and yellow mountain bike leaned against the wall, discordant with the antiquity of its surroundings. Like Madonna.

He climbed the marble steps worn to depression by countless footfalls. Outside the apartment door, Grey listened to the conversation and laughter from within, bracing himself for a crowd. He would know no one and few would speak English. Before knocking he hesitated, trying to determine if the man's voice nearest the door was Paolo's. It sounded like he was arguing with a woman about something. Grey imagined Paolo's hand gestures advancing in rhythm and intensity with the escalation of their voices, conducting the argument. He lifted his hand to knock. There was a break between music and discourse; all was quiet except the barely perceptible drone of an American television station, monotone, dissociative in contrast. It was only an instant but Grey paused, aware of both his Americanness and his tongue. He felt that when he entered he would not be able to speak.

The door swung open and caught Grey off guard—especially the doorknob. Grey found his tongue, his Americanness and the occasion to yell. "Fuuuuuuuuuck!"

"*Scuza, scuza.*" The middle-aged woman mirrored Grey's doubled-over body; they looked like two deferential geishas sharing a secret. She bent a little lower to see his face.

She switched to English and spoke with a strange accent that Grey was in no frame of mind to try and place. "I'm so sahry. Ahre you okahy?"

Grabbing his elbow, she lifted him to standing. As he surrendered in politeness, pain shot through his testicles into his stomach.

"Please pardon me," she said, directing him into the apartment. She sat him down in a small vanity chair next to the foyer table, just inside the door. When she bent over, her scarf slid from her shoulder, drawing an intense waft of perfume from her exposed cleavage. Grey's stomach lurched, as did apparently his expression because she repeated her English apology even louder than before. It was as though they had dropped a platter of china in a quiet restaurant; everyone within earshot stopped and looked. Grey forced an unconvincing smile. At once, Paolo came and stood in front of him, blocking his visibility from the rest of the room, mitigating attention.

"Brigitte, could you get Grey a glass of wine?" She hurried across the foyer and into the kitchen. In those three small steps she had already reset her scarf.

Paolo placed one hand on Grey's shoulder and contemplated him with a mixture of concern and humor. He smelled of fresh cigarette. "Talk about making an entrance. Here, take my glass; I'll intercept Brigitte. Just sit here till you feel better." Before leaving he leaned down to address Grey at his seated level. His voice was hushed, meant for Grey alone. "I'm assuming you don't mind drinking from my glass." He winked as he turned and followed Brigitte into the kitchen.

Conscious that others might notice him checking out Paolo's ass, Grey pretended to check out the room instead, redirecting his eyes up Paolo's back and continuing up the walls to the ceiling. From a large ornate rosette that dominated the small foyer hung a ponderous crystal chandelier that seemed too rococo for either the island or Paolo.

Ten minutes later Paolo and Brigitte led Grey around and introduced him to some of the guests. Thanks to the Berlitz primer he'd bought as a distraction for the plane ride, he managed the basic civilities. Afterwards, he and Brigitte stationed themselves in the frame of the pocket doors that divided the foyer and living room.

Brigitte smiled like an old acquaintance. Her regal elegance gave her the appearance of being in her mid-fifties although Grey thought she was probably younger. She was tall, an inch or two shorter than he. One of her eyebrows arched in supercilious intrigue as she began her investigation, "Paolo tells me that in America all doors open in. Probably that is why you were not hoping the door to hit you."

Grey smiled in response—"Something like that."—and changed the subject. "How do you know Paolo?"

The question launched Brigitte into storytelling, an art in which she proved to be expertly skilled. She had been close friends with Paolo's parents and had known him since he was born. She called herself an exile.

"If I am to leave France, I decide that I choose the most famous place in the world for French exiles." In 1950, "the dawn of the mid-century" as she called it, Brigitte gave birth out of wedlock. "I have only fourteen years and with this young I am a scandal, even to the French." Grey added up the years and was stunned by Brigitte's sixty-four. She wore her auburn hair straight, pulled back from her forehead with a simple black lacquered band. Her face was done but not overly so. It was not absent of wrinkles, but the few she had didn't age her as much as accentuate her features. But her body was the real deception. It was more than her chic thinness, more than her plunging lavender silk blouse, the scooped edge visible beneath her delicate scarf; every movement and gesture was natural and unrestrained, that of a woman in her prime. Grey had noticed this quality before in French women, not a denial of age but irreverence for the myth that with age a woman must relinquish her sexuality.

At fourteen Brigitte had left France and her family but not her family money. Somehow she had managed to hire a lawyer and propose an arrangement that would avoid family embarrassment, but at a cost: they would be responsible for her and her child's generous living expenses until both of them died. Contract in hand, Brigitte moved to Elba where she bought Paolo's apartment building. She never again set foot in France. Yet while she had forsaken France, she would never forsake the French palate. She leaned into him as she confided that the furnishings in all three apartments had been shipped from Paris because Italian design left much to be desired.

She named her daughter Sophie.

Sophie and Paolo's mother had grown up together and were best friends but they hadn't seen each other since the mid '80s. Brigitte said this was because Paolo's mother had cut off everyone after her husband died.

"She was so sad that she talks to no one. She blames the island." Brigitte stopped and looked across the room at Paolo. "No, she blames the sea. It taked her parents, the parents of her husband, and her husband also. After, she takes the childs to New York and Sophie moves to Paris. Sophie marries and has two childs, one grandchild and all eat dinner every of the Sundays with her grandparents who stay alive to make sure that I do not return and ruin everything another time."

Her story beckoned a multitude of questions. "You mean that all four of Paolo's grandparents drowned? And his father? At the same time?"

"The grandparents, yes, but the father is after." She explained that Paolo's grandmothers had grown up together in Padua and, at a wartime rally, had met their respective husbands who were attending university there. For some reason both couples were alienated from all four families. "In that time it was not wise to speak against Mussolini." Grey thought there was probably more to this but was enjoying Brigitte's exuberance and didn't want to interrupt.

The two couples moved together from Padua to Elba and opened a boat manufacturer that, to this day, was one of Elba's largest companies. Brigitte said when she first moved to the island, the foursome adopted her at once because, she boasted, "We exiles stick together." Within a year, each of the three women had her first and only child. "We was three families that becomed one." One day, several years later, the two men came home excited about the first manufacturing of a new boat design that, at the time, was supposed to revolutionize the fishing industry. Brigitte stayed with the kids while her four friends took the boat on a celebratory ride. They never came back and no one ever found either the boat or the bodies.

Brigitte's vocabulary and grammar were getting worse as she lost herself in memory. "The week next there is discovered a vice in the design."

Grey interrupted, "I think you mean flaw."

"Yes, a flaw, a big one. That boat should not never be builded."

She looked again to Paolo. "Paolo's poor mother and father have only eighteen years. Before they are friends but after they are lovers. I think this is difficult for my Sophie. She is a exile from her most close friends—a exile from exiles.

"So you raised Paolo's parents?"

"Yes and no. They have eighteen years—they are not childs but yes, they live with me. So much bad passed. They are childs who cannot herit money so the families that they never recounter take the money to guard for them until when they are more old. They never receive that money. I do not know if they try because the families treat them very bad." Brigitte paused as if she had remembered, or forgotten, something. Just as abruptly, she resumed her story, "Two years after, they marry and I helped for them to buy a house. They worked many years before they have money and Maria can to stop to have infants."

Grey was thankful to have this woman monopolize him so he wouldn't have to mingle, but he was also genuinely interested. "And the father, how did he die?"

Brigitte touched her shoulder; Grey thought she meant to again secure her scarf, but her hand remained resting on her collarbone.

"No one knows. It was another accident but it is a pretty day and the boat is not hurt. He drownded. A other fishingman finded the boat close to the shore. He lied on the ground twenty meters under the sea."

She drank her last sip of wine and then reached down to set her glass on the table. Her nails were impeccably manicured. French.

"The last time I seed Paolo was over ten years past before his mother taked him and his sister to New York. Now he returns home and he lives with me and manages my café."

"Well, I'm glad for you both but one thing confuses me." Brigitte's eyes were expectant for the required compliment. "You're far too young to have a great-grandchild; I would've thought you're not even old enough to be a grandmother." Grey winked with more than a hint of flirtation.

Brigitte rolled her eyes and crooked a devilish smile. "That is why they tell to you to have childs while you're young. Now you—I think you are a exile too. I want to listen of you but before, I need to bring a bottle of champagne. It is almost a new era."

47

Grey thought about Brigitte's last statement, of his being an exile. *Boy, did she hit the nail on the head.* He looked around him, taking in the apartment anew with the knowledge that Brigitte owned it. It now made sense. The small rooms were decidedly French—woods were dark and inlaid, fabrics were thick and cozy, paintings were oil; there was marble everywhere.

When Brigitte had not come back ten minutes later, Grey began to feel uncomfortable standing alone in the unfamiliar crowd.

Paolo had moved on to the group who sat watching television. Grey watched as he bantered with them, pulling at the arm of an unsmiling girl who resisted, dead weight against his efforts. At her side was a small white dog with a round furry face—a Bichon or a Maltese mix. Grey thought about John and Rothko and wondered how they were celebrating. When Paolo picked up the dog, the girl squealed.

"*Danielle, tu puoi essere pigra, ma Alfredo non dovrebbe stare sul divano tutta la notte.*"

She didn't stop whining until he gave the dog back. After Paolo left, she remained ensconced in the corner of the sofa with her magazine, clutching Alfredo at her side.

Grey walked over to the window, bypassing the TV crowd. He exchanged a stern-faced chin-down American acknowledgment with Paolo's eyebrow-raised chin-up how's-it-going nod.

Of the other houses on the piazza, most were dark; there were only three or four with open shutters. One of these framed the back of a couch upon which sat the backs of two heads, one bald, one bobbed. On the opposing wall was a smallish TV turned to the same channel the group beside him was watching, an American station, most likely CNN. It was showcasing millennium celebrations around the world. Grey thought of Scott.

In the center of the piazza, two boys, probably between eight and ten years old, were lining up bottles, one beside the other. The shorter of the two was the workhorse of the pair while the taller supervised. When they finished, the row of twelve bottles stretched about five feet wide. The taller boy pulled out a paper bag from under his coat and carefully unwrapped its contents. One by one, he dropped a rocket into each bottle.

Grey turned back to the TV. Paolo had convinced them to mute the sound. On the screen was a huge Ferris wheel against the London skyline. Scott had read about it when they were trying to decide where they would spend the millennium eve. "We could be on top of the world," he had said. He was pissed when he discovered all the tickets had been sold prior to its announcement in the press. "Fuckin' Brits," Scott had screamed into the phone after being kept on hold for over an hour. The newscaster was reporting some mechanical uncertainty. The scrolling headline news at the bottom of the screen read, *London's Eye will turn but with no one aboard.*

It was eleven-thirty. The television coverage switched to Paris. Brigitte brought up a 1959 vintage bottle of Dom Perignon (stressing, of course, that real champagne had to come from the Champagne region of France) that she bought the day of Sophie's first communion. Brigitte may have believed herself excommunicated but as she put it, "A pretty dress is a pretty dress." Upon seeing the indifference of Paolo's glasses, she whisked him back downstairs to retrieve her Baccarat flutes. Grey looked back at the TV. The reporter was interviewing the architectural illuminist responsible for designing the fireworks that, at midnight, would transform the Eiffel Tower into a glittering spectacle of light.

The entire party was now crowded around the TV. Everyone was talking, laughing or in the midst of some debate. Except Grey. He turned back to the window and lifted it open a couple of inches. The air carried a faint brininess. The two boys were sitting at opposite ends of their row of bottles. The five or so feet between them was far enough that they didn't have to raise their voices but not close enough for the secrets of mischievous boys. Their voices echoed.

The couch-glued girl whom Paolo had tried to entice into socializing appeared beside Grey and tapped him on the shoulder. She was much shorter than he had expected, about five-two, and for that height, more than a little wide through the hips. Her red and white checkered Keds matched her too-tight red T-shirt with *I* ♥ *SOHO* white lettering. In one arm she held Alfredo, in the other hand her open magazine.

Grey bent down, pulled his lower lip over his mouth and offered Alfredo his protruding chin. Alfredo knew an opportunity when he licked it and upshifted his tongue into high gear, moving from Grey's mouth to his nose. Grey shut his eyes and turned his head, giving Alfredo a go at his ear.

"He is *so* cute," Grey said; his eyes were still closed but he was pretty sure he was out of mouthshot from Alfredo.

From above, Danielle asked, "*E questo voi?*"

Danielle's magazine was *Metropolitan Home*; it was open to a full-page picture of Grey, Scott and Rothko in front of the bar of their condo. On the facing page, the 48-point font title read Early Adopters. Below it the blurb:

> The dazzling gentrification *of the meatpacking district has been phenomenal, even by New York standards. Neighborhoods that go from rags to riches follow the complex and unpredictable forces of urban renewal. But there is one common denominator: the trendsetters who take the risk on forlorn properties out of vision, affordability, or, in this case, obsession.*

The article began with a quote from Grey.

> "*The first time I visited Manhattan I happened upon Jane Street and made up my mind that one day I would live here.*"

Scott had pitched *Met Home* through a friend of his who was the current crush of the magazine's Head of Artistic Direction. They completed the shoot in September but were sure it wouldn't run before spring, if at all. Communication had been managed through Scott, so he must have known about the schedule change. Maybe this was to be a Christmas surprise.

"*Sì, è me.*"

The girl's face brightened as if his revelation were an unexpected Christmas gift. In this she found the flame of energy that before had been impossible to spark. She became the harbinger of party gossip, spreading the news faster than Paolo and Brigitte could pass around the fragile cranberry glass flutes. All heads turned to Grey—some for just a second, others longer. Upon crossing Danielle's path on their respective missions, Brigitte looked up from the magazine and found Grey in the crowd, flashing him a wry smile of admiration, one would-be designer to another. Paolo appeared to sense Grey's discomfort with the limelight and repeated a variation of his chin-up nod, this time slower with more intention, a look that said, *Relax, you're welcome here.*

The girl absconded into the kitchen to inform any stragglers as Paolo and Brigitte continued their distribution. The TV now showed Times Square. It was still light there but people had already started to congregate. Grey wondered what Scott and the boys were doing. He was certain they had planned something extravagant for the big moment but couldn't remember what. At five minutes to midnight everyone crowded into the living room. Paolo lifted his glass in toast. "*Ad un nuovo secolo di famiglia, amici, felicità e amore.*" As he spoke he turned to address each person in the room. When he reached Grey, Paolo paused and added, "*Vecchi e nuovi.*" With all glasses held high, Paolo began the countdown.

"*Dieci, Nove.*"

Everyone chimed in, "*Otto, Sette, Sei.*"

In the piazza the smaller boy was rapt, kneeling with his thumb atop his lighter, ready to go, while his accomplice also counted down. His fingers were disappearing one by one at a rate of about two fingers ahead of Paolo's.

"*Cinque, Quattro.*"

The two boys scrambled to light their respective six rockets. Upon lighting his last one, the smaller boy knocked over the bottle and in falling, it brought down two more. He froze while his partner in crime made a dash to escape, running from the bottles, rubbernecking over his shoulder to gauge the extent of the pyrotechnic mishap.

"*Tre, Due.*"

High in the sky, above the north side of the piazza, were the first explosions of a more substantial fireworks display, a twinkling geodome of a million red stars—probably the island's primary celebration. The boys' nine upright rockets began shooting into the air as the three felled ones crisscrossed the piazza. One of the three shot past the running boy, barely missing him. These rockets weren't nearly as spectacular as either the town's or those showcased on TV, but they were the millennium fireworks Grey would always remember.

"*Uno.*"

Grey turned back to toast with Paolo, Brigitte and the rest of the party. The champagne was slightly bitter, tasting more like sherry than champagne. Maybe its time had passed. The TV screen was back on Paris; through the flute's rose tint the Eiffel Tower did indeed look like a giant pink sparkler.

48

It was close to noon. Paolo and Grey had just left Paolo's building and were crossing the piazza. The boys' twelve bottles were still lined in the center; someone had re-stood the three that had fallen.

Brigitte had suggested the picnic, eager to discuss the *Met Home* article, which was all she could talk about after the midnight celebration had subsided. She wanted to know if Grey had connections to *Architectural Digest*. It was "more her." Not that *Metropolitan Home* wasn't nice and all—just too American. She told him that Elba was destined to become the new Mallorca. Grey didn't quite know what she meant but as Brigitte talked, he learned it had something to do with the highbrow tourism that she believed could be attracted through the exposure of a certain French Elbanian's style.

She had prepared a simple basket of picnic staples—china and oysters, crystal and Cassis, silver and quail—but at the last minute fell ill with a migraine and sent Paolo and Grey on their own.

It seemed strange for just the two of them, especially after Grey's outing by the *Met Home* article. Paolo quickly dispelled any discomfort. He handed the basket to Grey and dug his free hand into his pocket. "Let's stop first in the café so I can get a bottle of red wine; I'm not a big fan of Cassis."

Paolo pulled out his keys. "How long do you plan on staying here?"

"I'm not . . . uh . . . real sure. Maybe two weeks, maybe a month." Paolo was opening the door when Grey added, "I guess enough time to clear my head a bit."

Grey stayed in the doorway as Paolo went to the wine rack and considered his options before pulling out a stepladder from a hidden compartment at the foot of the bar.

"I've got a proposition for you." The word *proposition* threw Grey, causing his heart to race even though Paolo's tone was utterly professional. He sounded more like a businessman than a kid in his twenties.

Tiptoe on the ladder's top rung, Paolo grabbed a bottle from the uppermost row of the rack. "Well, really it's Brigitte's idea." Jumping from the five feet he had climbed, he landed with only a slight bend of his knees, more like a kid in his twenties than a businessman.

He was kneeling on the floor, pushing the stepladder back under the counter when he presented his proposal. "My mom's got a rental house here that needs a bit of help. It's a great location but I wanna do it over . . . I don't know, make it more attractive to tourists, I guess." Back at Grey's side, locking up, Paolo pulled the shade down over the glass door, its disclosure an oversight from the previous day's early closing. "Brigitte's lending me the money to fix it up and thought that maybe you'd be interested in trading some design ideas for free lodging. I'll give you a budget and you can go from there."

"Well, I'm really not an interior designer. I'm not sure I'd come up with anything different than you would."

They were outside; Paolo was locking up. He looked over his shoulder at Grey with a smirk. "Yeah, right. Look, I know you probably don't wanna spend your vacation working but I promised Brigitte I'd ask."

They strolled through the archway that led out from the piazza to the boardwalk. The day was brilliant, clear and windless. The harbor of white hulls and sails were motionless, inert upon the water. Grey was filled with a rush of childlike enthusiasm. Since he had given up his dream of architecture, he had never considered his love of design a skill for which people would pay. Also, such a project would be a plausible excuse. Scott might even buy this as a reason to spend a month away. All the more if he could get another spread out of it. Or a free vacation rental.

Grey answered with a tentative *yes*. "Maybe, where is it?"

On the cliff, the fort loomed above them. "It's walking distance. We can go there after lunch and I'll show you the place." Paolo bent over and picked up a stone. He inspected it like he was considering it for a keepsake, something Grey would do, and then skimmed it across the water. It skipped only once. "Hopefully after seeing it, you won't change you mind."

Grey felt the urge to call Scott and let him know, ask him for ideas. Maybe they could even work on it together.

They crossed town to the third harbor, to a protected part of the beach, not a hundred feet from where Grey, Miriam, Pete and Tom had met the two Texas bimbos. Grey remembered the girls had used fake names and smiled thinking about how angry Tom had been the next morning when he had to pay for their hotel room.

A natural finger of rock extended from the sand's grassy border to the beach. Like a giant snake, it slithered to the water's edge. Where they stopped, it was just high enough to lean against. Grey interlocked his fingers and reached his upturned palms over his head, twisting his body into the stretch. His loud yawn underscored their solitude. Paolo pulled from the basket a black *REI* blanket—obviously his and not Brigitte's. Without wind there was no surf; the water was as calm and glassy as a mountain lake.

"Is it always this warm in January?"

"Are you kidding? It's usually windy and at least ten degrees colder." He placed the basket in the middle of the blanket and grabbed the baguette that jutted from it. Breaking it in two, he handed half to Grey. "Celsius."

"Lucky us," Grey said, taking off his jacket. Grey noticed a book sticking out of Paolo's jacket pocket.

"Whatcha reading?"

"*Stranger in a Strange Land.* Have you ever read it?" Paolo handed the book to Grey. Grey found it odd that Paolo's hands were already beet red. Unfortunately, neither of them had brought sunscreen.

The book's cover image of a naked man meditating beneath the Martian sea made Grey uneasy. "Not since I was a kid and to be honest, back then I didn't really get what was going on."

"You should give it another try; it's amazing. He's got some wacko ideas, but he really gets what it's like to feel alienated by normalcy. It's one of the few books I reread on a regular basis."

Grey tossed the book back. "I'm lucky if I get to read one book a year, much less read a book I've already read."

As they were spreading the blanket, Grey stepped on a wound. "Brigitte said she's known you your whole life, that she knew your parents before y'all moved to New York."

Paolo stopped what he was doing.

Grey corrected himself. "I'm sorry. I mean before you and your mom moved to New York. I hope I'm not speaking out of line."

Paolo shook his head. He took off his shoes to weight two corners of the blanket. Grey did the same. "No, man, it's just that everyone here knows my past so I haven't talked about it in a while. D'ya mind if I open the wine first?"

As they ate, Paolo filled in the details of Brigitte's sketch. After his father's death, his mother had come unhinged. Brigitte had been correct in saying that she blamed the sea. She couldn't stand to be near it or even smell it in the air. She used what little money they had to move them to New York and found a job in a small Italian restaurant called *Due Amici*. The owner was a penny-pinching Sicilian immigrant and couldn't keep his wait staff because he required that they wash dishes as well. His mother had worked there thirteen years. She and the gruff owner had developed quite a reputation on Mulberry Street. So much so, a *Post* review of the restaurant had alluded to them as more than just *two friends*: *A Sicilian mom and pop or Signor y Signora restaurant that has been serving their traditional Italian fare for well over a decade.* But Paolo said that his mother had never remarried or, as far as he knew, ever even dated a man other than his father. He went on to say that his sister grew to love New York but that he always felt at odds with the city, like he didn't quite fit in. After he earned the college degree that he promised his mother, he returned to Elba.

Brigitte had somehow found time to bake a pear tart from which Paolo had cut two quarter-pie slices. "What does your mom think of you coming back here?"

"I don't know, it's weird—I thought she'd freak but . . . " Paolo hesitated, holding his fork over his pie. "It almost seemed like she expected it."

Grey took a bite of the pie. "Hath she come to vithit?"

Fork and pie hovered in front of Paolo's face as he studied the shoreline. The sea's calm was eerie. "No, she won't come here." He took his bite but continued to contemplate the seascape.

Grey lowered his voice in deference to Paolo's mood shift. "At least in Manhattan, she's gotten accustomed to being around water again."

Paolo did not look back at Grey as he responded, "She's never seen the water there."

"You're kidding. How's that possible?"

Paolo didn't answer.

The revelation's awkwardness blurred the lines of convention, the resulting silence disrupting the equilibrium of newly formed acquaintance. Grey further tipped the scale. "You never told me the other night what you came back to rediscover."

Paolo wrapped his arms around his knees and squeezed them into himself. When he turned to Grey, his eyes caught the reflection of the horizon between sea and sky, scoring the indistinguishable iris and pupil, splitting them in two. They were half domes of amber floating upon obsidian twins. In them, Grey saw the reflective eyes of another, the dream figure who both haunted and seduced.

"Maybe I didn't mean rediscover. Maybe I meant discover."

Grey couldn't look into his eyes without sinking into the dream and so it was now he who stared out to the sea.

49

After they repacked the basket, Grey leaned back against the rock. He rolled his coat for a pillow. Paolo lay on his side, his head propped in his hand. Sand spilled onto the black fleece from the indentation of his elbow near the blanket's edge.

With his free hand, Paolo reached for his glass that was on the basket between them. "Is that a Saint Anthony medal?"

Grey was enjoying the sun on his face and squinted his eyes open. "What?"

Before raising his glass to his mouth, Paolo tapped it to the base of his throat. "Your necklace?"

Grey had worn the necklace for so long he had forgotten it was there. It must have come out of his shirt when he had bent over to help spread the blanket. Grey lifted his hand to the medallion. "I don't know, I found it as a kid." He dropped the medallion back to his chest. "Why, who's Saint Anthony?"

Paolo put his glass on the basket. "You're kidding—you've never heard of Saint Anthony? You must not know many Catholics."

While still reclining, Grey tried to lift his head and take a sip. Unsuccessful, his coat fell from the rock and the wine spilled down his chin. He wiped his mouth with the back of his hand. "Not really—I grew up Methodist in the heart of the Baptist belt goin' to a Presbyterian high school. That was enough religion for me."

Paolo sat up, brushing the sand from his elbow. "Can I see it?"

Grey was surprised by the request. There had only been a handful of times he had taken it off. He sat up and rotated the chain to find the clasp. For a second he couldn't remember how to work it, but then it came undone. It felt odd to take it off after all these years. He handed it Paolo.

Paolo cupped the medallion in his palm, the chain hanging from his hand. He lifted it for closer inspection. "My father wore one all his life."

Grey recalled when he decided to first wear it. He had just returned from his European backpacking trip and was filing his passport in his firebox. For whatever reason, he emptied the contents of the blue velvet pouch where he kept random memorabilia: his high school ring, a childhood ID bracelet, his wisdom teeth, and the medallion. He fingered the medallion. It was almost black, oxidized from the untold years it lay buried in the suburbs of Memphis. He had never cleaned it. It felt old, European. The link from which it hung was just large enough to fit over the clasp of the necklace that Miriam had given him. He had worn it ever since.

"Where did you find it?" Paolo's hair fell forward around his face as he examined the medallion.

Grey moved closer to see over Paolo's shoulder. "My backyard, why?"

Undistracted by Grey's proximity, Paolo answered, "Because it looks like my dad's—a nautical St. Anthony's that's usually only worn by fishermen."

"So what's the deal with him? Why do people wear medals of him?"

Paolo continued his inspection. "He's supposed to help you find things that you lost." He looked up. "Although I can't say he ever helped my dad." Face to face, they were too close; Grey backed away. Paolo lifted the necklace to give it back. It hung between them. "Funny that something like this would end up in Memphis. Must've belonged to some Italian immigrant."

As Grey went to grab it, an involuntary shiver shot through his body. The medallion fell onto the sand beside the blanket. Paolo reached up and grabbed Grey's shoulder. "Wait, don't move—the island has a way of reclaiming its own." Paolo reached around Grey and retrieved the necklace from the sand. His chest pressed against Grey's arm.

"What does that mean?" Grey asked.

"It's just a saying. Here, turn around and let me put it on so you won't drop it again."

Paolo traced his finger across the base of Grey's hairline. "How'd you get this scar?" Again Grey shuddered, this time so violently that his head jutted forward causing the chain to choke him. He coughed.

"Are you getting a cold?" Paolo pulled Grey's head back to avoid losing the necklace a second time.

"Nah, just someone walking across my grave."

"What?" Paolo clasped the chain.

"Nothing." Grey tucked the chain back into his shirt.

Paolo got up and stretched as Grey had before and then climbed onto the rock beside them. He began to walk it like a tightrope.

Grey lay down on the blanket, his arms behind him, his head resting on his clasped hands. "I mean, it's just a saying as well, a Southern one."

"Sounds morbid." Paolo had walked a few feet away and his voice sounded different, deeper. It was remotely familiar.

"Not really. It just means—" Grey turned and was blinded by the afternoon sun that flooded around Paolo's body.

Paolo's holographic, faceless form spun around. "What's wrong, are you okay?" He jumped down from the rock.

Grey convinced Paolo that he was surprised by the intensity of the sun. But afterwards the conversation stalled and the two sat silent, staring out to the water.

"Did you ever go by a different name?"

Paolo had picked out some small stones and broken shells from the sand and had spread them on the blanket. He was grouping them by size and shape.

"That's a strange question. Why?"

Grey continued to look straight ahead. "I thought I heard someone call you another name at your party."

"Really? That's odd." Paolo had begun to place the shells next to one another in a serpentine line. "I go by my middle name." The white line bent upward and then reversed directions curving back on itself in a giant wave. "When we moved to New York, my mother started calling me Paolo because she said my first name, Giuseppe, was too ethnic." Underneath the wave, a little shell figure was standing atop a surfboard. Or a boat.

"It was also my father's name—I think that was more of her reason." The image vanished as he brushed the shells and rocks back into a small pile.

Grey's voice was deadpan. "Your father's name was Giuseppe?"

Paolo looked up. "Yeah, but he went by his middle name too. Anthony, like your saint." His voice sounded distant, like an airport announcer just audible above the dissonance. "But everybody called him Antonio."

A low surf broke the water's calm.

After a few monosyllabic exchanges, they agreed to head back. Grey watched as Paolo crossed the rock jetty to the downwind side. The wind had indeed picked up. The blanket billowed and snapped as he shook it free of sand.

It took only five minutes to reach the road that led back to the other side of town. They stopped. It was after two, and even though the sun was still warm, they had each put their coats back on.

"Do ya still wanna see the house?" Paolo asked.

As Grey nodded, the reality of the day shifted from under him. The blue sky faded to the black of the sea's embrace. The only sound was the sea lapping gently against the rowboat that was docked at the small pier. Grey shivered with the cold evening wind of a night long past penetrating his wet, exposed skin.

50

The following morning Grey was checking out when Brigitte appeared from nowhere. "I am very excited. I do not believe you are to help us." She was spewing ideas as they walked together to the house. Grey only responded when required.

The move-in process was perfunctory; Paolo was in a hurry because he needed to open the café. There was no need for physical contact, no need to elude his eyes. It helped that Brigitte was there as a buffer. After Paolo left she hung around for an hour, sharing her thoughts on how to create separate dining and living room spaces out of the large front room. "I do not understand why someone builds a house without a dining room."

"Brigitte, how old is Paolo?"

If Brigitte was suspicious, she showed no signs of it. "Hmmm, let me see. Maria and Antonio married in '68 and Paolo was ten years after. What is that? Twenty-one?"

Grey paced from one end of the room to the other, pretending to survey its full length. "And his parents, were they—"

Brigitte cut him off. "Did he tell you?"

Grey walked around to the sliding glass doors for a similar estimation of the room's width. He gave no hint of his racing heart. "What?"

"Maria has fifty years next month. Paolo told her and Juliana to come to Italy. 'She will not come to Elba but Paolo and Juliana compromised her on Rome." Grey was pondering his next question but then Brigitte spread her arms across the open expanse. "What do you consider of a banquette to divide the space?" The moment had passed.

Grey stood alone in the master bedroom. There was only one other bedroom in the house, one with two bare twin beds, the one where he and Pete had slept. He had never thought about where the children slept. Grey realized that for that night, they must have been here with their mother. He went to the window and looked back across the terrace; the outdoor faucet was in plain view. He dropped his head into his hands. His badly scuffed shoes were the same style wingtips that John had worn to his holiday party. After a few minutes he walked over, stripped the bed and carried the bedding to the smaller bedroom.

Even tucked under, the queen-size sheets were loose and gathered at the corners of the small mattress. Grey took off his clothes and lay down, wrapping the comforter around him. With the reflection of the setting sun, the peeling paint of the dilapidated ceiling softened like fading scars.

ROME

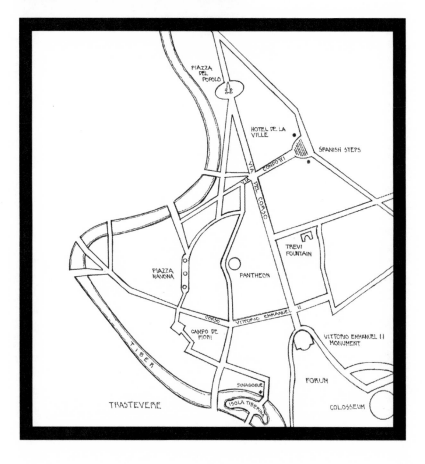

51

The date stamp on Scott's message was 2:34 A.M. It clearly wasn't a casual from-the-office response. In fact, it wasn't a response at all. Its subject line contained no *Re:* or *Fwd:* only, *i tried . . .*

Over the past month Grey had called Scott at least a dozen times and had sent him as many e-mails. Scott hadn't replied until now.

It was 10 A.M. Grey had either deleted or filed away his other messages. It had taken a while because of two sticky issues: Jane had a harassment complaint against one of the new Philadelphia reps, and the condo association had e-mailed him about whether or not they should pay for an exorbitant mold inspection. Apparently, mold was the new asbestos. Now, all that remained was Scott's.

"Paolo, can I get another?"

A porcelain cup flipped through the air like a flapjack, coming to rest on the saucer Paolo had picked up during the cup's flight. His other hand was already on the arm of the espresso press. "Can't seem to get through this morning, huh?"

They had forged a routine that would have never happened if not for the café's computer.

The morning after he moved into the house, Grey was physically and emotionally exhausted. He had reentered Antonio's life even though he was dead. Now Grey had to continue through the door that he and the hand of fate had pried open. There was no choice; he had committed. He would renovate the house but keep his distance. But to do so and manage his life during an extended leave from work required a computer and an Internet connection. Paolo had both.

When Paolo took over the café he bought the computer to quiet the bragging of Luigi, who owned Café Isla, Café Roma's primary competition. Café Isla attracted the college crowd, but even with no advertising, two or three people a week would trickle into Café Roma to surf the Internet or check e-mail. Over the past summer that number had grown to five or six. Even some of Paolo's regular clients who had never used a computer before asked him to show them how.

It would have been ridiculous for Grey not to take advantage Paolo's offer. Plus, there would be the immediate access to Paolo for quick decisions and approvals. Grey decided to ignore Paolo the person, the son of Antonio, and focus on Paolo the client. He would, as he had throughout most of his adult life, retreat to Grey the businessman and sales guy. It would be easy, or so he thought.

The first morning Grey used the computer, it crashed three times, the connection dropped twice and his back was so stiff from the barstool that it kept him from sleeping that night. The following day Grey decided to throw in a refurbishing of Paolo's Internet station for free. He convinced himself that a business-minded Grey would have done this for any customer.

On the third day, Grey asked, "So, what was your father like?"

Paolo looked up from the espresso machine. It was the first time since their picnic that they had talked about anything personal and from there, they began anew. "That's not an easy question to answer."

Every day from eight to nine Grey would use the computer for research, and to order supplies and other things he needed for the renovation. Often this was actually cheaper than buying from local distributors because, in the new competitive dot-com economy, most e-commerce sites were desperate to grow their international customer base so they threw in free shipping—even to Elba. While Grey surfed the Net, Paolo would ready the bar, steam them eggs, make Grey's one cappuccino to his two espressos, and then sit down to read the paper. Boundaries were crossed.

Their dynamic began as paternal, Grey posing concerned questions about Paolo's childhood. The more he learned, the less he discovered. Paolo's memories of his father were vague and distorted. He had died the year after Grey had met him, when Paolo was eight. All Paolo could remember was his calm presence. He said that when his father entered the room, the "spinning would stop."

"As a boy, I thought he was *waaaaaay* too serious. It wasn't until he was gone I realized how comforting this quality was. And magnetic—everyone was drawn to him. It made my mom crazy. He was always bringing home strangers he met on the street and she had to figure out how to stretch out dinner or sometimes even put them up for the night."

Any time Paolo disclosed something too close for comfort, Grey would change subjects. "And your sister?"

"Juliana's memories of him are different. She remembers him laughing and smelling of fish. And how he would pick us up and swing us around the room every day when he got home from work. I think I remember some of that but not so much. I don't know, maybe I just had a different connection."

One thing as confusing as it was comforting: from what Grey could gather, no one had ever suspected foul play either in his life or death. When Grey proposed the possibility of suicide to Brigitte, she was certain.

"No, it is not possible. On an island, to drown is bad luck. No one does it with purpose."

Brigitte emphasized Antonio's love for his family. "Antonio loved Maria and his childs more than most fathers because there was no more family. And because their love was borned of pain. He could never do that again to her. Or to the childs." More to herself than to Grey, she added, "How does a person move past a accident death that happens twice? Keeps taking. If I am her, I too will move and blame what cannot be blamed—to forget."

"It's children."

Brigitte raised her voice. "No, he never did anything to hurt Paolo and Juliana."

Grey wondered if Brigitte would have felt the same way had she known about Antonio's blatant disregard the night they had sex just outside Maria's window.

"No, I mean the plural of *child* is *children*."

It was in this first week that Grey convinced Paolo to let him fly both his mother and sister to Rome for his mother's birthday. Grey told the partial truth of the two tickets he won in an auction and promised that he would never be able to use them within the allowable timeframe. Paolo only agreed after Grey argued that it would be a fair trade if Grey or his friends could use the Elba house four weeks for free, no restrictions or expiration date.

The second week, the roles started reversing. Grey still hadn't heard back from Scott and there was no one else to whom he could turn—not even Jane; their friendship was too new and besides, she did work for him. But while he opened up a little, he was careful. One topic he never discussed was Scott. After Danielle's broadcast of the *Met Home* article, Paolo had asked, but he respected Grey's evasive response and had since left well enough alone.

The closest he came was one morning, when Scott still had not returned Grey's last e-mail, one in which Grey had groveled, *"Please say something, anything."*

Paolo asked, "What's up? You seem distracted."

"I don't know, I think a storm's a-brewin' on the home front."

"Anything you wanna talk about?"

Grey dodged. "Nah, but whaddya think about turning the olive grove into a tennis court?"

Paolo shook his head. "Funny." He inquired no further.

Day after day, over the course of the next week, Grey revealed pieces of his life. He started with work but then opened to more personal details.

When Paolo probed again about Elba's draw, Grey recounted selected snippets of his experience on the cruise and explained how he and Jane had deepened their friendship after working together for years. And then he almost slipped.

"When I first got off the boat I didn't recognize anything."

Paolo asked, "Is that why you asked about the Crystal? Was that where you stayed the first time you were here?"

Grey evaded specifics. "No, I meant the beaches. The first time here I never saw this side of the island. I spent the entire time on the other side, on the same beach where we picnicked the other day. Hey, come look at this island I'm thinking about for the kitchen and tell me if you like it."

After this close call, the honeymoon waned and their morning routine shifted into a comfortable, but less personal, exchange of two equals.

52

It was Wednesday. Grey sat in the Aeron desk chair he'd bought on eBay and was installing the additional memory chip he had just received in the mail. This was the final touch to the new Internet station that was going to blow Café Isla's out of the water. Grey had overhauled Paolo's computer, wiping the disk clean and reinstalling all the latest software (that he *borrowed* from Orion's Milan office). Also using his Orion connections, Grey was able to get Telecom Italia to assign Café Roma as Elba's beta trial of high-speed DSL. Luigi would be furious because DSL was not slated for the island until 2001, giving Paolo a full year monopoly. But the *pièce de résistance* was the cabinet encasing. Grey had convinced the cabinetmaker he hired for the renovation to throw it in for free. It was a mini-cubical, compact, with both charm and functionality, and it took up even less space than the card table it replaced. It had a drawer, a bookshelf above the computer, and three extended circular shelves: two on the right, one for the mouse, one for the espresso saucer and one on the left with a built-in ashtray.

On Monday, after the cabinet was delivered, Paolo was in a dither to see the renovation. Grey made him wait. This, added to Saturday's upcoming birthday party, fueled an infectious energy and boyish charm that grew with each passing day. The previous night Brigitte had dropped by the house and while assessing Grey's work, disclosed, "I never see Paolo so happy. You do not know how important this is."

"So, tonight's the night," Paolo said as he set down Grey's cappuccino. His unbridled gaiety was almost enough to make Grey log off and forget Scott's e-mail.

"Yep, but remember, not everything's done; there's a lot still on order."

Paolo responded with one of his now-familiar reverse nods, trying to stay cool while every body-language utterance screamed with mania.

Grey was clarifying, "I'm pretty sure you'll get an idea," when a new message popped up on the screen from Madge. He looked at his watch; it was the middle of the night in New York. He sensed that her new zeal as full-time employee might be a bit much. He would talk to her when he got back.

It was just a quick note to let him know that she and Jane were holding down the fort. She reassured him not to worry, that while they weren't getting along fine without him, they were making do and even becoming pretty good pals. Grey smiled; his absence was apparently good for office dynamics. Whether or not he was rationalizing, he had never before felt so comfortable that Orion could get along for a couple of weeks or even a month without him. Maybe even longer.

Madge signed off the message *Jean Gray*, which she had to explain to Grey's confused reply in a follow-up e-mail:

> *Never heard of Jane Grey but JEAN Gray is the most powerful*
> *X-Man—THE PHOENIX—who keeps the others in check!!!*
> *So that's what I'm doing boss-man ;-o*

Jane Grey, Jean Gray—too weird, he thought, surprised how good it felt to have a real-time exchange with home.

He deleted her e-mails, and again, the only one left was Scott's.

Grey watched Paolo walk back to the bar; his gait was different but had the same self-confidence as Antonio's. He clicked on *i tried . . .*

> *. . . to wait for u but once again u have chosen ur own world over ours.*
> *yesterday i spoke with a lawyer about separating our assets and he said*
> *that we should probably consider selling the flat. certainly one of us*
> *could buy out the other but i've a feeling u'll feel as strongly against*
> *this as i do.*
>
> *rothko is also an issue but i'm sure we'll be mature enough to figure this*
> *out. i doubt i'll buy another place soon so it would probably be easier if u*
> *took him.*

every thing else should be a straight 50/50 split. i've set up a meeting with a mediator recommended by brian and greg. it's on feb 14th--as appropriate day as any to end it don't ya think. i expect you can make it back by then.
- scott

ps the irony of ur sudden interest in my design contacts is not lost on me. nor is your 'secret' use of our rome vacation. go ahead and fly whoever u want out but know that u will need to reimburse me for half of the vacation's retail value (10K--i checked). i hope he's worth it.

"Must be a hurricane this time." Paolo's words were distant.

Grey managed a brusque response and then, without even bothering to take his empty cup to the bar, he logged off and left. His voice was low and monotone. "See you at eight."

53

Brigitte had offered to help Grey prepare dinner. When Grey left the café, he crossed the piazza and knocked on her door. With no wherewithal to make up a good lie, he told her that he needed some time alone and wanted to make dinner himself.

After nursing the pit in his stomach by roaming streets he had not yet walked and meandering stores new to him, Grey ended up at the top of Fort Falcone, staring out over the island. The fort was the highest point of the city and the view seemed to stretch across the Mediterranean's infinite reach. From this vista it wasn't hard to understand primitive cultures' idolatry of nature; here, one sensed the guiding hand of omnipotence. The fortress walls draped down the hill, crumbing from age and disuse. "It was once impregnable," Jane had said. It didn't look so impregnable anymore.

A few hours later Grey stood in front of the new Poggenpohl Island in the pristine, remodeled kitchen. He was still spinning on Scott's e-mail. This project was supposed to take Grey's mind off of Scott but for the last four weeks, he spent more time thinking about their relationship than he had during the last four years. Every design magazine or website he looked at made him want to call and ask Scott's opinion. They had grown so much together over the years; he couldn't figure out how or even when their relationship began to unravel. Two days before, Grey had sent Scott twelve long stem roses with a card that said, *Babe I miss you—I really do. Please understand I just need a little time.* And now this. *An equity split, my ass*, Grey fumed, grateful that he never put Scott on title. He tried to distract himself by focusing on the meal he was about to prepare.

The midday sun had already started to recede and the gnarled shadows of bare olive branches stretched across the sleek concrete counters. Grey had planned to make a stir-fry dish but the ingredients in front of him were Alessandro's, all the way down to the bottle of Brunello. He pulled a pasta pot down from the rack above the island.

"Whoa!" was all Paolo could muster in his first five minutes.

"Grey, I don't know what to say. Not in my wildest imagination would I have ever thought this house could be so . . . " Grey was uncorking the wine as Paolo ran his hand along the counter's smooth edge. "So hip."

Grey had chosen wisely. Within his first two days, he used Brigitte's network to find a mason, a carpenter and a seamstress. He also discovered a high-end home design company that had jumped on the "island life" speculative bandwagon and the previous year opened stores in Corsica, Sardinia and Elba. Apart from some modest Sardinian success, sales had been abysmal. Grey e-mailed the Milan-based owner with the link to the *Met Home* article and indicated he was going to try to get his new renovation published as well. Doors opened and prices were slashed. Even so, he splurged to get the quality and the timing he wanted. As far as Paolo would ever know, Grey miraculously came in at budget.

The primary theme of the house was what Grey would later term in *Conde Nast* as *flexible integration*. He told the writer that the basic concept had come to him in a dream. It was close to the truth.

For much of his first day in the house, he had lain in the small bedroom. The hours bled one into the other until the day began to wane. In the fading sunlight he watched sky, land and water merge into one and then become redefined by stars, electricity and the darkness in between.

Toward midnight Grey wrapped himself in the bedding and walked to the front room. The house was silent except for the soft whisper of the comforter dragging across the floor. His eyes were slow to adjust to the partial moon. He stayed in the hall doorway as the room formed around him, first a simple outline of empty space, then surfaces and objects. He took a folding chair from the table and placed it in front of the sliding doors that looked out on the terrace. There he sat. More hours came and went. He drifted in memories and fantasies, at times incorporating the actual surroundings and moment before him. Dawn's break shed a new dim light. The bedding fell from Grey as he stood, naked, and pressed his hands against the doors' glass. In its reflection both he and the room were shadowed by a mosaic of terrace stone.

Paolo lifted his glass to Grey. "You're un-friggin'-believable." They held each other's eyes until after the first sip when Paolo walked back into the living room. "Where'n the hell did ya come up with the idea for these floors?"

That second afternoon Grey started hammering up the terracotta floor. Beneath it was the bare concrete of the house's foundation. He called the fabrication firm he had used in New York and convinced them to guide his mason in the necessary additives and treatment to smooth the concrete. There was one point, after he had begun to jackhammer the holes, when he lost faith and thought he had gone too far. He almost changed his mind but the contractor said he would still need to refinish the floors to mask the jackhammer's damage.

It was the floors that tied it all together. Everyone talked about the retractable screens but the floor's embedded pathways were what opened up the house by creating an indoor/outdoor effect. Otherwise, even with the adjustable transparency of the screens' fabrics, the small spaces of the rooms would have seemed forced and confining.

Paolo leapt from stone to stone pretending he was crossing a river. On one he swayed as though he were trying to catch his balance. "It's amazing. I would've never thought to use the terrace stone inside."

The path wound from the front door, bending like a snake toward the middle of the room and then curved around to the back wall. Only at the end did it widen, stretching all the way across the threshold of the sliding doors for a seamless transition to the terrace beyond. At the same time the path's stone harmonized house and terrace, its curve produced a boot-shaped separation between the living and dining room side and the kitchen. The living room was sole-to-toe, narrowing to the dining room ankle.

Paolo stopped at the screen partition between the kitchen and foyer. Grey had adjusted the light so that it shone a deep violet. Except during parties this screen would likely be kept open, especially since Grey had kitchen cabinetry made that backed right up to it. But always having spatial efficiency in mind, he had designed the cabinet backs to be both functional and aesthetic. If one chose to close the screen, the cabinetry's rear panels could be popped off and then—

poof—instant cocktail bar.

"Wait, this isn't a real wall, is it? It's way too thin."

The screens were actually an afterthought, to further cut the room length-wise. The idea was born from Grey's experience sectioning hotel conference rooms with accordion curtains in order to cut the cost of sales training sessions. When shut, the screens receded into a pocket that Grey had scored into each sidewall but they could be pulled to isolate the front living room and foyer from the kitchen and dining room. He experimented with many different fabrics but chose an industrial grade metallic sheer because it had the widest contrast against the light; the adjustable halogens could take it from transparency to cobalt. It wasn't until after Grey had installed them that he realized there was also color fluctuation from the house's natural light: at morning an ice blue, at night indigo. On it, each point of the day reflected a meld of sky and sea.

Paolo disappeared down the hall. "I can't wait to see the rest of the house. What could you have possibly done with my box of a room?"

While Grey carried the elements of concrete, rock and vertical fabric into every room, he added variety by the different ways in which he incorporated them. He was whimsical with a narrow, two-inch wide stone line down the center of the hall that branched off into each room. In the bathroom, it became a Victorian Greek key border. In the small bedroom, it crisscrossed a large one-foot square grid onto the floor, creating a concrete tile effect. And in the master bedroom, it led to a huge circle of stone that dominated the floor's center like the Japanese flag.

Grey also repeated the screens' ceiling-tracked construction, using it to hang the shower curtain and, in the master, the white gauze that encircled the bed. Similarly, in the small bedroom, Grey used red silk to enshroud the queen-size trundle bed that replaced the two twins, smothering it with throw pillows sequined in the opulent colors of precious stones. Other details of the renovation reinforced the integration throughout the house. The stone's green and copper veins were effected in the tile and fixtures. The cabinetry was simple—stained gray-black, the color of the olive trees.

Paolo returned to the kitchen empty-glassed. "I *love* my bedroom; it's right out of *Arabian Nights*." He poured himself another. "This wine rocks—hey, what can I do to help?"

Around the dining table Grey had assembled a green vinyl banquette that opened to the terrace. *Assembled* because it wasn't a single unit but six modular chairs that together formed an L, the short arm dividing the dining room from the kitchen. Behind it, a reverse L of identical chairs in black suede became a couch for the living room.

"My God, how'd ya do this in four weeks?"

"To tell you the truth, I'm not quite sure. In New York this would have taken two years and cost twenty times as much."

They followed the stone path from dining to living room, from vinyl to suede. Paolo plopped down and stretched his arm out across the top of the couch, rubbing his hand across the tactile fabric. Grey continued, "Knowing the right people helps. Brigitte's contacts have been great. And who knew what a little *Met Home* article could do? Should we bring the wine and cheese in here?"

"I think you know me better than that by now."

As Paolo turned and watched Grey walk back to the kitchen, he slid his arm over the couch back to its vinyl twin. "These are great—sorta backward mirror images of each other."

"That's only how I arranged them tonight. It creates a clear delineation between the two rooms. You can put them any way you want." Grey raised his voice as though the kitchen were indeed a separate room as opposed to ten feet of open space away. "I have to give Brigitte the credit for the banquette-couch idea; I just added a modern twist."

He brought the decanter and wine glasses and set them on the coffee table in front of Paolo. "It works well this way but when you pull this other screen out . . . " Grey walked and unhooked the screen from its pocket. Paolo pulled his arm back from the banquette so the screen could slide between it and the couch. Grey pulled it three-quarters of the way out, stopping about two feet from the other screen. " . . . it gives you some visual privacy. You can pull it out as far as you want. You can even pull it all the way to the other one and completely split the rooms apart."

"Whoa, man, that is so cool." Paolo got up and backed away from the couch to see the effect of the blue transparent wall. He then walked over and poked the purple one. "You mean this one works just like that one."

"Yeah, just with different lighting. See those switches by the door? They control the lights on that screen, and these over here by the couch, control this one. Hey, while you're up, can you get the cheese platter that's sitting next to the fridge?"

After graciously conceding to a few more accolades for the screens, Grey toured Paolo through each room. Paolo was fascinated with every detail. He asked question upon question, gave praise upon praise. It was a full hour before they sat down to dinner.

54

"Grey, what can I say? I don't know how I can ever repay you." Paolo was seated at the table, facing the terrace; a white ceramic tureen of Alessandro's sauce sat steaming in front of him. Grey was turned away at the sink, draining the pasta.

"It's me who needs to thank you." Grey continued to talk as he emptied the spaghetti from the colander onto two plates and then, with the experience of a former waiter, balanced them on one arm and carried them to the table. "There's no way you can know how important these three weeks have been for me. I can't even begin to tell you."

"I think I know a little." Paolo smiled; the steam, now denser through the addition of that rising from his spaghetti, blurred his features.

Something in Paolo's tone or transfigured face blindsided Grey. His skin tingled and he felt as if his ears were plugged. He became aware of his breath and heartbeat. He reached for the tureen to pass it to Paolo but it slipped from his hand and banged against the table. "Shit." The exclamation was too extreme for the small accident.

Paolo grabbed the dish. "No worries; I can reach it."

As Paolo ladled the sauce onto his plate, Grey's world turned to slow motion. Paolo's words stretched like taffy. "Theeee-uuuss smee-eels aaaaa-maaaaa-zeeeeng. Whee-uuuuure diiii-uuuuud yooooo-uuuu luuu-uuuurn tooo cuu-uuk?"

This was not Grey's first panic attack. He recognized its onset and knew that he needed to continue the conversation to force himself out of his head. He struggled with his reply. "It's just a recipe from an Italian grocer on the outskirts of Chelsea. I'm sure it's no comparison to what you're used to."

Grey couldn't tell if he was slurring his words. When he tried to focus his attention elsewhere, he was distracted by the sweat rising on his forehead. A drop hung at the edge of his right eyebrow and was just about to run down the side of his face. He wiped it away and squeezed the top of his head, driving his thumb and middle fingers into his temples. "How was it moving to a different country at such a young age?"

Paolo either did not notice or ignored Grey's anxiety. Fork in right hand, knife in left, he began eating and talking, using his utensils for both. Like Brigitte, he was a natural storyteller. He recounted the awe of his family's journey to America when, having never traveled on anything other than foot, they went from ferry to bus to train to cab to airplane to subway. Spaghetti dropped from his fork onto his napkin-covered chest as he swung his arm to indicate the sea of people that towered over him when they arrived at JFK. As he continued the animated plight of an eight-year-old's world in upheaval, Grey's thirty-nine-year-old world began to calm. Both his breathing and heart slowed. He wiped his forehead a second time.

Throughout dinner, Paolo talked about what it was like for him to grow up in New York. His first impression was how small the sky was. "It seemed so much higher, so much further away." He soon adapted. His mother's boss all but adopted him and his sister, and the neighborhood kids were quick to befriend him as well mostly due to their reverence for his firsthand experience of a place about which their parents had filled them with lore.

Paolo told Grey how he thought New York was predominantly Italian until his third-grade class went on a field trip to the Museum of Natural History. "It was the first time I realized I was different. Afterwards, I became obsessed with everything Italian. I asked my neighbors what they knew; I checked out books and maps from the library. But I couldn't find much on Elba. So one day when I was ten, I skipped school and trucked—" Paolo stopped mid-sentence, "Is it trucked or truck?" then continued without waiting for Grey's answer. "I walked all the way up to the Italian consulate on Sixty-eighth. There was this older Italian man behind the desk—thick eyebrows, gray mustache, just like ya see in the movies. When he asked me why I was there, I told him I wanted to learn more about Italy, especially Elba. I gave him my name so he could check and see if he could find anything about my family. Then he took me to lunch."

"We walked to the park and got hotdogs at a stand by the Met. You know I think the stand is still there. Funny. Anyway, we sat by the lake and watched all these kids and their dads playing with their little boats. I was in awe. I'd never done anything like this. I mean, until then, I'd only left Little Italy once. And Mom wouldn't let us to go anywhere near water. I'll never forget it; he told me about growing up in a little town in Tuscany called Poggibonsi. I always thought he'd made it up but I went there in November. It's not so little anymore. Or pretty. It's sort of this industrial town—a blight by Tuscan standards. Anyway, the only thing that he knew about Elba was a famous palindrome supposedly attributed to Napoleon: *Able was I ere I saw Elba.* I'd never heard of a palindrome (or the word *ere* for that matter) and when he explained both to me I thought he said a palindrome *meant* the same thing forward and backward.

When we got back, my mother was waiting. (Of course, he'd asked me for my name just to call her.) The odd thing was she wasn't mad at all; she took me to get ice cream—outside of Little Italy. Well, a couple of blocks over, but still. You know that famous Chinatown ice cream factory? I forget the name but it's great. I remember asking her about the palindrome. She said she'd never heard of it. That night I laid in bed unable to sleep. I reversed the words in my head. *Elba saw I ere I was able.* In my ten-year-old Catholic, Hardy Boys' brain I knew the man was an angel who'd given me a secret message and that I needed to come to Elba to find myself. Before I could be *able.* In high school, when I learned that a palindrome didn't mean the same thing backwards and forward but was spelled the same both ways and that Napoleon obviously didn't come up with an English palindrome—duh—it didn't matter; my mind was set. And so, after graduation last spring, I came back."

Avoiding the picnic attack had forced Grey to listen with more intent than he listened to anyone in years. "Are you going to stay?"

Paolo used a wedge of bread to sop up the last bit of sauce on his plate and then reached for his wine glass. "I don't know; are you?"

After dinner, while the two of them were outside smoking, Paolo said, "Whoever repaired this terrace and rebuilt the grove walls did an incredible job."

"You know him; it was Marco, Luigi's son. He's gonna build a natural hot tub over there by the faucet when he gets the parts from Rome."

Paolo lit a cigarette, exhaling its smoke as he talked. "I still don't see how you did all this for just fifteen thousand dollars. What'd you do with the other stuff—sell it?"

"I wouldn't have done that without asking you first. There was only the table, a couple of lamps and chairs, that old La-Z-Boy and the twin beds. Marco's keeping them in his garage. I told him you'd let him know what you wanted to do with them. Oh, and that ancient behemoth console. You saw the small TV with a built-in VCR I got for the second bedroom. I also got a DVD player; a lot of people have them in the States now and if ya want to build a library of DVDs, it's far more convenient." Grey took a drag and turned his head away to keep the smoke from blowing in Paolo's face. "Oh, and I left the master bed because I thought, I don't know, I thought you would wanna keep it."

After stamping out his cigarette, Paolo bent over and picked up the filter. "Is it any good? Why would I want to keep it?" The question was rhetorical. "It's getting cold. You cooked; I'll clean."

Paolo washed; Grey dried. "What about you, what was your childhood like?"

Painting broad swaths of life growing up in a Memphis suburb, Grey told Paolo that he also felt like an outsider. "Not that I was from somewhere else, but I just didn't seemed to fit into the South. You can't get away from the race thing and I never really understood why skin color was such a big deal. I know race is more than melanin, but in the South, it's not. Except the only colors that matter are white and black. I couldn't take it and I literally planned my escape ever since I was a kid."

Later, while talking about their college years, Paolo again bumped against Grey's duplicity. "How old were you when you first came to Elba?"

"Around twenty-five. Hey, I wanna show you this idea I have."

Grey was wiping the counters while Paolo was kneeling on the sofa entertaining himself with the screen. He had pulled it halfway out and was playing with the switch, comparing all of the lighting possibilities. He had gone through the entire spectrum once or twice and was now tweaking it back and forth to find the exact spot where the screen went from transparent to opaque.

"This is so cool."

Grey came and sat down beside him. "It's actually a pretty simple concept."

In turning around, Paolo sat a little too close but didn't move away. "Simple for you maybe." He thrust his arms into the empty space before them. "So you didn't like our TV?"

"Yeah, right—it didn't even have a cable connection. But that's my idea—I was tryin' to figure out how to put a TV in here without muckin' up the space." Grey got up and pulled the wall screen all the way out so that it met the other one and closed off the living room. He walked to the front of the room, facing Paolo. "They have those projection TVs now. You could just put it over here and project it across the combined screens. Imagine the huge picture you'd have. Great for movies. Didn't have enough to cover it, but I bet prices drop substantially next year."

Paolo pulled his couch section over to where Grey was standing. He spun it around and sat down it like he was watching a movie. "Yeah, this'd be nice."

Grey flashed on an image of Antonio sitting in front of the console. He wondered if it was a real memory or just one of those fake ones that stems from too much reflection. He immediately pushed it out of his mind.

Paolo pretended he was eating popcorn from an imaginary bucket in his lap. "Boy, I wish my mom would come see this. She'd be blown away."

Grey got another cushion and pushed it toward Paolo who obediently lifted his legs so that Grey could scoot it under them. "On that note, Brigitte lent me her little mauve book for some of her contractor numbers." Grey pulled a third cushion over for himself and sat down between Paolo and the nonexistent projector as though the two were preparing for a home movie. "I found Sophie's number and asked her if she could fly down and join us this weekend. I remember Brigitte saying that she and your mom were good friends. I thought it'd be a nice surprise for both your mom and Brigitte."

Paolo dropped his feet from the makeshift ottoman to the floor and jerked around to face Grey. "Really? What did she say?"

Grey smiled. "She's coming."

Paolo leapt up, bent over and pressed Grey's face between the palms of his hands so hard that Grey's lips puckered. "You." He leaned down and kissed Grey on his misshapen mouth. "My God, you think of everything. She's gonna flip."

Grey knew the kiss was nothing more than gratitude. After all, this was Italy. He didn't care about the reason; he enjoyed the pure physicality of it, and the emotion that lingered. His smile broadened. "As they say where I come from, 'ain't nothing but a thang.' Now let me show you the *real* new TV." Paolo followed him into the hallway. "It's of a somewhat different scale."

A few minutes later they were sitting on the bed in the small bedroom. Grey had rented the movie *Billy Elliot* and it was still in the VCR when he turned on the TV. Paolo leaned back on his elbows. "This is such a great movie." Grey remained sitting upright, a respectable foot or so away. For twenty minutes, neither said a word.

Paolo dropped his head back. "I remember staring up at the ceiling of this room and dreaming all sorts of things."

Grey turned to Paolo. "So, have you found yourself—are you able?"

Paolo looked up at him. His eyes were dry and clear.

Grey reached down and put his hand against Paolo's chest. He desired more than Paolo's respect. "Do you wanna stay the night?"

Paolo put his own hand on top of Grey's, held it for a second and then lifted them both away. "No, I don't think I'm ready for that."

55

It was a sunny, cloudless day but still far too cold to be outside in the wind. Grey climbed up to the top deck to smoke. Wearing his neon blue fleece coat, he stood alone. The Italian mainland stretched in front of the boat on either side as far as he could see. Again he wondered how his first memory of the great distance between the coast and island could have been so wrong.

Before leaving, he had gone by the café to check his e-mail. There were three. The first was from Jane.

> *Breaking news—Larry's leaving, supposedly on his own volition.*
> *Said Orion's outgrown his leadership. How's that for an under-*
> *statement. I'll give you one guess who's replacing him. Yep, ole purple*
> *eyes himself. My sources tell me the board wants you for head of sales*
> *but Bob told them you already refused to move to California? Is that*
> *true?*
>
> *Anyway, it's all going down next week. Thought you'd want to know.*
> *-Jane*

The last two were both from Miriam.

> *Dear Grey,*
> *   How are you? Your mom probably told you I called. She said you*
> *were traveling for the holidays and I didn't want to disturb your*
> *vacation. Are you back yet? It's not a big deal and I know that, since*
> *we haven't talked in so long, you may think it was. But it's not . . . at*

least I don't think so. It's about Pete (BTW, he goes by Peter now). It's
not something I want to discuss over email so call me when you can.
No urgency, just when you can.

    I hope all is well with you. When I talked to your mom she was
actually nice to me. What's up with that? She says you're still single
and still living in New York. Is there seriously nothing upon the
horizon? Things are good with us. Rebecca and Isaac are both now in
school and I just got a job at Berkeley Seismology Labs. Can you
believe I'm actually going to use my degree? God, how time flies. In
case you don't have my number, it's 916-444-2278.

Hopefully soon,
Miriam

Her second e-mail was a correction.

Me again,
    Stupid automatic spell checker. Obliviously I meant to ask is there
no one on the horizon? Is there?
Miriam

PS Happy early birthday. What are you doing for the big Four-O?

After turning off the computer, he taped a note on its dark screen.

Paolo,
Sorry about last night. I hope I didn't offend you. I decided to head to
Rome a day early to get the apartment ready. Let's meet at the airport,
outside customs. Remember, American, flight 6603 from London.
Arrives 2:00 pm—I'll try to get there early. Sophie arrives forty
minutes later at 2:40 pm on Alitalia, flight AZ 333. Both gates
should be in Terminal B. Also, remember that Brigitte doesn't know
anything about this. We'll figure out how to orchestrate the surprise
after we see what time your mom's plane actually arrives.

I'm going to rent a cell and call you with the number later today so you

have it in case we miss each other.
-Grey

The ferry was now minutes from docking. Grey turned to the sea behind them; Elba still loomed large. He shivered as he inhaled another deep drag.

56

It was two o'clock. Maria's plane was ten minutes late and Sophie's supposedly on time.

Grey had spotted Paolo and Brigitte approaching and retreated deeper into the café. He leaned around the man standing at the table in front of him. They were still there. Even at this distance Grey could feel Paolo's excitement. Upon seeing him the embarrassment of his failed proposition resurfaced.

Paolo hadn't dressed up for the occasion (he wore jeans and a long-sleeved T-shirt) but he did look a bit more scrubbed than usual. Maybe he had cut his hair or had shortened his sideburns; it was hard to tell. Or was it just that he was so jumpy? Paolo couldn't sit more than five minutes without getting up and checking the arrivals board.

Brigitte wore an orange wool suit accented by a yellow and blue patterned scarf around her neck. This time the scarf was tied, the knot balanced upon one shoulder. She thumbed through some magazine, ignoring Paolo's impatience.

Grey recognized her at once. Not Maria, Juliana. He couldn't take his eyes off her as she turned her head from side to side, exchanging kisses with Brigitte. She looked exactly like Antonio. She was an inch or so shorter than Paolo but nevertheless crouched as they hugged so that her head pressed into her brother's chest. Their voices and laughter mixed in a spirited exchange that could be heard even from where Grey was sitting.

Paolo glanced at his watch and began scanning the crowd. It was time. Grey slipped from the back of the café and flipped open his cell phone so that it appeared as though he had just arrived.

"Ah, here he is, our gracious host for the weekend." Paolo kissed Grey's cheek with no indication of residual awkwardness.

Grey put his phone back in his pocket and grabbed both of Maria's bags. "Happy birthday, Mrs. . . . " He looked up into her face. Though he knew her name well—had seen it written on a random piece of mail the morning after he had slept with Antonio, over the years repeatedly searched the Internet for references to it and used it to secure her and Juliana's airline reservations—he had never said it out loud.

Maria's voice hadn't changed. "It's Viglietti." The *g* was silent; it didn't sound like he had imagined.

Grey was holding her bags and, with therefore no hand to offer, nodded instead. "Glad to make your acquaintance." It was 2:35 P.M. Grey led the group back toward the table where he'd been standing before they arrived. "Do you mind if I get a sandwich? I haven't eaten all day." As they walked over, Grey whispered to Paolo, "I just left Sophie a voicemail—I told her we'd be over here at this café."

Juliana snuck up behind them and linked her arm through Grey's. "What are you two whispering about? What other secrets are you keeping?" The sultriness of both her voice and her insinuation were meant to provoke.

Grey looked into her eyes; they were the same as her father's. "Other secrets?"

While she also smiled his smile, her Gen-Y flippancy was all her own. "Like where are we staying, for example?"

On closer inspection, though the color and luminosity of her eyes were Antonio's, they reflected less intensity. Hers challenged while his had vanquished.

As they waited for their food, Brigitte began regaling Maria with details of the house. "Maria, you need to come to see it—it is fabulous. It is the only house similar on the island. I am sure that people will rent it all season. I know you have bad reminders but much has changed. I don't mean to—"

A young girl materialized at Brigitte's side. "*Arrière-Grand-Mère!*"

Brigitte looked down, confused. "What are you—"

"Surprise!" Sophie was a larger woman, not fat but broad. She was taller than everyone but Grey, with whom she stood head to head. While she had not inherited Brigitte's frame, there had been definite stylistic influences—with a conservative edge. In her pink Oleg Cassini-style *ensemble* and white gloves, she appeared of an era when high fashion was requisite for travel. Upon her stylish bob of blond hair, a small hat tilted to one side.

"*Maman.*" Tears streamed down Sophie's face. The little girl, either frightened by her mother's crying or the unresponsiveness of her grandmother, started crying as well. It was a surprise much greater than anyone except Sophie had imagined. Standing next to her was an equally stylish elderly couple whom, judging by the extremity of both Brigitte's and Sophie's reactions, could only have been Brigitte's parents.

For about an hour the eight people spanning five generations stood around the small café table. There was also Grey, split between generations—the lost years, with only a tenuous connection to the family before him. Tenuous but stronger than they knew.

Tears were shed, laughter was enjoyed and introductions were made. Passersby would realize that this was a reunion of sorts, but they could have never imagined the time or distance that had been bridged.

57

With luggage, the small compartment could only fit two people. Juliana grabbed her brother as he was getting on the elevator with Grey. "Giuseppe, wait. I need to ask you something. Can you two go up first? Grey, you can tell Mom all my brother's little secrets." Paolo stepped out and Maria in. "Or yours," Juliana flirted.

The elevator was as slow as it was small. They were forced to stand shoulder to shoulder but neither spoke of the inconvenience. The three-story ride was oppressive. Grey broke the silence. "I must say I'm surprised that you hardly have any Italian accent. Did you grow up speaking English?"

Maria stared at the elevator's floor indicator above the door, its brass arm sweeping an arc, like a clock fast-forwarding through time. "No, I chose to leave my Italian behind."

In front of the apartment door, Grey searched his pockets for the keys. "Shoot, they must be in my coat downstairs." He smiled at Maria. "They'll be up in a minute."

Now, face to face, Maria addressed him for the first time since their meeting at the airport. "Do you mind if I ask you something?"

Though he had readied himself for this situation, his reply sounded too solicitous. "Sure."

"Have we met?" Had it not followed her previous question, it could have almost been a statement as she articulated each word evenly, failing to emphasize and lift the word *met*.

Grey shrugged. "It's likely; what's your restaurant's name? I eat in Little Italy all the time."

"No, I mean before." The depth of her stare made him squirm but he had prepared for this. He maintained his composure.

"Before when?"

Maria paused. He couldn't read her face; she either questioned his answer or answered her own next question. In the interim before either was sure, the elevator door opened and Paolo stepped out. Juliana's voice echoed from within, "Nice manners. Some Italian gentleman you are."

Paolo handed Grey his coat. Grey fumbled to find the keys all the while trying to ignore Maria's continued consideration.

Juliana walked past the modernist perfection of the expansive living room, past the Eames chairs and Noguchi coffee table, straight to and out the sliding glass doors to the terrace. "Get outta fuckin' town! Look at this view!"

58

It was a quiet night. The last time Grey had sat on the Spanish Steps was a week after his experience with Antonio. It had been the middle of a hot August day; throngs of college-age tourists were scattered from the top step to the bottom—chatting, reading, sunbathing, smoking—doing what college kids do on the Spanish Steps. As far as one could see, shoppers had lined the fashionable Via Condotti all the way to Via del Corso, the wide avenue that split Rome in two. Amidst the hubbub, Grey sat alone, lost in reflection.

Now at 1 A.M. on a cold January night, an almost imperceptible sliver of moon cast a dusty light. Few pedestrians walked Condotti. Fourteen years later Grey was again alone, lost in both time and spirit. What was he doing? He had no idea, but he had set a train in motion and now had to ride it to the end. But to what resolve and at what cost? He thought of Monte Carlo—the distinguished croupier, the power of the crowd, Bob. There, he had won through losing. That was impossible here. Black or red? He was no longer in Monte Carlo but back in the Hotel Riverview, in Jimmy's room. Jimmy was lying on his bed, his bloody hands clutching an invisible rosary.

"Do you mind if I join you?"

"*Ahhh-ahhh*." Grey jolted up.

"Sorry. I thought you heard me. I couldn't sleep and saw you from my window." Her voice was unapologetic.

Grey was not yet in the present. He saw Maria, a young woman on another sleepless night, watching him through her bedroom window.

"I'm sorry."

"About what?" She still had on the white pants suit she had worn on the plane.

"To keep you awake. You must be exhausted after your flight."

Maria looked out over the steps across Rome. For such a large city there were few lights. "I couldn't sleep tonight even if I were drugged." She wrapped her arms around herself and continued to gaze out over the steps.

"Grey, thank you for everything you've done for Paolo. For me. I'm not sure what I have done to deserve such good fortune." All the responses running through his head were tinged with guilt. He said nothing.

"I never thought I would come back here and never ever thought I would stay in a place like this." Gesturing toward the apartment, she added, "It's certainly not the Italy of my memories."

Maria sat down; her white pants would be dirty from the steps. He hesitated a moment and then joined her. She continued looking straight ahead. "Why are you doing this? You certainly don't need to . . . do you?"

He kept up his act, replying that it was he who was thankful—he, who Brigitte and Paolo had helped at a time when he had no one to whom he could turn. They'd given him a place to stay, a project to focus on and friendship that he desperately needed.

"Yes, I hear you've done amazing things with the house. It certainly had its flaws." She turned to him. Her eyes still absorbed. "But then, what home doesn't?"

Ten minutes and another protracted elevator ride later they were still alone together. Paolo and Juliana had long been asleep. Maria sat by the window in the open living room that separated the two bedrooms. She said she was not yet tired and wanted to read, but she hadn't brought a book from her room. Nor when Grey bid his goodnight had she picked up one of the magazines from the rack beside her chair. She just sat and stared out the window.

59

Grey closed the door behind him. On a night table that separated the double beds was a Tiffany two-headed reading lamp. The flowing bronze hair of the Elysian women intertwined to form the lamp's base—two of the muses, Grey thought. Paolo had left Grey's head on. Grey slipped out of his clothes and climbed into bed. Paolo was faced away, covers to his waist. His bare smooth back was tinted by a patchwork of Tiffany stain.

"Mom, isn't this spectacular?" Paolo, Juliana and Maria were on the terrace. Though the grapevines were bare, their intertwined branches provided a Gaudian canopy that shaded them from the morning sun.

Grey had risen early, much earlier. He rambled through empty streets as the sun rose and Rome came to life. This was the second time in two months he had thus experienced the awakening of a city. Rome was different from New York; there was no instant switch from secretive morning pleasure seekers to manic workday commuters. Here, the day unfurled with more grace, more dalliance than urgency. Before he knew it, stores were open and people were exuberantly exchanging morning salutations as they crammed into corner *pasticcerie*, sipping their espressos and smoking their first cigarettes of the day. Grey stood among them and ordered a selection of *cornetti* and *danesi*.

"I see you found the coffee; I hope it wasn't cold." He had just come from the kitchen carrying the platter of pastries.

As he set the tray on the table, Maria said, "Grey, thank you again. I keep wondering when the dream will end."

It was obvious from Paolo's and Juliana's reactions that their mother didn't usually make such puerile comments.

Grey imitated an ever-so-slight regal bow. "Well, one doesn't turn fifty every day." He raised his coffee mug. "Happy birthday, Mrs. Viglietti. Today's the actual day, isn't it?"

"I'm afraid it is and please, Grey, call me María. We're certainly close enough in age to do away with formalities." Maria lifted her mug as well, not in reply but to take a sip of coffee.

Sophie, a chip off the *bloc vieille*, had booked a luxurious suite at the Hotel De La Ville. It was just across the steps from their apartment, with a balcony that faced their terrace. At mid-morning, Brigitte came out and waved them over. It was to be a day of acquaintance.

Brigitte, at times, acted more like a little girl than Chloe, the great-granddaughter. She doted on her parents as though she had cherished them all her life. "*Je voudrais que tu rencontrais ma mère et mon père.*" To Grey, her French accent sounded perfect, with no signs of the quirky mix of Italian and English she had acquired on Elba.

Brigitte's mother and father, dressed all tweed and tartan, looked more British than French. They were impeccably gracious, straight out of a Merchant Ivory movie. You would have never guessed they were the parents who had disowned their child and banished her for over fifty years.

Brigitte introduced Grey and his *Met Home* article that she had brought with her and displayed on the coffee table with obsequious admiration. When Chloe had asked, "*Qui est l'autre homme sur la photo, votre frère?*" Brigitte was immediate in her response.

"*No très chère, c'est un ami.*" The subject was dropped and there was no further mention of either the article or Grey's affinity for interior design.

With a few gracious *no mercis* and *peut-être plus tards*, Grey and Paolo made their way to the door with the excuse of party errands. After the requisite farewell cheek kiss—two, not one—Brigitte's mother invited both of them to visit Paris, making a special point to tell Grey, "*Vous pouvez également amener votre compagnon si vous voulez?*"

Juliana yelled across the room, "Wait, I'm goin'! You don't think I'm gonna miss a chance to tool around Rome with you two hotties? Just give me a sec."

Grey whispered to Paolo while they were in the hall waiting for Juliana to come from the bathroom, "Did Brigitte's mother invite me to come to Paris with Scott?"

Paolo whispered back, "Yeah, when they decided to tear down the walls, they must've hired a bulldozer."

60

To three New Yorkers, Rome was not overwhelming—it was quaint. They walked everywhere, drawing attention from both genders and all ages. Grey was in his West Village look of Levis and a black turtleneck. Paolo, hair pulled back in a blue bandana, was more edgy East Village retro, with faded-thigh jeans and a red-striped, four-button cuff, protruding-collar shirt. Juliana straddled Upper East and West Sides in her magenta rhinestone-studded Manolo Blahniks and below-the-ankle elkskin coat that opened over copious amounts of her own skin and essentially-placed swathes of black silk.

They had barely made it into the street when Juliana nudged her way between Grey and Paolo and linked her arms through theirs. "Mom thinks there's something goin' on between you two."

Neither replied.

She pulled her arms tight, forcing them closer together and whispered, "I hope there is because I think it would be cool to have a gay brother, especially if his boyfriend is as cute and as nice as this hunka hunka burnin' love."

Grey smiled in spite of himself and looked over at Paolo who had a silly, deer-in-the-headlights look, the likes of which Grey hadn't seen on him in the entire month they had spent together. In that month neither Grey nor Paolo had ever overtly discussed either of their sexualities and here Juliana brought them both into question the instant the three of them were alone. Grey started with a nervous snicker which, when Paolo joined in, progressed to an all-out belly laugh. The two were laughing so hard they had to stop and back up against a storefront so people could pass.

Juliana dropped their arms. "What? It's not that funny. I mean you are gay, right?"

Grey finished the chortle that had risen in his throat and then nodded his head. "Yes, Scott's my boyfriend and though we're going through a tough time, there's nothing going on between your brother and me. He's been a great friend, that's all."

Paolo looked relieved.

Juliana was adorably shameless. "Damn. Will ya still invite me over to see your place?"

It was the second of many comments that Juliana made throughout the day that would cause Grey to laugh and to which Juliana, each time, would respond, "Why are you laughing? Really, I'm not that funny."

In reality there were few errands to do. Grey had taken care of everything. He had found a *sous* caterer who purchased, marinated, cut and chopped, readying everything necessary to prepare a gourmet meal in under an hour. He had also already bought the flowers and selected the music. All they needed to do was to pick up some wine. So, the three of them toured. Of course there was the Coliseum, Trevi Fountain, the Pantheon and Navona, after which there was lunch in Campo de' Fiori. In the afternoon they shopped. Rather, Juliana shopped while Grey and Paolo waited on the elegant chaises of several women's clothing stores, nodding or raising a speculative eyebrow when Juliana emerged wearing this shoe or that skirt.

At the end of the day they were gelato-ing in Trastevere when Grey realized it was almost five and the caterer would arrive in less than an hour. Earlier at the Pantheon, Paolo had bought a couple of disposable cameras for the birthday party but when "just this one picture" turned into ten, they decided to use one of the cameras to chronicle their day together. They had one picture left, so on the way back, as they were crossing a bridge that led to a small isle in the middle of the Tiber, Paolo stopped a pedestrian and asked if he would take a picture of them. The man was a cleric of some sort, dressed in a long brown frock. Paolo was talking him through the complexity of the single button camera. When the man bent to examine the intimidating button from a closer angle, the top of his head came into view revealing his male pattern balding. As Paolo rushed back to join them, Juliana leaned into Grey and whispered, "A fuckin' friar—not something you see every day."

The picture caught Grey just before he laughed, with a smile that was almost giddy. It was a great photo except that his pupils came out red. Juliana, with her hand in front of her mouth, was obviously whispering something to him. Beside them was Paolo with his arm around Juliana and his hand resting on Grey's shoulder. He too was smiling wide but his eyes were closed. Behind was the river and the little island whose name Grey did not yet know. If you looked closely you could see the hospital's emergency entrance. It would be one of the handfuls of pictures that Grey would always display rather than keep hidden in the throngs of photo albums tucked away on the top shelf of his office closet. At some point he bought a special pen to blacken his pupils. Everyone who saw it said that Grey looked different but they assumed it was his smile, not his eyes— as dark as Paolo's if his had been open. Few days went by that he didn't at least glance at it and, whenever he did, it never failed to transport him.

61

They arrived home right as the caterer was delivering the cook-by-numbers meal. She was a large bubbly German woman who told him she had moved to Italy for the love of life that Germans lacked. Grey spent a half-hour with her, going over the cooking instructions which were detailed down to when to put the appetizers in the oven, not only in time for the guests to eat but in time to fill the apartment with aroma so, as she said, "zay vould exshperience ze meal from ze moment zay entered ze door." Every direction was detailed and bulleted. She may have come to Italy for the *joie de vivre* but she mixed in a healthy dollop of German discipline.

Grey opened the door to Paolo standing naked by his bed. He faced Grey in full frontal nudity. The muscular sinew was as Grey remembered his father's. Paolo made no sign of embarrassment nor did he attempt to cover himself.

"You don't mind if I jump in the shower first, do ya?"

Grey's hand was still on the doorknob. "No, go ahead. I need to get the table ready." He backed out and shut the door behind him. He went to the window and stood, his hands resting on the back of the same chair where Maria had sat the night before. Behind him, the table had already been set.

"Beneath this beautiful sunset, on this beautiful veranda, in this beautiful apartment, and before he gets a chance to do yet another wonderful thing, I would like us to raise our glasses to Grey. He has touched us all."

Everyone followed as Maria raised her champagne. Glasses clinked. Grey was sitting lengthwise across the table but she bent forward to make sure her glass met his.

It was one of those Italian sunsets you see on postcards and in photography books, a terrestrial sea of red tile suffused by the sky's deepening hues, broken only by wisps of blue-purple clouds. The tile, the clouds, the sky, all reached out across the horizon, one atop the other, like the layers of an intricate cake winding between the river, reflecting the infinite gradations of the red and yellow spectra, folds of icing so sumptuous you wanted to reach out and scoop a fingerful.

Grey scooted his chair out from the table. "I'm gonna start the lamb. It should only take a few minutes."

"I am able to help you." Brigitte had already stood up so there was no point in refusing.

Tonight everyone wore color except Brigitte. Maria had traded her white pants suit for a green one; Sophie was again in pink, her color; Juliana debuted a stunning lavender dress she had purchased during their afternoon of shopping; Paolo still had on his red-striped shirt and Grey also wore a red shirt, one Juliana had made him buy to assuage her shopper's remorse. Brigitte was draped in black, a full-length gown that, from the front, revealed her usual healthy scoop of cleavage. From behind, it plunged even farther, down almost to her waist. All lines were long and straight, including the two from the scarf she wore Isadora Duncan-style so it fell down her back, outlining her exposed spine. She must have employed a variety of hair products to tease her hair up into Edwardian levels of height and volume.

She waited until the kitchen door was closed. "In a million years I can not imagine we all together." She walked to the counter where the salad ingredients sat in an unnested set of banded Yelloware mixing bowls, and pulled from the a shelf a large white ceramic tureen, the same one Grey had bought for Elba. Pouring the lettuce from the largest of the bowls into the tureen, she said, "Tomorrow I go with my parents and Sophie to Paris. I do not believe that I am free to return." She picked through the lettuce and removed some questionable leaves. "You will visit?"

Grey checked the oven temperature indicator. "Wait, are you moving?"

"No, but they are old." Brigitte grabbed the smallest bowl of caramelized walnuts. Again she examined and took out one or two for good measure. "And Chloe is young. There is much to share."

The preheating light was still on. He searched the utensil drawer for a temperature gauge. "Why didn't they come tonight?"

Brigitte placed a walnut in her mouth, further convoluting her strange accent. "They have little time; not many peoples have the joy of a great-child. Maybe now they are happy that I had a child at fourteen years."

Her smile was unconvincing, more so as there was a bit of walnut between her front two teeth.

Widening his mouth in a cartoonish grin, he pointed to his own teeth. Pushing with her tongue, she freed the walnut and licked it away. With most people, this would have been crude; Brigitte managed to make it sexy. Grey opened the oven and put in the tray of skewers. "Have you forgiven them?"

Brigitte continued her selective addition of ingredients, bowl by bowl. "Forgiveness is such an American concept."

"Oh, and in Europe you never get mad at each other?"

She reached for the juice glass in which the caterer had poured oil and vinegar. "No, I am serious. Not like America, we are old. We see'd so much unforgivable that we now do not stop to forgive. We keep going." She held up the glass. "Like this here—why do you think she mixed it? Everyone knows oil separates from vinegar."

Grey picked up the baguette. "I don't know. I guess to get the correct proportions. Do you think everybody will want the bread heated?"

Brigitte poured the dressing onto the salad. "Exactly—some things are not how you like them but the difference is able to mix together. I mean as long as there is not too much vinegar." She picked out and tasted a watercress stalk doused with dressing and then pushed up the delicate sleeves of her dress, burying her arms elbow-deep into the salad. "They did pay for Sophie and me."

Grey was still holding the baguette.

"Oh, the bread—Italian bread." She pursed her lips, causing a wrinkle that spread across her face. "Heat it." She returned to her salad.

"Anyway, I do not know how long I go and I hope that you are able to stay in my apartment. I hope that you are able help me with some new design ideas I have. I know I am finding new things in Clignancourt. Maybe we are able together to change things. A little more Provençal. I know that you prefer modern but I am an old Frenchwoman, no?"

Grey was bent over, peering into the bottom oven to check on the squash. "*Non!*" he said, attempting both a French accent and sarcasm. He failed at both;

Brigitte showed no hint of amusement. As he was crossing to the refrigerator, he replied, "Really, that is so generous, but I think I'm going to head back soon." He pulled out a second bottle of Veuve Clicquot and brandished the orange label in her direction. "From the Champagne region."

Brigitte was at the sink, washing up. She raised her voice just a notch to be heard above the running water. "I thought you decided to stay some more. Do we bring the salad before or after?"

Grey winked at her, closing both of his eyes; winking was a skill he had never mastered. "When in Rome . . . "

62

A massive bird's-eye maple table was centered between the kitchen and an inlaid Biedermeier china cabinet that Brigitte had oohed and aahed over since she set foot in the apartment, even though it wasn't French. Worse, it was German. Flanking the china cabinet were two Fortuny sconces that matched the Scheherazade chandelier above the table. Leaning floor to ceiling against the wall next to the kitchen was a twelve-by-five-foot, gilded Art Nouveau café mirror. The mottled wood, the silk-shrouded light and the age-splotched mirror distinguished the turn-of-the-century dining room from the mid-century living room far more than any wall ever could. It was a room that evoked the past.

They had removed the table's three leaves so it was more intimate. Now it was round, a little larger than the chandelier. The seating order was Maria, Brigitte, Paolo, Juliana, Grey, Sophie. Grey was nervous; he was not good at dinner parties, especially one where he was an intruder in a familial setting, a voyeur into shared experiences in which he played no part. Throughout the meal, he tried to exchange niceties with Sophie but her attention was focused on the birthday girl from whom she had been so long estranged through distance, time and faded circumstance.

Juliana made up for Sophie's distraction; she adopted Grey as her confidant. When she was not chiding her brother about his self-detachment from the family, she was whispering not-so-sweet nothings in Grey's ear. On Brigitte's heightened obsession over everything Paris: "Boy, now that Brigitte's fully regained her Frenchness, she's gonna be insufferable." On Sophie's size and bone structure: "That unknown father must have been one big German. Maybe that blond hair's actually real." Scott would love Juliana.

Dominating the conversation were Brigitte and Sophie. With selective remembrances, they led the party back in time. Brigitte recalled Maria's mother who, eight-months pregnant, had gone house hunting arm-in-arm with the terrified five-month-pregnant, fourteen-year-old French girl. Eyes scorned or turned away as they walked through the town and across the piazza to the building where in four months, she would give birth to Sophie. When the owner refused to consider any offer from Brigitte, Maria's mother had suggested that an unfortunate downturn in the boating needs of the island could require the dismissal of several employees. The proprietor, whose son worked at Maria's parents' plant, huffed and asked to have Brigitte's lawyer contact him. Later that night, when Brigitte and Grey were alone in the kitchen lighting the cake's candles, this story had been further embellished by Brigitte's revelation that Antonio's nine-month-pregnant mother had also been present and had threatened the man that if he shut the door on them, she would give birth on his doorstep.

Nostalgia, shunned for so long, now enlivened Maria. "So, Sophie and I aren't the only fiftieth birthdays." She raised her wine glass a second time. "To a wonderful home that has provided unwavering protection . . . " She faltered; her voice lost its emphasis. Her final words were muffled. "To the most important people in my life." Before glasses were raised, Maria regained her fortitude and turned to Brigitte. "And to its owner, who has cared for and been there for me and my children throughout our lives."

Then Sophie began to tell story upon story of their childhood. Some were garnished with elaborate detail while others were kept short. These were times that, if dwelled upon, would need to include Antonio. She was careful to paint a picture of their youth that did not ignore him but neither brought him clearly into view. Still, Grey hung on each nuance, each shadow.

Even Juliana quieted during this journey, the early experiences of her mother's life long kept secret from her. She and Paolo sat rapt as characters were introduced and mysteries unraveled. Several times during dinner, Grey watched Paolo to see his reaction at the mention of this or that person whom Grey recognized as a customer from the café. But Paolo's face was that of an enchanted listener so caught up in the story that the players all remained distant, bounded in the realm of the past. Tonight Paolo was visiting their world, not the other way around.

Sophie told one story about a grade-school nun who had rapped their knuckles at every imagined infraction. The two adult women rolled their eyes about what, as children, they shared in shame: that she was reprimanding them for the secularity of their respective births. Sophie turned from Maria to the table. "She had these big brown spots on her hands and we used to laugh through our tears that she was jealous of our smooth, clear skin."

Maria held up the backs of her hands for everyone to see. "Look at mine now; they're probably worse than hers." They were not bespeckled like the nun of their story but were permanently pruned by overexposure to the water and chemical saturation from years of dishwashing. She still wore her wedding ring; it was a smooth band against the wrinkles. To it, the abrasive dishwater had either been impenetrable or added to its luster.

After the obligatory birthday song, everyone remained at the table while Maria cut the cake.

Sophie pulled out a small square present from her purse. Adorning its red glossy wrapping paper was a beautiful cluster of white ribbon with streamers that draped like one of Brigitte's scarves. "I think it's about time to open gifts, yes?"

Maria was coy, "I wish you wou—" but Juliana didn't let her finish.

"Wait, Paolo, can you go get ours?"

Paolo pulled his chair from the table. "Why don't we do cake and presents in the living room by the fire."

Brigitte and Sophie sat on the couch, next to Maria; Juliana and Paolo, on the floor; and Grey, a few feet away, in one of the chairs that faced the window. Maria removed the ribbon from Sophie's present and laid it to the side. Instead of ripping the package open, she took her time and peeled the tape with care, leaving the paper unmarred.

Sophie downplayed the gift's significance. "It's really nothing. I'm not sure you'll even remember."

Once the paper was folded and laid by the ribbon, Maria opened the box. She pulled out an old forty-five record—"I Am Woman" by Helen Reddy.

Maria lifted her hand to her mouth and swallowed her words. "Do I remember?" She turned and embraced Sophie. For over a full minute they rocked in silence. Apparently, in the early '70s it had been sort of a theme song for the two girls. They had listened to it every day for over a year. At twenty-three, when Sophie decided to move to Paris, Maria had given it to her as a going-away present.

When they released each other, Sophie's black mascara had smudged beneath her eyes. "Did you see the card?" Maria picked up the envelope from the bottom of the box. The card was a typical touristy card with an airbrushed Eiffel Tower. As she opened it an old yellowed postcard fell out; on it, a picture of the main Portoferraio harbor. The boardwalk was less developed but the photo didn't look a quarter of a century old.

"I can't believe you saved this." Maria picked it up, turned it over and read,

> *"Vanno là e forti 'roar' come potete.*
> *Voi amico per sempre, Maria"*

Paolo interpreted. "Grey, the card says, 'Go there and roar as loud as you can,'" lifting his fingers in quotes at the word *roar*.

In the Eiffel Tower card, Sophie had written her belated response:

> *Come hear me roar.*
> *Still your friend forever, Sophie.*

Maria put down the cards. She reached over and grabbed Sophie's smooth unblemished hands. They were still worthy of envy. Sophie's bottom lip quivered. "I mean it, I'm buying you a ticket to come to Paris in May for my birthday. Will you?"

Maria smiled and nodded her head as the women hugged another time.

Next was Paolo, who pulled a packet from under the coffee table. The wrapping—old-timey yellow kraftpaper bound with twine and a blue penny-size wax seal where the strings crossed—was itself beautiful enough to be the gift.

Maria smiled. "Franco."

63

As long as even Brigitte could remember, Franco had been the owner of a small leather goods store in Portoferraio. Over the years he had updated his selection of merchandise to include modern-day organization items like address books and photo albums, but he had never altered his signature Victorian wrapping, free with each purchase, no matter how small.

Paolo handed his mother the pair of scissors that he had brought from the kitchen. "Mom, it isn't what you think, and we want to preface it by telling you how much we both love you, and if you don't want the gift right now, we'll keep it for you until you do."

After Paolo's skittish disclaimer, Maria seemed unsettled and took her time unwrapping the present. She was particularly careful not to break the wax seal, leaving the cut string stuck to the paper as she unfolded its corners. In it were two things: a framed picture and another wrapped package the exact same size. A present within a present. Grey recognized the photograph at once; it was just as he remembered. Maria's sad eyes peered from the frame.

It was her wedding picture.

Brigitte and Sophie scooted over to make room for Juliana and Paolo, who sat on either side of their mother with their arms around her.

Paolo's voice was soft. "Juliana found the restorer in New York; she shipped them to me; and Franco wrapped them."

Maria did not look up. She and everyone else knew that the second package contained the matching wedding picture of Antonio. Juliana chose her words carefully to avoid an actual reference to her father. "Mom, we know you'll probably wanna wait to open the other one, but we just wanted you to have both of them."

Maria laid the pictures down on the table and raised her head. Her face was blank and her eyes clear. "I love you both so very much." It was sincere, but spoken without emotion. Her hugs with each of them were as moderated as her words.

The energy in the room shifted; perhaps they had pushed her too far.

Everyone waited. Grey stared at the wrapped photograph that sat on the coffee table in front of him. His heart beat in his throat and a tear dripped onto his right cheek. Another hung on his left eyelash. Paolo noticed and reached across the table to grab Grey's hand. Maria's eyes followed Paolo's hand to Grey's, and then up to his face. The tear had fallen and he was able to see her clearly, without its distortion. Her eyes did not condemn nor did they approve; they still questioned.

It was Brigitte who broke the tension. "Well, I have fear that my gift is also of the past. I say the same as Paolo's when he says, 'if you don't want it now' and 'I love you.'" She handed Maria a manila envelope.

Maria looked at the envelope and then at Grey. Grey answered her unspoken request. "Do you mind if I go outside to smoke?"

It was cold and, in the immediacy of his exodus, Grey had left his coat inside. There was a new moon and Rome lay flat against the darkness, its scant lights like stars, their relative distance imperceptible. The only indication of additional dimension was the river. While you couldn't see the water at night, its total absence of light cut a serpentine path into the skyline.

Fifteen minutes later Grey returned to a more animated group than he had left. Paolo and Juliana were talking in excited tones, trying to convince their mother of something. Maria looked up. "Grey, please rejoin us."

He replied, "I'll be right back," and continued on to the bathroom.

When he returned, Maria was saying, "I'm not ruling it out, but it makes no sense to waste a nonrefundable ticket and, besides, I can't—I have to go back to work on Friday." She leaned over and asked Brigitte, "Can Paolo and Juliana represent me? They can go check it out, and I'll call or fax or do whatever I need to do from New York."

In the next ten minutes Grey learned of Brigitte's gift. Because of her *exile*, Brigitte had developed a deep understanding of both French and Italian estate law. She knew it was next to impossible to pass on an inheritance to someone other than the person named in the will. She asked a lawyer to do some checking in Padua, and sure enough, he discovered that there was a mysterious bank account in Maria's name. He had also found one in Antonio's, but she wouldn't mention that until later. Maria needed to either go to Padua or authorize an immediate family member to claim the account.

Paolo and Juliana were enthralled—Paolo, with the potential of discovering more about their ancestry and Juliana, with the accounts themselves. It would be easy for them to go because Juliana wasn't leaving for another two weeks. But Maria was scheduled to return to New York in the morning. They urged their mother to cancel her flight.

With the decision to go without her, Paolo and Juliana were abuzz in planning.

Maria was hugging Brigitte. "Brigitte, I can't believe this. What if my inheritance is there? I'll finally get to pay you back for all the money you've given us over the years. What made you think of this after all this time?"

Brigitte nodded toward Grey. "Something more to thank for Grey. The first day we meet he asks me of you and I remember you never receive your heritance." Maria turned to Grey with a look of gratitude tinged with rekindled suspicion.

It was nearing midnight and the evening was winding down. Everyone was tired and Maria, Brigitte and Sophie all had morning flights. The goodbyes were drawn out, most of all Brigitte's. She had decided to return with her parents and Sophie to Paris for a week and begged Maria to reconsider staying longer. "I return next weekend. We have more time together, yes?" When she hugged Grey, she whispered in his ear, "I hope that you remain. Please consider what I ask tonight. Let us discuss it more when I return."

The threshold's final goodbyes should have been easy but there was an unexpected snag. Sophie, to whom Grey had spoken very little, was thanking him for inviting her. As she kissed his cheek, she asked, "Is Grey a common name in America; I've never heard it before."

Before Grey could answer, Maria, who had been talking with Brigitte, spun around abruptly and said, "Oh, I have." She turned to Grey. "But only once."

64

As soon as the elevator doors closed Grey excused himself to the bedroom. Ten minutes later, when Paolo entered, Grey was putting on his coat.

"Where're ya going?" he asked.

Grey replied, "Just for a walk; I need some fresh air."

"Can I tag along?"

They went some blocks without saying anything. The city was more alive at street level but after they left the Spanish Steps, pedestrians were fewer, and most hurried past them in transit.

Grey spoke first. "Your mom seemed to have a good time."

"That's an understatement if I ever heard one. I've never in my life seen her smile about, much less talk about, her past. I mean, tonight we learned five times more than we ever knew before."

Grey searched his pocket for his cigarettes. "Except about your father."

He offered one to Paolo. "That's different, but who knows, maybe she'll get there."

They turned briefly onto Via del Corso. In the distance Vittorio dominated its hilltop setting, lighting up the dark sky. The memorial never ceased to impress Grey, a monument glossed over in the travel guides yet it made U.S. landmarks pale in comparison. They turned down a small street, toward the river, similar to the route they had taken earlier in the afternoon.

Grey lit Paolo's cigarette, and then his own. He exhaled his first drag. "Why's it different—especially if it was an accident? Maybe she knows something you don't."

Paolo stopped, taken aback by Grey's implication. His expression was stringent and interrogating, like his mother's. "No, it's the other way around."

In that look, Grey was shocked by an idea that had never occurred to him. Maybe it wasn't Maria who saw him, but Paolo, a six-year-old boy, who watched from his parents' bedroom window and saw his father having sex with another man. A memory that haunted him his whole life to the point that it forced him into exile.

Grey's face must have reflected some of this because Paolo added as they started walking again, "No, I wasn't there when he drowned or anything like that. But I know, beyond a shadow of a doubt my father died of natural causes."

Grey was uncertain of what Paolo was saying but, by his tone, he was pretty sure that it didn't include the memory he had just feared. As they neared Navona, they encountered more and more people, mostly teenagers, enjoying their Saturday night. Grey and Paolo turned from both the river and crowd, cutting beside the piazza. Once they were alone again, Grey probed further. "How can you know for sure? You were only eight."

They entered the plaza of the Pantheon. The temple was ominous at night; its shadow engulfed them like an eclipse.

"How do you know how old I was, and why the hell are you so curious about this? No one has ever questioned his death. Mourned yes, blamed yes, but never questioned."

It was so black Grey couldn't even see Paolo's face, only the red cigarette ash hanging at his side. "Blamed?"

Paolo's disembodied voice blared in anger. "Goddammit, Grey! I've told you that my mother blames the sea, Elba, blames something—anything—but to be honest, I don't know exactly what or who she blames because, as you yourself have witnessed, my father is off-limits. Why you have this morbid curiosity is beyond me, but if you have to know, I'll tell you, but only if you promise never to tell any of them."

At last they came to the other side of the plaza, out from the darkness.

Grey grabbed Paolo's shoulder. "Hey, I'm sorry; I didn't mean to push. I don't know why I want to know, I really don't." It was Grey's second blatant lie.

Paolo pulled his shoulder away. They walked for a while in silence until they came to the old Jewish ghetto, the history of which they had discussed during their afternoon together. Outside the synagogue, two policemen were talking.

Paolo had told them when they passed it earlier that the police were there day and night, a twenty-four hour vigilance enforced ever since an early '80s terrorist attack.

At the river, Paolo spoke. His voice was now calm. "Actually, maybe I should talk about it; it'd be good to tell someone."

They turned toward the small island, the backdrop of the picture the friar had snapped. "I'm pretty sure I know how my father died because it may be the same way I'll die."

Grey did not respond. He knew that he needed to let Paolo tell his story at his own pace. As they started across the river, Paolo continued, "When I got my physical in college, they discovered I have a condition I inherited from my father. There're a few symptoms, most so minor people never get 'em checked out, and so they never know about it. I guess I'm lucky because, now that I know, I can avoid risky activities."

They stopped in the middle of the bridge. "You know, this is the oldest bridge in Rome. It was built before Christ." Paolo pointed his chin toward the isle. "That's Isola Tiberina. Supposedly it's been the gateway to the city ever since Rome was founded. Legend has it that it's actually the hull of some medicine god's ship that sank during a great flood. When the floods receded, the ship surfaced here, grounded and abandoned. Both the god and his seamen vanished."

Paolo paused, leaned over the rail and stared down into the river. His voice echoed from its surface "The boat was left in honor of him and filled with the sands of passing time. That's the reason for the island's shape and why it's believed to be a place of healing. There's been a hospital here since Renaissance times."

Grey didn't comment nor did he look over at Paolo. The two men remained staring out to island until at last Paolo spoke again. "Wanna walk around it? There're stairs down the other side."

"Sure."

Paolo continued his disclosure. "Most men with this disease—oh, and only men get it; it's passed through the Y-chromosome—die of a sudden heart attack or stroke caused by a lack of oxygen that, for a normal person, would cause nothing more than shortness of breath."

They had crossed the island and were now on the opposite side, from which stairs did indeed lead down to a walkway around the island's edge. Earlier in the day Grey had not even noticed it.

"When I found out, I remembered my dad's obsession with the sea. Really, I only remembered bits and pieces of the arguments that he and Mom had about his diving. It was sorta just a vague memory until, after Brigitte told me about how my grandparents died, I woke up one night with a clear flashback of my mother yelling at him down the street as he walked toward the beach. She screamed, 'You're never going to find them.' "

They strolled alone down the walkway, the river just a foot or so below. Midway down the island, Paolo continued, "So you see, I've put two and two together."

Ahead of them the river gurgled. It got louder as they approached the island's tip. There was a break in the water, a submerged wall of some sort or a small spillway. For such a small disturbance, its sound, when they were right next to it, was loud enough to drown their conversation. The turbulent water was a rude disturbance of the Tiber's quiet repose.

They rounded the island to the darker side. In the shadows, farther down, two lovers were engrossed and backed deeper into the bridge's arch.

Grey offered Paolo another cigarette. "Couldn't he just have been a carrier?"

Paolo shook his head. "You are really too much. I tell you that I have a disease that's probably terminal and all you can ask about's my fuckin' father. Why the fuck do you care? What's he to you?"

Paolo threw his cigarette down and started walking back.

Grey followed him. "Wait, listen."

Paolo swung around at the island's tip. "No, you listen. OK Sherlock, one side effect of this stupid disease is a heat rash that you get, especially on your hands and feet. I never got it before coming back here. Now look at my hands; they look like an eighty-year-old's." Paolo didn't raise his hands for Grey's inspection. "Maybe it's Elba—I don't know. But I remember my father' hands were always covered in red splotches. I was disgusted by them and wouldn't let him touch me. I would cry as though he were some sort of monster. There, are you satisfied? But then I guess this could be a coincidence as well, and my father really did kill himself. He fuckin' drowned himself to escape his wife and

kids who adored him. Now, if there're no more questions, I think I'll head back."
Paolo pushed Grey aside and started running.

Grey ran after him. He was much faster and caught up to Paolo just past the spillway. When he reached for him, Paolo lunged to the side and lost his footing. Grey grabbed his shirtsleeve but it wasn't enough. Paolo fell into the river.

65

Grey didn't pause to think. He dove forward out in front of where Paolo had slipped. The icy coldness stopped his breath. For an instant he lost all sensation but it was not like before; there was no beauty, only fear. When he surfaced, Paolo was right behind him, struggling to swim to the side. Grey wasn't able see the spillway but its deafening rush couldn't be more than a few feet ahead. Against the current he rolled over and with both arms, reached behind him and grabbed Paolo around the waist, wrapping him in the curve of his body. Upstream, the lights of Trastevere reflected on the river's tranquil surface. Paolo went limp in his arms.

The wall caught him at the middle of his back and spun them around so that they slid headfirst down its slope. There was a sense of friction followed by the soundless thud of the shallow river bottom. Then they were back on the surface. Grey wouldn't remember the rest, whether he swam or if the river was shallow enough to wade, but somehow he made it back and pulled them onto the embankment. All he remembered was Paolo's dead weight in his arms and his lifeless body splayed on the concrete.

Grey straddled him, using his knees as support so as not to put any pressure on Paolo's lungs or abdomen. Paolo's eyes darted wildly back and forth. Grey deepened his voice and whispered in authoritative command, "Breathe slowly." Paolo responded in spasms while Grey demonstrated with slow inhales, repeating the word *breathe* on each exaggerated exhale. Finally, Paolo's shallow gasping slowed and his breath synchronized with Grey's.

They continued breathing in unison until Paolo said, "I'm okay."

Paolo closed his eyes to deflect a drop of water that had fallen from Grey's hair. Before he could open them again, Grey's lips were upon his. Paolo jerked his head to the side.

Grey lifted himself to standing. From behind there were footsteps and then, "*Sta bene?*" The young man was a child, not even twenty. His maroon corduroy coat was unbuttoned, as was his shirt underneath, exposing a two-inch vertical strip of smooth hairless skin from his neck down to his unfastened belt buckle. A good thirty yards away, running up to join them, was the even younger waifish girl with whom he had been making out under the bridge. She had long blond hair and a short black miniskirt. Slowing her stride was not only her restrictive couture but also her cumbersome chaussure—black high-heeled, knee-high patent leather boots. Before she had time to catch her breath, Paolo was back on his feet, forcing the lovers a smile of assurance. "*Non è niente.*"

The cabdriver first needed to be convinced of why he should defile his cab with two drenched passengers and second, wanted to know how they came to be wet in the first place. There was eye rolling and then laughter and then, shrugging his shoulders, he waved them in. On the drive back he continued to ask questions. Paolo replied with short, clipped responses.

66

"Do you mind if I shower first?" They were Paolo's first words to Grey since the aborted kiss.

"Sure," Grey replied. Paolo went into the bathroom and shut the door.

Grey took off his coat and twisted around to see himself in the dresser mirror. His shirt was soaked with blood. It was a surface scrape but it covered most of his back. He changed into a pair of sweats and an old T-shirt. In the kitchen he found a plastic grocery bag, stuffed the bloody shirt into it and hid it in an unused compartment of his suitcase. He then went and hung his other wet clothes on the terrace railing. As fortune would have it, his new wallet had not fallen out of his pants, but at that moment, the last thing Grey felt was fortunate. Emptying the wallet's contents, he laid each item separately on the table to dry. To weight the bills from blowing away, he used rocks from the larger topiary pots. His underwear was no longer very wet but he managed to wring some water from his pants. It dripped to the steps below. He hung them on their rail without pausing to think what the posh neighbors or boutique owners would think.

When he returned to the room, Paolo was sitting on the bed wearing one of the plush terrycloth robes hospitably hung beside the shower.

"Can I ask you a question or do you wanna take a shower first?"

Grey sat on his bed. "Sure, go ahead."

"Who am I to you?"

"What do you mean?"

"Grey, ever since I met you, you've told me stories of this person and that friend, some homeless guy who died a horrible death, the kid who walks your dog, everybody but your boyfriend."

Grey tried to keep his mind quiet, free of analysis. He wanted to really hear Paolo, listen with his whole being as he had done the night of the panic attack. He owed him at least that.

"But the funny thing is you haven't really told me who they all are to you and how they fit into the weird struggle you have, this search for . . . for what?"

Paolo's voice muffled as he looked into his lap. "I can't figure it out. You seem to have a good job, a great home and friends who care a lot about you." He was considering the palms of his hands, turning them over one at a time with each point—left, then right, then left again. "I don't know what your relationship's like, but you seem to wanna drift through life, waiting for something better. I mean you want something better to happen *to* you because you're sure as hell not gonna go after it. That would be too . . . too what . . . too tacky, like our old console TV."

While Grey was doing his best not to react, this last comment hit him hard; it sounded just like his condemnation of Scott and their friends. Paolo apologized, but kept going. "Hey, I didn't mean that but I don't know; it's almost like you think giving up control of your life is some pure, in-the-moment, way of living that'll . . . what? What is it that you want and why are you so bummed that you haven't got it? Most people don't have half of what you do and they don't go through life numb like they're in some sort of dream."

Paolo raised his head and was angrier than before but he kept his voice low. "Let me correct myself, most non-Americans don't. It's one of the things I could never understand there, another reason why I came back. The *fucking* American Dream. Americans are always comparing themselves against some romantic ideal, always so obsessed with it, you forget that life is passing every instant, every second of every day. And you wonder why your old people, locked away in some retirement home, are sad and lonely. You fear that when you get there yourselves, you'll never've reached that ideal, never lived your American Dream. And the scary thing is is that you're right."

Paolo crossed his legs, foot on knee. He was naked underneath his robe but Grey didn't notice. "But that's my soapbox; not yours. And your dream's different."

He leaned into the space between the two beds, spreading his elbows calf to ankle, resting his chin on top of the knuckles of his clasped hands. "Your dream's not a dull suburban white picket fence; yours is some other bizarre script where all of us—everyone you meet—play some character, some role which you don't let us in on. We are either overly structured and cold, or passionately experiencing every second of every day without a care in the world. And then we disappoint you by growing up, selling out our ideals, or crucifying ourselves. And there's no room for any of us, or you for that matter, to be anything in between."

"So I just wanna know what my role's supposed to be? Am I supposed to be your midlife-crisis lover?" Paolo lifted his head from his hands and thrust his arms forward at Grey, a conductor commanding his crescendo. "And for that matter, who is my father? Midlife-crisis lover's father, who committed tragic unexplained suicide that sent midlife-crisis lover searching for the meaning of life. Which I'm supposed to find in you?"

Grey fought the blinding urge to do exactly what Paolo accused of him, recede and drift away, like he did from Scott, like he did from everyone, even from himself. But his dream had died; what was there to drift to? The pain and humiliation of Paolo's words flooded over him, but he held on. He made it through.

"I'm not sure what to say. I'm glad to see you're using your psych degree." It was meant as a joke but in his dismay it came out barbed. "Let me ask you a question. How have you found people different here?"

Paolo reclined onto the bed but stayed on his side, facing Grey. "I found that, here, people aren't totally self-absorbed with some preconceived notion of how their lives should be. They have problems, they lose their job, their wife leaves them, they get some terminal disease . . . but they don't stop and say, 'Didn't turn out like I planned, or didn't plan, so that's it; I'll just dream about a better life from here on out.' Look at Brigitte. Even my mother. She may be avoiding some painful memories but I can tell you, she hasn't shut the rest of the world out."

Paolo waited for a response. They looked at one another, each with an expression the other didn't understand. At last Grey got up and walked toward the bathroom. Over his shoulder he said, "Well, I am an American; what can I say?" He shut the door and turned on the shower.

Ten minutes later Grey came out wearing the same clothes. His hair was wet and combed back. Paolo was lying on the bed still dressed in his robe. Grey went to the closet and got a sweater. "I'm gonna take another walk."

"Wait!" Paolo caught Grey at the front door of the apartment and spun him around. This close, without shoes, the top of his head came right below Grey's brow. He grabbed Grey's elbows. Grey didn't resist but his blank expression offered no encouragement.

"Grey, ya know what I think? I think you're terrified of life. You're a scared little boy who, for some reason locked his emotions away and retreated to a sort of dream state where he never has to live a compromised life, where he never has to risk being hurt. Who watches us all from the safe seclusion of his crow's nest, his perfect glass penthouse, with a secret desire that one of us will climb up and wake him. And lead him back."

Paolo reached out and placed the bridge of his hand under Grey's down-turned chin, lifting it so that they were face-to-face. It was more intimate than a gesture between friends. "If you really know me, you know how much your friendship means to me, how much you mean to me. God, you've been incredible. In a month you've done so much for me and Brigitte and now my family. You've changed our lives forever. And yes, I've been confused by my feelings for you." He put his hands on his Grey's shoulders. Neither acknowledged that his robe fell open. "My attraction."

Paolo leaned in and kissed him, his lips slightly opening onto Grey's. It lasted no longer than a second before they both pulled away. "But in this, you've got far more to figure out than I do. A single kiss won't do it. You've got to wake up and find the way on your own."

After Grey left and Paolo returned to his room and turned off his light, the unnoticed light from under Maria and Juliana's door flickered off as well.

67

The streets were deserted, even Via del Corso. Grey walked its length. He stood for what seemed like an eternity at the base of Vittorio and stared up into its symmetric grandeur. Then he wandered. For two hours he walked streets both known and unknown. He knew he would find his way back; there was always the river. At one point he happened onto the Trevi fountain. Even it was desolate except for a solitary American woman about his age. She faced away from the fountain and pitched a coin over her shoulder.

Packing silently in the dark, Grey was careful not to disturb Paolo.

After carrying his bags out, he lingered at the bedroom door. Paolo lay in his bed, faced away. The covers were pulled to his shoulders and all that was visible was his thick mass of hair.

"Where are you going?"

Grey was too tired to be surprised. He turned to find Maria behind him. She wore the same robe as Paolo had; there must have also been one in her bathroom. It was not yet dawn, still too dark to see her expression.

Paolo stirred in his bed and started to roll over.

Grey closed the door, grabbed his large suitcase and rolled it to the front of the apartment. "I'm headin' home."

Maria picked up his small one and followed him. "I thought you were staying."

"I changed my mind."

They stood at the front door, the suitcases between them. The kitchen's night-light was just enough to see her confusion.

"And what're you gonna do?" Grey asked.

"What do you mean?"

Grey no longer feared engaging her in a real conversation. "Seems like Brigitte's started a theme of returning from exile. Looks like I'm following suit. What about you?"

Maria turned into the living room and walked toward the terrace. "I can't." Rome was invisible, the city inseparable from the river. "And anyway, they told me the ticket's non-changeable."

"How about we trade tickets? Mine's for two weeks out. I'm pretty sure I can convince United to swap them. I'll pay any change fees since I have to change mine anyway."

Grey was still behind her, but in the glass, in their ghostly reflection, there was no distance; she was just larger. They were Chagallian lovers, floating over Rome.

Maria opened the door and walked onto the terrace with Grey behind her. He had almost forgotten about the clothes and wallet he'd left there overnight. His underwear had fallen onto the terrace slate. She bent over and picked it up.

Handing it to him, she asked "So what happened last night?"

He put the underwear down on the table, picked up his wallet and started collecting the dry bills. "We stupidly went for a plunge in the river and froze our butts off." Maria flinched at the word *river*. Grey walked over to a topiary pot and dropped the stones in. "Paolo will tell you." After putting the money back into his wallet, he joined her back at the rail. "If you stay."

A young Italian couple dressed in their Sunday best were approaching the top of the step. She carried a newborn baby and he, a single lit candle.

Maria's comment was soft, inward. "Today's Candlemas."

Upon the first step the man reached his free hand beneath the woman's elbow for support.

"I was married on Candlemas. The day after my nineteenth birthday."

Maria's voice deepened into the memories through which she was about to drift. She sounded as she had the first time Grey heard her speak, the calm prescient young wife and mother who questioned her husband's decision to let four strangers stay the night. At the bottom of the steps the family turned and disappeared.

"The year after my parents died."

"Brigitte told me." Grey turned to her but she stayed staring out over the tiled rooftops that were beginning to take shape in the shadows of the day's new light. For the next twenty minutes she didn't look at him but remained immersed in different place and time.

"When I was young I would sit on the beach and stare out to the sea for hours, dreaming the dreams of young girls. I felt the sea knew my every thought, washed away my deepest fears. Would help me realize my every desire. It was my secret friend, infinite and wise. Silly huh?"

"Not at all; some of the most advanced civilizations, including the one before us, were built by men who believed the sea was a god."

They sat for a moment in silence. Grey feared he'd broken her spell but then she continued.

"I guess it was my God, more so than the emptiness I felt when I was in church listening to words I didn't understand from an old man who seemed to despise the life that courses through our veins. When they drowned, everything changed. The sea betrayed me. My God betrayed me."

The freezer's icemaker emptied and refilled its tray with fresh water. She waited for its pour to complete, for the return of the silence.

"That night Antonio and I slept at Brigitte's. She lit candles and we prayed together. I promised everything—my dreams, my life, my soul—in exchange for their safe return. I fell asleep with my hands clasped together so tight that my fingers would be bruised in the morning.

"I dreamt I was in the stairwell of Brigitte's building, standing at the foot of the steps. It was darker than usual, the sconces looked the same but they weren't electric. Candles flickered beneath their silk shades. Outside I could hear a storm swirling and became afraid. As soon as I locked the front door, I heard a knock. I hesitated but then it came again. They shouted for me to let them in. I grabbed the handle but it stuck; the lock jammed. I tried to free the latch but it wouldn't budge. They begged for me to save them. Water started pouring in under the door. I slipped and fell but held on to the knob. Their pleading was now frantic. The water covered the floor and began to fill the stairwell. I struggled but its rush was too strong. I could no longer stand yet I held on tight to the doorknob. I tried to turn it, force the lock, but I didn't have either the leverage or the strength. My shoulder ached with the strain; the metal slid against my palm. The water over-whelmed me and lifted me with its rise. I stopped struggling and let it take me. The screaming stopped; all sound stopped. The last thing I remember was being under water, hanging upside down. My hand was numb, but still I held on. Although the water stung in my eyes, I could see clearly as if, instead of blurring, the water magnified every detail. My fingers were white against the gold brass of the knob, my arm floating, alabaster in the water's dull gray. My patterned dress and long hair fluttered around me like the tentacles of a giant jellyfish. I knew that any moment it would all be over, the candles would burn out. Suddenly the lock unjammed, the knob turned and the door opened. I shut my eyes and let go.

"When I awoke I was gasping for air, my face wet with tears. I knew they were gone. I felt empty, weightless, and Antonio wrapped me in his arms. If he had let go, I would have floated away. That night we made love for the first time. It saved me. He saved me.

"The dream came back, always the same, always ending with me floating silently up through the flooded atrium, never breaking the water's surface.

"Six months later we married on Candlemas. The church was ablaze. Candles lined the walls and everyone held one. It had to have been beautiful but all I could think of were the candles we held in their funeral procession. I hadn't walked it all but had stopped at the crest of the hill. I couldn't face the sea. I didn't take the boat with Brigitte and Antonio to watch the four weighted caskets disap-pear beneath the waves. When I found a candle in Antonio's pocket the next day, I asked Brigitte. She told me that after the priest finished his prayer, Antonio had not cast his candle into the water like everyone else but kept it lit even after he rowed them back to shore. With it still burning, he returned to the sea alone.

"When the same priest announced us man and bride, Antonio leaned into me and whispered, 'I swear I'll find them.' The wedding party followed us back to Brigitte's and Antonio carried me over the threshold. He opened the door without a key—either he or Brigitte had removed the lock."

At the start of her monologue, Grey's heart was pounding; he thought he might finally discover the truth. But as her story unfolded, he stopped listening for connections to his past but rather listened to a woman who needed to purge her demons.

"After we married, Antonio would take his rowboat out at least once a week. He scoured the coastline inch by inch.

"So you see, it was my fault that my husband died."

"You can't believe that," Grey blurted.

She went on as if she hadn't heard him. The only hint of acknowledgement was that she moved for the first time since she had begun her story. It was slight; Grey would have missed it had he not been so intent. With her left thumb she pushed her wedding ring around her finger.

"When he died, the dream came back but it was worse. It started with the atrium filled with water. There was no storm, no screaming—just black, inky water. Although I could see nothing, I knew the lockless door was swung open to the utter obscurity of the sea. To oblivion.

"It took us two weeks to move. I had the same dream every night until we got to New York."

"Did the move help?"

Grey's question broke her trance but not her story. The floodgates were open; she would continue to the end.

"I survived. I wouldn't've on Elba." Maria walked over to the couch.

Grey followed. "I doubt that."

She sat down and picked up her wedding picture. Grey remained standing.

Looking into her own distant, sad eyes, she said, "Yes, the survival instinct is strong. We insulate ourselves, build safe borders against pain. In this exile we do indeed survive. But at what cost?"

"Maria, I can't imagine your pain but obviously you conquered it and raised two wonderful children in the process."

She put the picture back down on table but propped it up and continued to study it. "When I look at them I see him. They live their lives without fear, without limitations. New York gave them this."

"That's certainly not the New York I know."

"Back then, Little Italy was magical. Everyone helped me; you can't imagine. There I could forge ahead without the weight of the past. It's one of my favorite things about America—you don't hang onto yesterday. Each day is completely new. My nightmares vanished as soon as we landed and over time, so did most of the memories—good and bad. Now they've come flooding back."

Grey sat down on the couch beside her. "What was he like?"

Maria smiled and turned to Grey. There was no judgment but there was something else, something he couldn't put his finger on.

"He was pure."

She glanced at the still-wrapped photo that sat beside her standing one.

"I don't mean he was perfect; he was far from it. But his every action, every word, reflected some inner light he had. Some beacon of—I don't know how else to say it but pure love."

Maria picked her photo up, placed it down on top of his and put the stacked pair beneath the table with the other presents.

"But he was not an easy man to be married to. He saw no boundaries. He opened his heart to everyone, every stray cat or dog or even strangers in need of . . . " Maria turned and looked directly at Grey. " . . . whatever.

"When I lost him, I lost his light. I lost my second God." Grey realized that the something else in her eyes was forgiveness. He grabbed her hand; she let it be grabbed.

"On New Year's Eve I dreamt that I was back on Elba, sitting on the beach and staring out to the sea. It was no longer dark and terrifying but the beautiful incandescent sea of my youth. From behind, he whispered in my ear, 'I've found them Mari—they're safe.' As I turned to see him, I was blinded by his light. I just caught his eyes, his incredible shining eyes. And then I felt him touch me, not my skin but deeper inside me. And then suddenly his light was in me, obliterating everything, shining through my every pore.

"It's as though he's resurrected my soul."

They sat for a few minutes holding hands, both allowing silent tears to flow. She then looked up into his eyes. Her face was now an older version of the one he remembered, that of a beautiful strong woman who loved and feared and lived. "Are you sure we can switch tickets?"

Grey reached in his pocket and pulled out his cell phone. A half-hour later Maria and Grey were back on the couch having coffee.

"Hey, I'm gonna get outta here before they wake up. Don't wanna do the whole explaining thing."

Maria nodded. "I, of all people, understand."

Grey glanced at the presents and neatly folded wrapping paper under the table in front of them. "I didn't get you anything."

"You've got to be kidding." He had never seen her laugh. Her eyes smiled.

He lifted his hands to the chain under his shirt. The clasp was so simple now. He pulled it from around his neck.

It hung between them.

Maria went pale. "Where did you—"

He reached over, gently pulled her hand from her mouth and placed the medallion in her open palm. He told her the truth. "When I was a kid, I found it in my backyard. Paolo told me your husband wore one like it. I was going to stop wearing it anyway and so I thought . . . "

Maria looked into her hand. When she lifted her head, tears had again welled in her eyes. His too. Grey leaned in first but they met in the middle.

68

It was nearing eight—Juliana and Paolo would be up any minute. Maria reached under the table and picked up the two photos. She stood hers back up and stared into its reflection. The unwrapped one remained in her lap. She ran her hand across the rough kraftpaper and inhaled deeply, breaking the string and pulling it from the paper. Cracking the seal in two. The blue wax fell to the floor as she tore the paper from the frame.

69

"Scott, I'm on my way home. I should get in tonight around ten. You were right—I was an asshole for running off, but I had to come back to find out how far I'd drifted. Instead, I found out how far I'd sunk. I can't explain it over the phone, but . . . look, we should talk before going to a lawyer. I don't know if it will make a difference, but we can't end it like this.

"Given the situation, you're probably going to think that what I'm getting ready to ask is selfish, and I can't say that I would blame you, but is there anyway you can take this week off? I've got to go to California and I want you to come with me. It's totally up your alley—big knockdown-dragout with Bob. I'm finally taking your advice. I know it's last minute but you can name the hotel and choose every restaurant. If you can't, let's plan something extravagant for the weekend. Maybe the Berkshires. We never have been back. What better place to figure everything out—to figure us out. Think about it. I'll see you tonight. Love you . . . I really do love you."

The plane had fully boarded and though the flight was more than half full, Grey was the only one in his row. He looked across the two empty seats and wondered if fate had anticipated his journey's end and intervened on his behalf. Across the aisle, a woman was talking about seeing some poor drunk robbed at the Florence train station. Grey listened in. " . . . the day after Christmas . . . so wasted that he couldn't feel the watch being taken from his wrist." Sure enough, he was the drunk. He didn't correct her; there was no point. For her it was a good story, a recent vacation memory. For him it was as far away as Elba was below.

He dialed Miriam's number and stared out into a bank of gray—one of the day's few clouds, but through which, for whatever reason, the pilot chose to ascend. It blanketed his window. "Can I speak to your mommy?" The plane passed into clear skies, revealing an unobstructed view from the South of France to the Amalfi Coast. "Miriam, this is Grey. I'm great but I can't talk now; I'm on a plane. I just wanted to let you know I am going to be in the Bay Area next week and was hoping we could get together. No, business—my company's headquarters are out there." He found Corsica and Sardinia and followed the coast up to Elba. He could barely make it out. From this height it was just a speck. "I know I should have but every time I've been out, I'm usually swamped with work. Yeah, I'm pretty sure Tuesday night will work. I'll make it work." He ran his hand across the new journal he'd bought at Franco's shop. It was almost identical to the one Miriam first gave him. He was tired of cheap spiral notebooks; he missed the symbolism and feel of craftsmanship. "Is everything okay?" He scanned the last entry he'd written on the ferry from Elba to Rome, after his first failed seduction of Paolo.

> *Am I destined always to live in exile, subjugated to the recesses of my mind and the pages of my journals?*

"OK, well next week then. I have to say it's great to hear your voice. We've got so much to catch up on. Wait, I missed that; what'd you say?" He took a pen from his coat pocket and laughed. "Of course I remember him—what an asshole! Where the hell'd ya run into him?" The woman across the aisle shot him a reprimanding glare. Out of his peripheral vision, he saw her do a double take. "Hey, speaking of Tom, you'll never guess where I've just come from." He clicked open the pen—"No, Elba."—and wrote:

> *What does it mean*

He hesitated. "It's a long, story. I'll tell you on Tuesday."

Grey studied his words, remembering another long-ago interrupted and unformed entry that made him question everything. The pen hovered above the page. "No, it's five. It's New York that's six hours behind; you're nine. I hope it's not too early for you." With his left hand, Grey counted back the hours, his thumb starting with his pinkie and touching each of his fingers, repeating the sequence until he stopped on his ring finger that bore no ring. Six hours. He realized that Maria's vision of Antonio could have been at the exact same time as his own. His chipper voice belied his distraction. "No. I mean yeah, today's the day—I'm now officially over the hill." He finished his quandary:

to be resurrected?

"I wish I could say it was just your typical midlife crisis but it goes back way further." Grey rolled the pen back and forth in his palm. It was one of those cheap promotional pens, blue with yellow lettering. It read: *Café Roma.* He'd had a batch made for Paolo's Internet station. "Unfortunately nothing that cliché. I think so—you tell me after we talk. Yeah, me neither. 'Til Tuesday then." As he was putting the airphone into the seat back into front of him, he noticed a book that he didn't recognize in the carry-on bag at his feet. He pulled it out. It was Paolo's copy of *Stranger in a Strange Land.* The image of the naked man meditating beneath the sea now seemed less erotic than it did prophetic. On the inside cover was written:

Grey,
Life doesn't have to be so alienating and lonely. Hope some day you'll
make it down to Earth and join us.
- Paolo

Grey closed it and put it in the empty seat next to him. He returned his attention to the journal. He sat staring at his last entry for some time. The pen tip rested on the paper, creating a small blotch of ink from its prolonged contact. At last he turned the page. At its center was a tiny dot where the stain had soaked through. Over it, he penned his final entry, the last one he would ever make.

February 2, 2000.
Ere I saw Elba there was just sea and sky. I pray that, after all these years,
I am able.

Grey turned back to the window. The winter sun was about to set. The steel blue of the open sky lay upon the deeper slate of the Mediterranean that stretched beneath it. The horizon was again unbroken. Elba was gone.

THE END

ACKNOWLEDGEMENTS

For a business guy with no background in creative writing, attempting a novel is an arduous task; completing it, a near impossibility. It is said that the hardest thing about writing a novel is finishing it. Truer words were never spoken. There are so many people who encouraged me, nudged and prodded, cajoled and threatened—whatever it took. I truly appreciate each and every one of you. If I've forgotten anyone in the below list, forgive me—you all know how I am.

First to: Kristy Lin Billuni and Dennis Billuni, my daughter/father editorial team whose guidance went far beyond the editorial. I also need to thank those who provided secondary editorial assistance: Vikas Arora, Marisa Arrona, Maia Ettinger, David Gershan, Tracie Klein, Diane Perro, Gilles Perroy, Leslie Stern, and Sheila Von Driska.

For additional creative and proof work: Sheila Von Driska for zillions of things, not the least of which was her cover design; Tracie Klein for the cover photo; Duane Cramer for the headshot photo; Fernando Martin del Campo for the map inserts; and Pie La Rocca, Marco Gazzetta, and Mathieu Sureau for Italian and French translation.

Others who gave me inspiration and honest assessment were: Duchamp and Tennessee Banks, Loretta Barrett, Kate Antheil Boyd, Dave Brunetti, Rick Canvel, Leslie Caplan, Alejandro Celis, Dan Bunker, Brigitte Benharrous, Ron Christensen, David Chustz, Jorge A. Colunga, Kim Daus-Edwards, Charles Decker, Mavis DeWees, John Dye, Kevin Edwards, Carol Lee Flinders, Harvey Frank, Kirk Froggatt, Bob Garrison, Katchen Gerig, Jennifer Glos, Michelle Glover, Kim Green, Erich Hendrickson, Gary Higgins, Carole Hines, Nick Hodulik, John Houghtling, Nina Katz, Krandall Kraus, Renee Lekan, Matt Leum, Helen Lin, Adam McLaughlin, Tim Meager, Gilles Mésana, Chris Miller, Kevin Morgan, Camilla Newhagen, Heide Oberndorf, David Ottenhouse, Alan Pellman, Tom Perrault, Joe Piazza, Douglas Plummer, Monica Pressley, Paige Reynolds, Mary Jane Ryan, Ed Salvato, Mary Beth Sammons, Carol Sanford, Christopher Schelling, Anita Schiller, Robert Shepard, Matthew Siedhoff, Weston Stander, Kevin Smokler, Charlie Stratton, Laura Strickland, Kathe Sweeney, Alex Teague, Deanna Teoh, Cameron Tuttle, Claudia Welss, and Julie Young

Finally I want to thank my partner Nick Rubashkin who was there with me every step of the way. Full moons forever.

THE AUTHOR

Drew Banks (drewbanks.com) is a businessman and author. In both his business writing and fiction, Drew deconstructs behavioral patterns in an attempt to explore causal motivations and deterrents. While Drew's first two business books, *Beyond Spin* (beyondspin.com) and *Customer.Community* (customer-community.com), examine organizational implications of various social psychologies, he is drawn to fiction as a more intimate medium for delving beneath the surface of the individual. *Able Was I* (ablewasi.net) is his first novel.

Printed in the United States
137064LV00003B/117/A